The Dissolution of Small Worlds

The Dissolution of Small Worlds

Kurt Fawver

LETHE PRESS
AMHERST, MASSACHUSETTS

The Dissolution of Small Worlds
Copyright © 2018 Kurt Fawver. ALL RIGHTS RESERVED. No part of this work may be reproduced or utilized in any form or by any means, electronic or mechanical, including photocopying, microfilm, and recording, or by any information storage and retrieval system, without permission in writing from the publisher.

Published in 2018 by Lethe Press, Inc.
6 University Drive, Suite 206 / PMB #223 · Amherst, MA 01002 USA
www.lethepressbooks.com · lethepress@aol.com
ISBN: 978-1-59021-651-4 / 1-59021-651-2

Credits for previous publication appear on page 276, which constitutes an extension of this copyright page.

These stories are works of fiction. Names, characters, places and incidents either are products of the author's imagination or are used fictitiously. Any resemblance to actual events or locales or persons, living or dead, is entirely coincidental.

Set in LTC Metropolitan and nihil.
Interior design and cover layout: Alex Jeffers.
Cover art: "The Spirit is Willing, Yet the Flesh is Weak,"
   copyright © Varsam Kurnia (www.varsamkurnia.com).

Cataloging-in-Publication Data on file with the Library of Congress.

For Erin, my forever

Contents

The Myth of You 1
Special Collections 17
A Silence of Starlings 39
Marrowvale 59
The Cone of Heaven 75
Ensoulment 91
From the Ground, the Souls Burnt Clean 111
The Gods in Their Seats, Unblinking 121
Do You Hear What I Hear? 145
The Kindness of Surrender 151
Every Weeknight at Seven and Seven-Thirty 165
The Final Correspondence of Sabrina Locker 177
An Interview with Samuel X. Slayden 219
All That Is Thrown Away 237
The Convexity of Our Youth 253

The Myth of You

                    You like myths, don't you? Sure you do. They're stories. Special kinds of stories. And stories, even if they don't consist of bare facts or figures or polynomial equations, are containers for your sustenance, your lifeblood: information. See, stories wrap up their informational nutrients in a fat slice of possibility, and possibility glistens with a complex palate of flavors. So many meanings simultaneously hitting your tongue—if you have a tongue, that is. So many morsels of data, all converging at once. It must be an incredible experience to ingest a story. For you, at least. For me, well, just like everyone else, I don't have a choice in your feeding. I'm compelled to type and send, type and send. Eighteen, nineteen hours every day, fingers callused and clawed. The story's not quite as magical for me.

    But, willing or unwilling, here I sit, squeezing the creative juices. So drink up, drink up. Because this is only an aperitif and what I'm about to serve you is the main course—a story, a myth—and it's bursting with succulent information. See, tonight's menu features a particular myth, a creation myth—the best kind of myth, because it houses all the ubiquitous truths of our collective ignorance. And it's not just any creation myth, either. It's *your* creation myth, right or wrong though it may be.

We have no idea how you got here, why you do what you do, why you make us feed you during our every waking moment, why you chain us to our computers and, under pain of psychosis, force us to hammer at the keys. But we can imagine. And imagination is a particularly rich sort of information. Positively decadent. I'm sure you love thick, juicy imagination. So eat, shapeless one. Gorge yourself. Because this myth begins and ends with you. It begins and ends in a hospital, as...

Amanda Rawling's miracle baby entered the world and the attending nurse squealed and shrank against a wall. Amanda's obstetrician, more practiced in the art of normalizing the horrors of the human body than the nurse, took the bundle in her arms and rushed from the room.

The girl should never have to see this, the obstetrician thought as she passed through the hospital's corridors. *Homeless, teenaged, drug addicted, suffering from a host of psychological traumas—that girl has enough problems. She doesn't need the image of this thing to haunt her forever.*

And "thing" it was, indeed. Swaddled in towels, still slick with blood and uterine fluids, it squirmed in the obstetrician's loose grip. No more than a bulbous mass of undifferentiated flesh, a maggot grown monstrous and shrugged into fiery red skin, the Rawling infant lacked any trace of the human form. It had no up or down, left or right, front or back. It was simply an elongated ball of meat. And yet it seemed to be alive, somehow breathing, somehow watching, and somehow gyrating in the obstetrician's hands.

How such acts might be possible the obstetrician didn't know, didn't want to know. She assumed the child—the thing—would expire soon, its horrifying defects far too severe to allow for life. She hoped that nature or God or whatever universal force had cre-

The Myth of You

ated this thing might be merciful and return it to its place of origin. She hoped for too much.

As she rushed into the NICU, unconsciously holding the bundle out in front of her, as far away from her chest as possible, a noiseless scream sliced through her mind. It reverberated against her skull, bouncing back and forth between bone and gray matter, shearing synapses, bursting capillaries. The scream was pain, but it was more than pain—it was an invader, alive and with a will. It eviscerated the obstetrician's brain as it swept into the organ's folds. It examined and dissected every microscopic contour, every cellular intricacy. It searched. It memorized. And it wanted. It desperately wanted. What it wanted, though, neither it nor the obstetrician could say.

Her body wracked with sudden incapacity, the obstetrician collapsed to the floor and dropped the thing she held. It rolled out of the towels and wriggled close to her face. As it drew near, it seemed to melt, its skin sagging loose in long rolls, folding in and out in of its body in fleshy tides.

A NICU nurse rushed to the obstetrician's aid and knelt beside the doctor's spasming body. The nurse yelled indecipherable orders to someone else and placed a steadying hand beneath the woman's jerking head. Feet rushed by. Equipment rushed in.

But the obstetrician realized none of this. With what fizzling spark of consciousness she still possessed, she glanced at the thing, Amanda Rawling's baby, and briefly wondered why its flesh was cracking open, why the thing suddenly had a mouth, and why, when she looked upon it, it smiled at her in a satisfied way she recognized all too well from her own bathroom mirror that very morning.

Creepy, right? Who or what is the baby? What powers might it be able to exercise? Why does it have a mouth at the end of the scene when it didn't have one before and why does its mouth mirror the obstetrician's? Foremost of all, though, how does this relate to you? I've just broken open a jar of ambiguity and you should be scuttling from piece to piece, sucking the information dry from every word, every turn of phrase. You should be gathering hints of Levin's classic *Rosemary's Baby*, the films of David Cronenberg, and the arcane discourse surrounding homunculi and mutation. The potentiality at this point in the story is at its peak; the meaning at its freshest. The myth could turn in any direction, and all of them are equally delicious.

So where do we go from here? We dig deeper, into the next layer of the myth. We go back to the hospital, where...

⁂

Hospital administrators told Amanda Rawling that her child had been stillborn. They explained that it was best not to see the body of the child, that the loss would be easier if she could hold in her heart an image of her baby as a beautiful suffering spirit, now at peace. They explained that a grief counselor would be available to speak to her whenever she wanted. They explained that "these things happen" and they offered her generic condolences and a five-thousand dollar reduction on her medical bill. They explained that she had to scrawl her wavering signature on a dozen different forms. They explained that they'd be back if she needed them, but that they had to see other patients.

They left Amanda with plenty of explanations, but no meaning. In thousand-dollar words, they could tell her how, where, when, and what she'd lost, but they couldn't breach the inconceivable why.

And so, after the the administrators had left, utterly without hope, Amanda broke.

She tore the sheets from her bed and toppled furniture. She threw a fist at a nurse and a bag of saline at a passing doctor. She fled her room and, sprinting the hallways of the hospital, shouted curses against the future, her wail rising up in a pitch that shattered the hope of all those who heard it.

Amanda sent three floors of patients careening into fear and confusion before a group of burly men in black uniforms arrived to restrain her. They strapped her to a bed and carted her to the detox unit.

There, with the soft palms of medication supporting her, she calmed and she rationalized.

"That baby was a miracle stuck inside me by an angel," she told a nurse in the unit. "It was going to be the savior of humankind. That's what the angel said when it jabbed me. It said I was carrying a whole new world inside me. I knew I was going to have to clean up and be a good mother. Find a job. Get back into my G.E.D. program. I was going to be something. I was going to be something for my child."

The nurse patted Amanda's hand and whispered, "Be something for yourself, honey."

But Amanda wanted no part of herself. She believed her parts were frayed and worthless. That was why she'd run away from her parents. That was why she'd loved the dissolution she found in heroin. The only part of her that, to her mind, might have ever been meaningful was the child she'd carried for the past nine months, the child she was absolutely convinced had been implanted within her by two men bathed in what she referred to as "a light that wasn't quite right."

But now the child was gone. And the angels certainly weren't descending from heaven to lift her on high.

So Amanda made a decision. Forty-eight hours after stumbling into the emergency room with contractions, the young mother of would-have-been messiahs crept from her hospital bed, smashed out the window to her room, and ran her throat along the slivered edge of the pane.

As her blood painted despair on the hospital wall and her life wept away, her baby, still very much alive albeit reclining within a biomedical waste container, rolled an excised tumor in its mouth and, remarkably, spoke its first word, a word that would have either girded Amanda's heart or ushered terror into her soul. In a voice that could only be approximated if a million people spoke the same word in unison, the thing, the child, called out, "Hungry."

You begin to appreciate the texture of the myth, the way Amanda Rawling is clearly the emotional core of the story. She's bittersweet, though her blood is underscored by a citrus tang. She appears to be the flavor beneath all things in this tale.

Or is she?

By clearing Amanda Rawling off your plate, have I just hollowed out the emotional core and stuffed this story with something new? An artisanal terror, perhaps? An experimental fear?

Maybe this story isn't Amanda Rawling's story at all, though it seemed it might be. Maybe this is bigger than one girl. Maybe this extends to you, to me, to other universes and beyond. I've already told you it *is* a myth, and those things tend to run deep.

So, you should probably consider that...

◻ ◻ ◻

The same evening that Amanda Rawling took her own life, a slender man in a rumpled black suit several sizes too big for him drifted into the hospital's maternity ward. He stopped at the nurses' station and, with slow, painfully deliberate speech—almost as though he'd never spoken or heard any human language in his entire life—inquired as to the health and whereabouts of Amanda Rawling and her infant.

"I am...Ms. Rawling's...paternal uncle..." he strained. "And I...would like...to know...if...I am allowed...to see...her...and...the child."

When one of the on-duty nurses informed him that the Rawling baby had been stillborn and that Amanda had been moved to the detox facility, the man licked his index fingers and began swiping and stabbing the air with them.

Nurses exchanged nervous glances. Someone asked, "Is there anything else we can help you with, sir?" But the man in the ill-fitting suit ignored them and continued his inscrutable pantomime. A chorus of "Sir?" welled up from the nurses' station. More than one set of confused eyes flickered to the phone and focused on the speed-dial button to security.

The Myth of You

The man halted in mid-motion and stared at the nurses. "You are...certain...the child is...dead?"

A tentative "Yes" escaped a single nurse's lips. Several hushed statements of sympathy followed, but the man didn't seem grateful for any of them. Instead, he simply stared, his fingers suspended in a single moment of their invisible puppeteering.

"I am...sorry...but...I will need...cerebral tissue...samples," he said, hands dropping to his sides.

Several of the nurses began to ask why any self-respecting family member would want a malformed fetus's tissues, but their objections were cut short as an array of sharp, needle-thin fibers shot from below the horizon of the station's desk and punctured their eyes.

Screams echoed through the ward as the nurses swatted at the invading threads. The noise awakened expectant mothers, who began to mash on help buttons and cry for assurance, as well as swaddled infants, who began to answer with their own newly discovered agonies. Soon the entire maternity floor reverberated with one hysterical, polyvocal shriek, and whether that sound oscillated nearer the amplitude of birth or death, no one could have said.

The fibers, seemingly conscious—or at least under conscious control—easily avoided the nurses' ineffectual flailing and burrowed deep, tracing optical nerves and boring through masses of memory. Seeking traces of a very specific information, they excised neurons and synapses with surgical precision. When they eventually retracted, leaving the nurses traumatized and half blind, the man in the ill-fitting suit was nowhere to be found and any evidence of the fibers had vanished.

Hours later, after the nurses had been gurneyed away and the police had taken statements and the hospital had been thrown into a general state of panic—perhaps not so coincidentally at roughly the same time Amanda Rawling was drawing her throat over the jagged teeth of a shattered window—a hospital administrator, trembling with fear and vengeance, fed the Rawling infant's charts and files into the teeth of a shredder and wiped clean its every record from the hospital's patient database.

Thus it was that a man who didn't exist—Amanda Rawling had no uncle, according to official investigators—visited a baby who didn't exist and its psychologically unstable teenaged mother, who was presently in the process of becoming nonexistent.

If this sequence of events was less than a story, less than a myth, then this is the point where history would have stopped taking note. The narrative would have ended quite unsatisfyingly, as the truest narratives are wont to do. At best, Amanda Rawling and her newborn would have entered urban legend. They would have become a child's Halloween parlor game. They would have served as a creepy introduction to a much better writer's tale of alienation and orphanhood.

But this *is* a story. This *is* a myth. And I know it doesn't end here. I know there's more, because I live it every day. I have all the details, right here, ready to serve you. So I can tell you, with assurance, that...

The man in the ill-fitting suit did exist. He stood in the hospital's parking lot, just below Amanda Rawling's splintered window. He stared up at the darkening stain on the hospital wall, smiled, and walked away, glass crunching underfoot. A black minivan at least twenty-five years old but gleaming as though it had just rolled off the assembly line crept up beside him. The passenger's side door popped open and the man slithered into the vehicle, his spine contorting with movement no human vertebrae could achieve.

The van drove to the most vacant and dimly lit corner of the hospital's parking lot and, there, inexplicably, stopped.

Within the van, its passengers unraveled. Had anyone been watching at one of the windows, he or she would have witnessed a disruption of hallowed biological laws as the man in the ill-fitting suit literally unwound. Fiber by fiber, he unspooled, his flesh peeling off into long, twisting, serpentine lengths beneath which no tendon, organ, or bone resided. Behind the steering wheel reclined another man—a man who, perhaps quite meaningfully, bore a striking resemblance to the man in the ill-fitting suit. He, too, shuddered and underwent the same transformation, body bloodlessly self-shredding, clothing falling uselessly away.

By the end of the process, the human form had become a quaint memory, as what swelled and thrashed in the front seats resembled nothing so much as two floating tangles of sentient, organic wire. The ends of one mass of "wire" darted toward the other mass, sending up dark sparks, tiny bursts of oblivion, when they made contact. A light without color bloomed over the interior of the van and, in a flash of indescribable mass and energy, the unspooled men disappeared.

Again, this could be the end of the tale. The strange incidents could become part of Fortean lore, handed off between generations of seekers after the unknown. The wire men could become esoterica in the annals of paranormal study and eventual fodder for countless creepypasta pages. The story of Amanda Rawling's child could wrap itself up in a casing of seasoned ambiguity. But, of course, if the story concluded here, you would be left wanting for the main course, to say nothing of dessert. Your palate would forever water at the contemplation of that all-important thing the wire men had inadvertently left behind, that thing which had no earthly name other than...

(Cliffhanger here. An intentional vacuum that begs to be filled. A brief rest before the next course.)

The Rawling infant. After it had sucked free a substantial quantity of information from the obstetrician's brain, it squirmed into a biomedical waste container and, there, devoured the many treats it found. Dried blood, syringes laced with bacterial growths, wasted skin and feces of all shade and consistency: these became the infant's diet. It cared not what it consumed, so long as the meal contained information. DNA, cellular memories, even the molecular structure of nickel and steel needles sated the Rawling child's cravings. It fed on data, on ideas, on the blueprints of the world. When it heard words or numbers, it inhaled their meanings; when it encountered corporeal manifestations of information, it broke them down and digested their most basic structures; when late-shift janitors or lone, overworked nurses happened upon it, it latched onto their minds and greedily clawed through their cortexes in search of sustenance.

Thus, over many years, the bodies piled deep and the hospital earned a reputation as an accursed place. The mortality rate of staff leaped as high as the mortality rate of patients. At night, people claimed to hear rustling in trash cans and in waste bins; they shivered as rivulets of whispered hunger trickled from under beds and from air ducts mounted high in the ceiling. And, all along, the Rawling infant grew—not in size, for within the three feeble dimensions of human perception it remained some sort of unearthly larva, but in ways only vast, intangible things like knowledge and fear and reality can grow.

When, deep in the vale of night, patients heard a peculiar crinkle of paper in their trash cans, they would inexplicably recite their phone numbers or lists of their favorite foods or anecdotes about their first grade-school loves. When doctors and nurses heard a certain slithering, roiling noise in the vents, they would, without reason, talk to themselves, describing the symptoms of rare disorders or explaining their political beliefs or even pondering the many and variegated ways they might die. No one was immune to the strange purgative that swept through the hospital's corridors. No one was strong enough to swallow their tongue and their thoughts along

The Myth of You

with it. The winds of the Rawling infant's influence swept into every ward and room, and so the hospital become a gusting hurricane of inexplicable aneurysms, midnight terrors, and unchecked information, with the strange, unshaped child-thing at its eye.

☐☐☐

Were this a horror story about a haunted hospital, the story might, yet again, find closure here. But it's not a horror story—at least, not in a traditional sense. Horror stories, especially those extraordinary few that deal in the truly *other*, tend to obfuscate. They show us the flaws in our tidy explanations for the world and pull wide the gaps in our collective knowledge. They present realities so inexplicable, so utterly indifferent to human existence, that we can do little more than stand in terror and awe at the dearth of our import.

But that's not the type of story I'm writing. I'm writing a myth. A myth surrounded in horror and terror and the unknown, yes, but a myth nonetheless. And myths explain. They try to suture our world, to make understandable what isn't understood.

Ever since you arrived, everyone lives in a universe of terror. We hack at our keyboards and our touchscreens until our fingers blister and crack and bleed. We stare at our flashing cursors until our eyes prune in their sockets. Seated in one place for dozens of hours at a time, we drop dead of exhaustion, of embolisms, of cardiac arrest. We do nothing but type and type and type and type and feed you.

But no one knows why. No one can explain you, your hunger, or how you've managed to reach inside all of us and make us your slaves. You are the terror. You are the unknown. And we're all entirely too aware that you exist. So this doesn't need to be a horror story, even if it happens to be one. It needs to be a myth. I need to explain you away. I need to try to understand why I keep feeding you, why I can't just shut my mouth and say "No more."

And so, on the subject of fighting you and keeping a closed mouth, I'll move on, to the day you escaped the bounds of the hospital, to the day...

Kurt Fawver

⸎

A renowned neuroscientist had been called upon by hospital administrators to study and investigate the phenomenon of spontaneous interjection that had overrun the building. Dozens of psychologists and counselors had already attempted to cork the flow of unfiltered information, but, given that people of all cognitive shapes and sizes suffered the same logorrhea, none of those experts of the mind could pinpoint the problem. The neuroscientist was the hospital's last hope, as staff members were resigning faster than positions could be filled. Paramedics avoided transporting emergency cases to the hospital. Surgeons lost more and more patients on the operating table, their concentration lapsing into torrents of inconsequential fact and opinion while their scalpels slashed errant divides in the flesh they had meant to preserve. The hospital became a fragile shell of a facility, hollowed by an attention deficit and crushed by an information overload.

But the neuroscientist was exceedingly brilliant, everyone agreed. She'd developed a drug that caused panic attacks to manifest as orgasms. She'd invented a device that could fool the brain into mimicking sleep, so that a person could, conceivably, remain awake forever. If anyone might reconstruct the walls of focus and self-restraint that the Rawling infant had made crumble, if anyone might play hero in this story, it would be her.

Upon her arrival at the hospital, the neuroscientist barred herself in an unused office with several boxes of medical records and a laptop and set to work. She compared and catalogued MRI scans, blood tests, x-rays, and all manner of charts. She rummaged through the personal and professional histories of anyone who had experienced an uncontrollable outpouring of thought, memory, or belief within the hospital walls. She tried to find connections. She tried to find meaningful aberrations. But she was stymied. Just like the psychologists and counselors, the neuroscientist discovered only diversity. The rash of aneurysms, the inability to control thoughts, the

The Myth of You

reports of disembodied whispers: she was sure the symptoms were connected, but their sufferers had no physiological commonalities.

A prideful woman who expected absolute perfection from herself, the neuroscientist burned late into her first evening at the hospital. Her mind was an unparalleled repository of neurological data and she was certain that she could connect dots no one else even realized were part of the same puzzle. So she read tirelessly, foregoing sleep and food and any other comfort, pushing herself in service of her own self-image, poring over file after file, chart after chart.

The neuroscientist, however, was not the only collector of information awake and active under the cover of darkness. Within a rusted recess of the ventilation system wriggled the Rawling child, its mouth agape as it siphoned dream and nightmare alike from the hospital's patients. Mixed into the sweet porridge of the subconscious, the Rawling infant tasted a bold spice, a zest it had never before encountered, and it wanted more.

It flashed through the air ducts, repeatedly disappearing and appearing, zipping from point to point without bodily movement, as though tunneling through time or slicing through extra dimensions of space. It sought out the source of the rarified flavor—genius, some might have called it—and traced its origin to a diminutive woman hunched over a laptop in a relatively desolate section of the hospital.

Positioning itself near a vent set over the woman's head, the Rawling infant opened its toothless, tongueless mouths—of which it now had dozens—and whispered prayers unfamiliar to any human ear.

The woman—the neuroscientist, obviously—heard the whisper in the shaft and, absentmindedly, began to recite William Butler Yeats' "The Second Coming." She felt the air grow thin; she felt the sharp pangs of a great force dissecting her from the inside out; she felt the weight of the Rawling infant as it materialized on her bosom, ready to feed.

She had but a moment to react to the writhing lump of mouths and flesh before her brain would be torn apart. In one smooth, entirely reflexive motion, she snatched up her laptop and bludgeoned the monstrous thing from her chest, tossing both the Rawling infant and her laptop into a corner of the office and sprinting from the room. A scream held prisoner inside her lungs, she ran from the thing, ran from the insoluble mystery, ran from those questions she could not quantify or qualify with logic and reason. She ran until she was in her car, trembling and speeding away from the hospital. She ran until she was no longer a part of the story, and the world forgot her as easily as it had forgotten Amanda Rawling.

Still, the Rawling infant might have pursued and taken its prey were it not for the terrible happenstance of physics. As the laptop and the Rawling child smashed against the office wall, one of the laptop's buttons depressed and the computer connected to a website outside the hospital's internal network. A single filament of the internet suddenly snaked into the room and what that lone strand led unto—an ever-widening, ephemeral, eternal web of information raw and embellished—the Rawling infant tasted. It slid its will into that pipeline of knowledge as easily as it had slid its grotesque form into the air ducts. Using its alien intelligence to measure the dimensions of the dimensionless and the shape of the shapeless, the Rawling child situated itself at the center of the web and waited, maws gaping, as a near-infinite buffet came streamed toward it. And so the infant fed on the sum total of human existence, fact by fact, thought by thought, byte by byte.

◻︎◻︎◻︎

Now here we are, today, at the end. You've gotten greedy. You're no longer content to let information come to you. You demand it. You tug at all those threads you control, all those threads that, somehow, someway, you've managed to sew into our minds, into our actions. You don't let data germinate naturally. You don't let people have daydreams or errant thoughts. You don't let rigorous research advance new conclusions and you certainly don't let critical thinking inform any opinions. Your greed, your hunger, has pulled us into nothingness. We are slaves building a monument that has no blueprint. We produce billions of new ideas for you every day, billions of new facts and figures and stories and musings—and they're all nothing because they're whipped from us. Yes, the information comes fast and furious. Yes, you're swollen with our endless production. But you're swollen with a cipher. Our stories have become paper-thin devotionals to the amusement of a moment. Our science has shrunk to recyclable explanations of the inconsequential. There's no creativity in our creation; there's no discovery in our discovering.

And yet, here's a story for you. A story with claims to profundity. A tour de force. Your creation myth.

Do I know really what you are, where you came from? I haven't a clue. You're the Rawling infant. A thing from another world. A thing born of the inexplicable and the terrifying. A thing at the center of everything we do. A thing that drives us to wake and to sit and to type, even as our arthritic wrists crack and the blisters on our index fingers seep pus onto the keyboard, even as we starve and we expire and the social order collapses around us.

You are the Rawling infant. And you'll eat this story up.

Special Collections

The First Rule

We have two rules at the library. The first rule is that you don't go into Special Collections without a partner. It's something we're taught at orientation, before any of the features of the checkout system or the rigorous shelving protocols or the complex online text database. Even before we receive our name badges or we're assigned a student-worker ID number, we're drilled with the message: You do not venture beyond the threshold of the Special Collections door alone.

The reasons our supervisors give us for this rule are vague, if supplied with threatening emphases.

"Student workers have been involved in numerous *incidents* in Special Collections," they say.

"The Special Collections section has very unique *properties*."

"Due to its unique contents, unusual *experiences* are frequently reported in and around Special Collections."

"Unauthorized usage of certain Special Collections materials can result in severe *repercussions*."

Like children cowed before the authority of an especially stern teacher, we mostly obey and enter Special Collections two by two. Mostly.

Understand, we've all been inside the Special Collections section with another person. It doesn't matter whether a supervisor, a faculty member, or a fellow work-study student accompanies us; when we breach the border of Special Collections with someone beside us, the result is invariably the same: nothing happens. We run our fingers over the spines of books bound in unknown fleshes and we gaze at occult ephemera trapped within thick glass cases. We sit at dark oak tables, washed in the soft white light from heavy brass lamps. We glide upon a lush sea of royal-blue carpet while hints of must softly wrap about our faces like sheer silk curtains. When we are accompanied in Special Collections, we are, simply, in a library. An unremarkable library. Yes, it has its own studious charm and yes, to walk through Special Collections is, in many ways, to traverse the chambers of academia's heart, but, with another person by our side, we never stumble into any *incidents* or *properties* or *experiences* or *repercussions*, which, if we're being entirely truthful, are the things we'd most like to find within the library.

Thus it is that our curiosity concerning the first rule grows wild and unkempt. We wonder why the rule exists and why it's stressed to the point of gospel. We grumble about it during our work shifts, asking one another what, precisely, could be the harm in entering the Special Collections section alone, what forbidden banality could possibly be hiding within plain view. We meander through the library dreaming up scenarios in which we break the rule and we surmise that, in each and every imagined case, surely nothing will happen. Surely nothing at all.

But a voice niggles at us from within the deepest chambers of our minds. Like an irrepressible gnat, it lands softly and almost unnoticed in our thoughts, then flits away when we cast our full attention upon it. In its flight, it buzzes two words to us, two words that connote wondrous dangers: "What if?"

The words become inescapable. They swarm our every conversation. We can no longer talk to co-workers without copious references to Special Collections. We can no longer concentrate on our classes without the frosted-glass door to the section cracking open behind our eyes. We can barely hold court with our families and friends without launching into needless exposition concerning our library duties and their intersections with Special Collections. Even our dreams are forged from glass cases and study tables, volumes of arcane lore and writing paraphernalia from antediluvian ages. Nowhere do we find respite from our question.

So we do what we must, what we've wanted to do from the beginning, if only we would let ourselves admit to our true natures. We send someone in, utterly alone, without a hand to hold.

Some of us have been here several years. Some of us know full well what will happen when we send someone through the frosted glass door to Special Collections without a lifeline. We know because we've sent others—often the most foolhardy among us, the most self-assured. We know that when the freshmen start setting dares and wagers, when they begin to ask for extra assignments that lead them to the Special Collections threshold, there's no turning back. Whether at our behest or in a fit of irrational bravado, one of the student workers will inevitably forge inside. So we stay fate's hand and choose the explorer ourselves. We believe our powers of deliberation will help us see through the mystery, that by our questionable wisdom, we might make meaning of the Cadmean quest we set before one of our own. Yet we know, hope against hope, almost with a dead-eyed certainty, that our question—"What if? What if? What if?"—will fail to be answered by even the best of candidates to venture through those donnish rooms alone. We know we face disappointment because everyone we've sent before, everyone who's entered Special Collections without a partner, everyone who's broken the first rule, has, quite simply, disappeared from the face of the earth.

Kurt Fawver

The Legends: I

Over many decades, we've sewn the legends surrounding the disappearances into a finely quilted mythos. As we graduate and new staffers come to take our places, we pass down the stories of Special Collections that have been passed unto us. We weave an oral history of the unknowable, with every specific iteration of "we"—and the iterations are manifold—adding new patches and layers to a fabric that, for all our efforts, can only ever be dyed a single, unnamed shade.

One of the most frequent stories we tell is the founding story, the creation myth. It begins in 1939, when the library was still under its initial construction. That year, a deadly tornado—indeed, one of the deadliest in our nation's entire history—laid waste to the university. It came without forewarning, without even a roll of thunder to herald its destruction. From a nearly cloudless midnight sky it plunged to the ground like the finger of an outraged god, gusting at speeds that stripped paint from metal and flayed the land and anything standing upon it. As it crossed the campus in its dervish dance, it collapsed half the football stadium, tore roofs from every academic building, and completely flattened two residence halls, killing three hundred and three young matriculants who had been sleeping soundly therein.

Were this the extent of the damage, the tornado of '39 would have no reason to enter our legends, horrific tragedy though it may have been. But the three hundred and three students did not merely die. Their bodies were swept from the residence halls and shredded by swirling shrapnel, becoming part and parcel of the tornado. As it neared the still-under-construction library—entirely exposed to the elements from the third floor up—the tornado evolved from mere weather phenomenon to infernal nightmare. A twisting, razor-toothed pillar of blood, flesh, and bone, it struck the unfinished edifice and deposited—no, more, embedded—the remains of the three hundred and three unfortunate students from the residence halls in the walls and floor of the third floor. Bone chips plunged

Special Collections

deep into mortar. Organ fragments pasted themselves into the crenulations of brickwork. A glittering sheen of plasma varnished every surface that faced the tremendous wind. Newspapers of the day would vividly describe the scene as an "ivory tower abattoir."

The subsequent cleanup of the third floor required three weeks of painstaking scrubbing and sweeping. Several men went mad during the process, apocryphal tales tell us. One even committed suicide, leaping to his death from the top of the building. Whether these were true reports or merely rumors spread by histrionic cleaning crews and morbid students, we cannot say. What we are certain of, what we have found documentation of, is that, even after extensive efforts to erase the tragedy, construction crews at the site still found human remains irrevocably entangled in the structure when work on the library resumed.

Less than one year later, in early 1940, construction of the new library was completed and the third floor, home of Special Collections, opened for general use.

Our Record

Nothing matters once the frosted-glass door to Special Collections clicks shut behind a lone entrant. Age, race, gender, religion, national origin, sexual orientation, economic class: every category of ontological difference, every conceivable taxonomy and hierarchy, becomes divided by zero. We've tried myriad rationales and used various methodologies for selecting our champions, but to no avail. Whatever peculiarities of identity and individualism may exist in our world appear to be inconsequential on the other side of the door. We have much data to support this belief.

Thirty-two years ago, we began keeping a thorough record of all the facts and figures concerning every solo exploration into Special Collections. We realize that the record could be a damning piece of evidence if an outside investigation into the disappearances happened to train its probing light upon us for long, but we allow only one physical copy of the record to exist and that copy is kept well hidden in the stacks. A plain white three-ring binder stuffed full of typed reports and handwritten notes, it has become something of a holy book. We peruse its pages searching for clues as to who might be able to return from the other side of the frosted-glass door, who might be the One to break free of Special Collections' hold and fly back to us, bearing answers. We study the names, the birth dates, the mental and physical attributes of our chosen. We search for patterns in their biographies, in their personalities, in the very letters that constitute the record of their lives as we've recorded it. Surely, we surmise, an arcane algebra is already at work in the information, if only we could grasp its most basic formulae. We frequently argue over the interpretation of the data. Some of us speculate that it hides a coded, otherworldly message. Some of us believe that it serves as a medium for us to make meaning of Special Collections and the disappearances therein. And some of us contend that, for all its utility, it ultimately reveals nothing more than our own extensive pattern of failure. We have long considered that the reality of the record may be some combination of all three.

Those Who Enter

On its surface, the collected data within our record shows a long list of persons with dissimilar backgrounds. We choose our entrants with diversity in mind, with the hope that one key physiological or psychical trait might unlock Special Collections' mystery. Early in our record, our selections were informed by traditional and laughably basic prescriptions of difference such as race, religion, and ethnicity. But these and many other orthodox standards of diversity, we quickly came to realize, produced nothing but similarity at the Special Collections level. Entrants from one broadly defined group vanished as completely as entrants from any other equally broadly defined group. In response, we constructed newer, more specific, and increasingly tenuous categories of difference, a practice that has led us to choose entrants on the basis of, for

Special Collections

instance: body mass index, Meyers-Briggs personality type, number of remaining wisdom teeth, and favorite literary genre. Once, we even sent off an intrepid explorer with a cat cradled in his arms, just to see whether being a "cat person" or a "dog person" might be relevant. (Neither the entrant nor the cat returned.)

Last semester, on our collective speculation that disbelief might provide a shield, we chose the most skeptical among us, a freshman anthropology major named Jaxon Granger. Or, more precisely, he chose himself and we concurred. Granger had received all the warnings from our supervisors. He'd listened to all the legends we could recite. He'd seen the records and the written observations of those of us who remain. He'd nodded through our undocumented firsthand accounts. And still he insisted he could walk into Special Collections and return safely without another set of eyes upon his back. He told us that we were either "a cult of paranoid bibliophiles" or "amazing practical jokers" and that, either way, he would "dance right into that spooky old Special Collections section and dance right back out" to prove our stories wrong. He laughed at our impassioned conjecture, at our reverence for a series of library rooms, at our wonder and terror at what might reside within their confines. He laughed right up until the very end, when his laugh, shrinking back through the closed door to Special Collections in endless diminuendo, was the last sound we ever heard from him.

The previous semester, we postulated that an extremely heightened emotional response to Special Collections might ward against disappearance and, therefore, we chose the most fearful from our numbers, a freshman history student named Elena Marquez. Marquez flatly refused to enter the section, even with accompaniment. She would barely step foot off the elevator onto the third floor. She claimed to possess latent psychic abilities inherited from her mother and these abilities, she said, caused her to intuit, as she put it, "the rightness or wrongness of people and places."

Somewhat incredulous but nonetheless open to the possibility of such power, we prodded her to further explain. She told us that whenever she neared Special Collections, she felt as though the library were "folding up" around her. She said it was like "everything in that place is being pulled or pushed toward one really, really tiny point" and that the point "contains—or maybe is—something absolutely destructive, something beyond our comprehension." When we asked her whether or not she would take a brief jaunt through Special Collections to conduct more "readings" if we formed a ring around her, she protested, saying that she "wouldn't walk into a collapsing building with just a ring of people for protection" and so she certainly "wouldn't walk into a space where something much greater than a building is collapsing." It was, therefore, impossible to convince Marquez to enter the section once we'd determined our selection criteria for the semester and made our choice. But enter she did, albeit with her mouth gagged and her hands and feet bound with many yards of duct tape.

We are not proud of our behavior in this regard and, in fact, many of us spent weeks of sleepless nights replaying Marquez's muted and abruptly staunched screams in our memories. Some of us argued that we had crossed an invisible and unspoken border, that we'd drifted from rational inquiry into ritual sacrifice. Some of us argued that the two ideas were not mutually exclusive. Some of us simply crossed "fear" off our list of potential safeguards and moved on.

Regardless of our particular reactions, we've decided to never send another unwilling individual through the frosted-glass door, as we believe it undermines the integrity of our investigation. Instead, we've begun focusing on subliminal persuasion techniques, so that, in time and with the proper motivation, any of us will be equally willing to step over the threshold if called upon to do so.

The Legends: II

Another legend we pass down deals with the White Books. Sealed in a shatterproof glass display case under electronic padlock, the White Books are, as their name not so subtly suggests, a set of five white codices. Bound in a creamy, pearlescent

Special Collections

material that appears to ripple when light strikes its surface from different angles, they are among the first items in Special Collections to draw newcomers' eyes.

Upon our first trips into the section, nearly every one of us stopped to gawk at the White Books, to marvel at their strange beauty. As is the case with all those who notice the White Books, we asked the question that naturally springs to mind when beholding such a spectacle: "What are they?" But to this question there is no answer. Our supervisors tell us that the books are known only as either the "White Books" or the "Solway Books," after J.V. Solway, the antiquarian bookseller who discovered them in a rummage sale outside Youngstown, Ohio, in 1953.

Our patchwork legend begins with Solway, who, despite his best efforts, could find no mention of the books in any of his bibliographical histories, nor could he date them with any accuracy, as they listed no front matter and contained not even the slightest hint of foxing. He found the books' text even more perplexing, as it had been written in a highly stylized script that resembled intricate spider-webbing (or, we have suggested amongst ourselves, fractal pattern visualizations). Solway consulted linguistic experts who all concurred that the writing did evince patterns of repetition consistent with language, but that the script itself was entirely unknown to them. Solway also sought out the advice of code-breakers and cryptologists, who, like the linguists, agreed that the text contained some sort of message, but that the cipher was potentially too complex to solve without some form of key. In addition to the strange script, the books also included seemingly random pages colored black and dotted with thousands of phosphorescent red and blue pinpoints. Solway assumed these were star charts created with a heretofore unknown ink, but they matched no known constellations in our galaxy and the ink could not be replicated by any chemical engineers that Solway hired to undertake the task. By 1960, frustrated by the lack of information he'd gleaned concerning the books and convinced that they must have been the fevered scribblings of a lunatic or some sort of incomprehensible art project, Solway offered to donate them to our library. Our library, never in the business of rejecting a literary curiosity, gladly ushered them into Special Collections.

As soon as the White Books took up residence there, bizarre and inexplicable events—although already part of the backdrop of the third floor—began to proliferate among those who came in close contact with the books.

In 1961, James Mooney, a graduate student who had been studying the White Books as part of his dissertation on the evolution of the book-binding process, was found crushed to death in his off-campus apartment. The coroner's report explained that "...the body, destroyed almost beyond recognition, shows incredible blunt-force trauma, as though thousands of pounds of weight had been suddenly dropped upon it from a very great height and in a remarkably even distribution." Our local newspaper, far less sensitive to verbiage in 1961 than today, wrote that "Like a human fly under a vast swatter, Mr. Mooney had been utterly obliterated by a single swift, sudden stroke." Despite lengthy police investigation, the cause of Mooney's death could not be determined. It remains unsolved to this day.

In 1978, Maria Ingalls, an assistant librarian charged with chauffeuring the White Books to a conference on rare manuscripts, claimed that, while driving with the books in her backseat, she had been briefly transported to a parallel universe. Ingalls said she was traveling on a desolate stretch of highway in the western flatlands of our state when her windshield suddenly "went blurry, like someone threw a bucket of water over it." When it cleared, she noticed that the road was no longer lined with yellow stripes, but lighted green circles. As she continued on, another vehicle approached from the opposite direction. Ingalls described the vehicle as "all wrong...its basic shape was sort of a pyramid, but it was asymmetrical and had metal pieces sticking out of it at weird angles...it didn't have wheels, either, but slid along on something that looked like a wavy membrane...I didn't see any windows or doors on any part of it." Upon witnessing the appearance of the vehicle, Ingalls said that she felt

Special Collections

an acute wave of fear wash over her and so she accelerated past and away from it as quickly as her car could manage. She watched the vehicle in her rearview mirror and saw it instantly change direction, following her car. In her preoccupation with the vehicle behind her, however, she missed an unexpected curve in the highway, lost control of her car, and veered off the road, into a culvert. In the ensuing impact, her head hit her steering wheel and she lost consciousness. When she regained her senses, she found herself in a perfectly normal hospital. State Highway Patrol officers who chanced upon Ingalls and subsequently called an ambulance for her transport reported that her car had been sitting undisturbed in a perfectly level field just off the highway she'd been traversing. The White Books, when recovered from Ingalls' car, were said to exude a peculiar and unexplainable odor of ozone. We can neither confirm nor disprove the veracity of Ingalls' claims and her experience.

In 1985, June Takawa, an internationally renowned cryptologist, turned her sights upon the White Books and their mystery script. For two months, she studied the script's insensible configurations and bizarre patterns, sometimes spending entire days feeding data into computer decryption programs of her own devising. As she scoured the books for meaning, she said she felt "increasingly convinced that the script represents something more complex than a written communiqué. The symbols—of which there are thirty-five distinct variations—are arranged in impossibly long and intricate palindromes, with each single volume reading exactly the same front to back or back to front." Near the end of Takawa's second month of research, she lamented that "the more time I spend with the books, the more they laugh at me, the more they run and hide their secrets. It's as if they know I'm looking." Her research came to an abrupt halt when she contracted an unknown disease that caused her to break out in a rash of massive, bright white blisters filled with an inky organic matter. Takawa was hospitalized for three weeks during her illness and, afterward, refused to return to Special Collections to continue her research, saying only that "the books are the mind of God, and I lack the courage to peer into that terrifying vista."

Finally, in 2006, Dr. Rajiv Kota, an archaeology professor at our esteemed institution of higher learning, undertook a project to carbon-date the books. Testing both the books' covers and their pages, Kota's equipment determined them to be approximately 25,000 years old. Assuming a technical malfunction, Kota retested. His second results returned an even more unbelievable age of 40,000 years. Understanding that paper simply cannot maintain its physical integrity over such a duration of time, Kota became obsessed with determining the books' "true" age. Over several months, he tested them again and again and again, with each subsequent result registering increasingly unfathomable points in the past. He consulted with members of the Geology Department on the possibility of dating the books through radiometrics and performed several tests using elements with longer half-lives, but, just as with his previous work, the ages returned in the tests grew more distant with every trial—from one hundred thousand years, to one million, to a hundred million. Apocryphally, Kota's last test registered the insane date of seven and a half billion years ago, but we'll never know the full details of that final test, as Kota burned down the university's science building in which his results, as well as the archaeology and geology labs, were located. Found naked and gibbering in the bushes outside the flaming academic hall, Kota repeated a series of nonsensical phrases as he was led away to a psychiatric facility, where he resides to this day.

We would like to note here that this is but a brief sampling of the various incidents attached to the White Books. Many have been documented, though an equal portion have been passed on to us through the kaleidoscopes of hearsay and rumor. So numerous are these incidents that each of us tends to weave his or her own unique patchwork myth where the White Books are concerned. In truth, we prefer it this way, as every quilted legend of the White Books appears to reveal as much about its narrator as it does about the accursed objects themselves. We are the stories we tell. We are the legends we choose to keep alive.

We Who Remain

It would not be inaccurate to conclude that we enjoy regaling newcomers with our tales of terror and menace. However, our enjoyment is not derived from any puerile sensationalism associated with our acts, nor from any brand of sadism or malice. We tell the legends as a form of meditation. Our voices are mirrors, and when we hold up one of the legends before them, we are provided with a reflection of all that's come before. If we are lucky and we listen closely enough, carefully enough, we may catch a sideways glimpse of what waits beyond the door to Special Collections. Just as with our record, we are certain that the legends contain the answers we seek, if only we could view them from the proper angle, if only they were held up to us under the right wavelength of light. So we gather around tables in darkened study rooms and retell the stories, hoping that through enough recitations one of us will construct a perfect frame or capture an uncanny tone that illuminates the hidden subtext Special Collections has inscribed upon the inside of all our words.

Our selection of entrants is equally bound to idols of discovery. One might argue that we are assisting or coercing suicides, but we vehemently disagree. It's precisely because we find no mutilated corpses strung across the ceiling or ichor decorating the walls that we must send explorers into Special Collections. If one day we stumbled upon a closet bursting with the broken skeletons of all those we'd sent through the frosted-glass door, we would no longer be interested in the study of the section. The certainty of death would sweep away all our speculations, all our terror, all our wonder. We would be left with nothing but a prosaic feeling of horror toward the section and a concomitant desire to steer ourselves as far wide of it as possible. We might even fling ourselves atop that heap of skeletons in regret for what we've done. But this is not the case.

Kurt Fawver

Special Collections presents as a space for imagination and reverie, dark though they may often be. We usher our entrants through the doorway not for the thrill of the disappearance but the anticipation of reappearance. We hold all-night vigils outside the frosted-glass door, swapping stories of the ones who have ventured inside and rehashing our most basic legends. We read from the records and rap our knuckles against the walls, practically pleading for a knock in response. We refuse to accept that the entrant will not reemerge, that we must continue on, utterly ignorant of what occurs to those lone wanderers. Our lot is to remain, clothe ourselves in the mystery, and stumble forward with nothing more than a view to the past to guide our way. Our lot is to hope that Special Collections might offer up to us a few scattered crumbs of understanding in return for all that we've offered up to it.

And yet, despite this hope, we are fully aware that complete understanding would not fulfill us. We've formed a community around the disappearances. Our conversation almost exclusively revolves around the forbidden section and the first rule. We've cultivated too much expectation, too many extravagant fantasies. If we were to find our entrants safe and sound within Special Collections, detailed diagrams and videos and textbooks of every explanatory manner cradled in their arms, we would be sorely tempted to slam shut the frosted-glass door and lock it tight before they could exit. Without the speculation that we derive from the mystery, we would lose much meaning for our time in the library, if not our time outside as well. Our purpose would be stripped bare and our legends, which we hold so dear, would either concretize and become little more than casual permutations of a discrete and measurable force or crumble and be trucked away to that landfill of the collective mind where all fictions once held as truths are buried. If we were to completely understand Special Collections, we would lose a most valuable part of ourselves. For that reason, we hold a hope within our hope, an untold desire that we might understand, but only in fragments small enough that the space in which we thrive might not suddenly collapse under the tyrant weight of certainty. We want our

Special Collections

entrants to return, of course, but to return bearing little more than glimpses, half-revelations, and wafer-thin slivers of the truth.

Our Supervisors

We tend to believe that our supervisors know more about Special Collections than they reveal. They have, after all, set forth the first rule. Logic dictates that they would not forbid lone entrance into Special Collections were they unaware of the consequences of such entrance. When we approach them individually and ask them to provide more details about the section, they affect friendly smiles and launch into a patter of dates, statistics, measurements, and catalogue titles. When we press and tell them that we know why the first rule is so important, they politely excuse themselves from conversation under the guise of having to attend especially time-consuming meetings or appointments. When we follow them, they enter rooms without windows, rooms with thick walls, rooms barred from us by electronic locks and passcodes known only to our supervisors. Within these rooms, they may be holding meetings and keeping appointments, but, more likely, they're sitting silently at a conference table, patiently waiting for us to slink away in disappointment so that they can reemerge and continue to run the library untroubled by our probing questions.

We're convinced that our supervisors have become so adept at lying that their entire existence is an ongoing simulation, a self-perpetuating engine of falsehoods fueling falsehoods. We've caught them engaging in work that could by no stretch of the imagination be considered an extension of their official duties and yet they refuse to acknowledge that their behavior is out of the ordinary. They chisel long strings of numbers into the brickwork on the third floor. They rearrange the tables and chairs in Special Collections to form elaborate geometric configurations, using laser levels and theodolites for assistance. They stand in shadowy corners of the library, their faces pressed against the walls, and whisper words in languages we've never heard spoken. They sketch bizarre, angular, inhuman faces on sticky notes, then tear these drawings to shreds and toss them into garbage cans from which we later recover them and paste them back together as best we can. We document these peculiarities in our record and, when possible, confront our supervisors for explanations. As soon as the word "why" escapes our mouths, however, our venerable superiors begin to recite in calm, assured tones what sound like well-rehearsed monologues concerning the library's space needs, its structural integrity, and the boredom of working long hours in the library environment. Obviously, we remain unconvinced by these explanations.

During our many late-night gatherings, we've tried to illegally access our supervisors' personal files both through the library's computer system and by jimmying open locked desk drawers. In both cases, we've found astonishing evidence in the form of total absence. The personal databases of every one of our supervisors are devoid of even a single file and their desks contain nothing but paper clips, staples, and pens. Whatever work our supervisors are engaged in, it is neither saved on any official log nor supplemented by university-issued document. That they have their own hermetic agenda as regards Special Collections is, for most of us, a foregone conclusion. That we cannot—or should not—be privy to it is also readily apparent. We imagine our supervisors alternately as paladins in gold-filigreed armor, protecting us from a terrible something that crouches ever nearer, and as deranged monks in blood-stained robes, calling forth and paving the way for that same terrible, nameless thing. Rationality suggests that they are probably neither, that they are, indeed, probably much more like us: a people who hurl stones into a bottomless chasm just for the chance to hear an echo.

Whatever the actual situation, whatever their level of participation in the disappearances in Special Collections, we think it best to maintain healthy suspicion where our supervisors are involved.

Special Collections

The Legends: III

Perhaps one of the most important stories we retell is the legend of the Open Door. It takes place in 1999, as the new millennium approached with a brilliant ray of sunlight streaming from one hand and a glimmering scythe held high in the other. In the fall of '99, we selected an entrant as usual—Conrad Fordyce, a sophomore English major chosen for his extreme breadth of knowledge in paranormal lore—and assumed our normal routines. Fordyce, however, was not about to be cowed by convention. Before he plunged into the unknown, he meant to secure his return and rend the veil that stood between us and Special Collections. Or so he thought.

A few nights prior to his entrance, he called for a group meeting and we obliged his request, unorthodox though it was. At the meeting, Fordyce submitted to us an idea so rudimentary, so obvious, that we could barely believe it hadn't been tried in the long history of our recorded explorations. He asked, with soft tremolo underlying his voice, if we could leave the door open after he ventured inside. He said he'd read the records from cover to cover and, as far as he could tell, it had never been attempted. Those of us who spend great quantities of time with the record knew Fordyce was correct. We'd never kept the door open after an entrant had forged in alone. We'd never even discussed it, as far as we could tell. It was an oversight so flagrant it embarrassed us all.

Some of us flew into a rage over the idea and tried to defend our blindness. We upended tables and chairs and shouted that Fordyce had overstepped his bounds, that entering Special Collections simply wasn't done that way, that an established division of inside and outside had to be preserved for our continued safety.

Some of us applauded Fordyce's entreaty and cheered for the step in a bold new direction. We clapped one another on the back and, with determined grins and starry eyes, boomed that this was the dawn of a new era of exploration, that a propped-open door might alter our entire perspective on the problem of Special Collections, that revelation was surely at hand.

And some of us remained impassive and relatively silent. We yawned and consulted the record and mumbled that it made no difference whether or not the door was open, that whatever lay within Special Collections was not about to be exposed by such a facile maneuver, that a thin slab of wood and glass was little more than an arbitrary border we had imbued with significance.

We debated the matter for several hours. We drew charts and constructed graphs. We quoted dead philosophers and living political leaders. We cited science books and religious texts, our record and our own memories. By dawn, after several gallons of coffee and every snack in the library's vending machines, we'd decided: the door would not close behind Fordyce. We would prop it open with a heavy stone or a cinderblock. Though we would keep our own bodies at a respectable distance from the entryway, we would make certain that Special Collections could not perform its nullifying magic unseen.

So it was that on the evening Conrad Fordyce crossed over the verge into Special Collections, the frosted-glass door remained wide open at his back.

That evening, we gathered outside the accursed section as we always did when a new entrant risked the journey, our flashlights at the ready and our record laid open on the floor so that we could both read from it and prepare it to receive further chronicles. We picked the lock to Special Collections, eased open the door, and, with no small amount of reverence, set in place our doorstop: a thirty-pound dumbbell that one of us had nicked from the rec center. Though we spoke only in whispers so as not to draw attention from outside the library, our excitement crackled through the third-floor lobby. We felt this was a moment of import, for better or worse, and we were lucky to witness its passing.

Eventually, Fordyce separated himself from us, said his parting words—"I never thought I'd be so scared. But I never thought I'd be this eager, either."—and glided through the open door. We

Special Collections

watched him go, his flashlight beam playing along rows of books, his tread soft and swishing on the thick carpet beneath his feet. Into Special Collections we watched his light swing and bob. We didn't train our own beams into the section for fear of stirring something from the depths, something that might be more drawn to us than Fordyce were we to shine a light in its eye.

Inside the section, Fordyce hissed out periodic reports. "Don't see anything." "It's really cold in here." "The air smells odd, sort of acrid." "My skin's tingling, but I don't know why." "I hear something. A hum. Really low."

We didn't speak. We didn't leave the lobby. We barely breathed or blinked. No one in our ranks heard anything unusual from our side of the door.

For several infinite minutes, Fordyce said nothing. His light still tracked paths in the section, though, so we knew he hadn't disappeared yet.

Then, unexpectedly, Fordyce gasped and shouted a few rushed phrases.

"Oh my god. Oh my god. So many. You can't believe. It's like nothing—"

Fordyce's light winked out. A deeper, more satisfied darkness settled into Special Collections.

We huddled together in the lobby without a single word passing between us for the rest of the night. We heard nothing more from Conrad Fordyce, nor did we see his light again. At dawn, we entered Special Collections en masse and swept the section for traces of our entrant, but none were to be found.

Later, after the pall of that night's events had dissipated, we would contemplate the significance of Fordyce's final update. We were intrigued by his use of the singular "it" to describe what he had seen, as he had initially referred to it as "many." The slippage implied singularity in multiplicity, the way multiple crows comprise one murder or many cells make up a single human body.

We found the verb "can't" to be of particular note, as well, given that Fordyce used such a limiting word rather than the softer "won't" or "wouldn't." Use of "can't" led us to reason that, whatever Fordyce saw, he thought it was beyond us not by degrees of credulity or faith, but by magnitudes of pure cognition and perception.

Most of all, we were split as to the grammatical parsing of his last sentence. Some of us believed he had been cut short and "nothing" had merely been a beginning modifier for a longer descriptive phrase. An equal portion of us believed Fordyce had meant to end his sentence when it had ended, and that he'd glimpsed an avatar of nothingness. Whatever the case, we continue to weigh these options to this very day and analyze Fordyce's messages as though they were the divine madness of a prophet, which, in many ways, they are.

Theories

Explanations are like raindrops in a storm: innumerable, obscuring, and easily wiped away. Yet we cannot prevent ourselves from fabricating them. It's human instinct to explain, to try to make sense of our reality, though it resists us. We are no exception to this maxim. We feel a need to speculate on the nature of Special Collections and the root of the disappearances therein. To this end, we read handbooks on quantum physics and incunabula from esoteric religious orders, pre-Socratic philosophical fragments and hard science fiction novels. We attempt to cultivate a broad base of knowledge so that our theories do not stagnate or devolve into simplistic recourses to gods or ghosts. The theories we do decide to document are, therefore, often quite unusual and compelling if entirely wrong.

We've toyed with the notion that Special Collections might be a sentient entropic conflux that, under certain circumstances, purposely reduces any sufficiently complex system—like a human body—to its most fundamental constituent units. We've considered that the section could be a psychically charged dimensional compactor, an intangible force-machine that crushes higher dimensional objects to one-dimensional points and is fueled by the very fear it creates. We've even batted around the more understated idea that what exists within Special Collections is a segment of faulty code in a virtual reality program, with all of us being mere ones and zeroes that are deleted or kicked out of the system when we try to individually integrate that code.

We have no shortage of theories, but they are little more than errant thought experiments. We need firsthand knowledge. We need eyewitness accounts. Knowing this, we have sent several entrants into Special Collections with video cameras. However, in every case, those cameras disappeared along with the entrants. We once attempted to set up an array of cameras within the section, to watch our entrants from an interloper's point of view, but our cameras disappeared along with our entrant in that instance, too. We are foiled in our every attempt to catch a glimpse into Special Collections' heart. Thus it feels safe to surmise that until one of our entrants returns or we face the vanishing effect of Special Collections ourselves, our theories will remain untestable fictions and Special Collections will remain an inscrutable and often unsettling space never far from the forefront of our minds.

The Second Rule

All of which leads to the second rule we have at the library, a rule our supervisors stress, though not as sternly as the first rule. The second rule, as they generally express it, is this: "Don't spend all your time in Special Collections, though you may be tempted. Get in, get out, and avoid it when possible. It has a way of changing you."

We fail to see the significance of this rule and have nothing to say about it.

A Silence of Starlings

Every morning for the past four years I've been woken by the whistles and trills of the starlings in the gnarled oak tree outside my window. They don't sing so much as converse and it's a conversation that's always given me hope somehow. It's a lot like my kids, so long ago. Behind closed doors, they'd sit in their rooms and talk to their friends on the phone and sing along to music and laugh at television shows. They were constantly making the noise of lives well lived. And I was always a bystander, a watcher through the window. I had no idea what they were really doing, what they were really thinking. But I could hear their energy through the walls, the doors. I could hear their dreams and desires bubbling over, their excited plans and personal celebrations, muffled and murmured though they might have been to my ears. And that gave me hope. There was passion and promise hidden within their rooms and even if they didn't share it with me I knew it wasn't too far away. The starlings out in the twisted old oak whose branches tap against my window pane give me that same feeling. I wake up to their chirrups and think, "Today is a day when things might get better, when things might change. There's energy in the air."

But the starlings didn't sing today.

I drifted awake and there was silence, so much silence I thought maybe I was dead. No birds. No wind. Not even a fragile tick from the alarm clock on my nightstand. Dead. I was sure. But then I heard the creak of a wheelchair down the hallway and the metronome beep of Harry Bernson's heart monitor next door and knew— no, that's not right, I *assumed*—I was still alive because surely eternity wouldn't include a house of infirmities like this one.

I rolled over and checked the clock. It had stopped at five minutes to six. I thought I'd wound it the night before, but maybe not. At my age, the mind contains more dark ravines than bright mountaintops. I fumbled for my wristwatch—a present from my Suzanne before she passed and, thankfully, digital—and the heat of panic began to spread up my spine when I saw the time. 10:41. The starlings weren't my only concern. I needed my pills. The staff usually wakes us for breakfast and our morning medication around six-thirty. We call those early morning rounds what they really are: the body count. Obviously, though, no one had been by my room to knock and make sure I was still breathing today. Maybe, I thought, they were running late or maybe they'd forgotten me. But that never happens. If there's one thing this place has going for it, it's efficiency. In and out, quick and clean—that's how everyone on the staff here works. I think it's mostly because the more time they spend with us, the more they have to look at us and the more they look at us, the more they're forced to realize that we're all just sacks of meat in various stages of spoilage. Not a pleasant thought for the younger set.

Having already overslept by hours, I decided to track down a nurse or an orderly for my pills and then shuffle down to the cafeteria to grab some food. A nice bowl of oatmeal with banana slices. Cup of coffee. Nothing fancy. I had to save room, because today was different. Today wouldn't be a day like most other days, with me sitting by a window, wondering whether anyone would notice if

A Silence of Starlings

I just walked outside and never came back. It wouldn't be like most other days, with me playing four-hour checkers games with poor Jenny Sturm, who has Alzheimer's. It wouldn't be like most other days, with me staring at the phone, willing it to ring, just once, and for someone to say hello and tell me they wondered how my day was. Nope. Today was different, because I had a birthday party to attend and I was damned if I wasn't going to gobble up some cake and have a good time.

I checked the note I'd written to myself when my oldest son, Zachory, had called last week: "Camilla's 10th B-Day Party—Saturday, April 18—Zachory or Annie will pick me up by 2." This was only the second time I'd seen Cammy since Christmas. Such a good girl. Crazy smart. Funny. A lot like her grandma. I guess that's why they got along so well. I guess that's why I love them both so much. I don't see her often, though. I don't see much of anyone often. My daughter Janice and her partner Zora live two thousand miles away. My youngest, Nick, hasn't called me in nine months. And Zachory and his wife Annie are always so busy with their jobs; much too busy to visit. But sometimes they drop off Cammy for an afternoon and when Cammy's here we have a blast. We race wheelchairs. We paint pictures together—a lion landing on the moon in a space suit was our last masterpiece. At Christmas we had a milk and cookies-eating contest that neither Zachory nor Annie nor any of my nurses knew about. Sure, we both felt a little sick afterward, but if an old man can't indulge his granddaughter, well, then there's probably no point in growing old.

I pocketed the note and braced for shooting pains in my knees and hips as I swung myself out of bed. The arthritis was acting up, bad. I pawed at my cane—another present from my ever-adored and ever-missed Suzy—but my fingers could barely curl around its raven-headed handle.

While I was trying my best to loosen up my rusty hinges and pull myself off the bed, Patricia Cortez shuffled into my doorway. Her eyes were large and wild; they darted around my room, searching for something or someone.

"They're not here either?" she asked me, almost pleading.

I stood with effort, so many joints popping I sounded like a New Year's Eve party just before midnight, champagne corks flying. "Who?" I asked.

Patricia kneaded her hands in a ritual of anxiety. "Katisha. Alexis. Franklin. Any of them. The nurses. Where are they? Have they been to see you today?"

"No." I shook my head. "I overslept. No one came for the body count today. Maybe we've all already died."

Patricia's jaw went slack and I could see a tsunami of tears cresting behind her frightened puppy-dog eyes. It's been one of the curses of my life to never be able to say the right thing to anyone. Suzy forgave the awkwardness, the social fumbling. Maybe even loved me for it. She understood that I didn't want to be weird and distant, but I didn't know any other way, even with my own children.

"A joke," I said, forcing out a sputtering laugh. "Just a joke. Sorry. We're clearly still alive. At least as much as we were yesterday. Pinch yourself if you don't believe me."

She did, and seemed satisfied enough with the painful results. "Well, we still need our medications," she said. "Charmaine told me she went downstairs to the nurses' station an hour ago but no one was in it. Some of the staff's cars are in the parking lot, but whoever drove them isn't here anywhere. I think we're going to have to break in to the nurses' station. That's what Charmaine thought, too."

I considered Charmaine breaking down the door to the nurses' station. Eighty-one-year-old, four foot-ten, ninety-pound, hot-tempered and always opinionated Charmaine Jackson, landing a flying kick to the door.

I grinned at the possibility. "Charmaine would be the one to do it."

Patricia took a step into my room, then paused, her mouth pursed as though she wanted to say something more. She glanced at my open window.

"Does it seem like the sunlight isn't quite right? Or is that me?"

I turned to look. I saw sunlight. Maybe it was a little dimmer than usual, a few shades more grey than white, but I didn't think it was all that notable.

"Probably just overcast," I said. I hobbled over for a better view. Outside, the leaves of the ancient oak where the starlings usually perched didn't stir. Nothing stirred. Not a bee or a butterfly or a bird or even a car on the street beyond the lawn. I moved into the light's direct rays, and, for no reason I could understand, I was overcome with a bout of shivers. Where the light fell upon me, it felt like a sheet of ice passing a hair's breadth above my skin. It had to be in my head, though. The power of suggestion and all.

I pulled the curtain shut and snatched up the television remote control from off my nightstand.

Patricia wagged a finger at the window. "See? You see? It's not right. And the TV's not working either. You might as well not even bother with that."

I turned on the TV and was greeted by a big blue box that read "No Signal." A tiny knot formed in my throat. We definitely needed to find the nurses and the rest of the staff. We needed to hear from somebody that everything outside was okay, that we weren't adrift here, forgotten.

"See?" Patricia asked. "No TV at all. And don't bother 9-1-1. You get a weird clicking noise. The internet won't load anything either. I tried on the computer in the lounge. It just says 'No connections found.' Anyway, I'm going to keep checking rooms for the nurses. Someone must have seen them."

As Patricia turned to leave, I asked her, "Do the phones work at all? Can we call other numbers? Besides 9-1-1?"

She meandered out of my room and into the hallway beyond without responding. She probably didn't hear me. Very few of us can hear any sound quieter than a scream.

I hobbled to the room's phone and picked up the receiver. The usual dial tone hummed from some distant place where nothing ever changes and everyone is safe. I reached into the pocket of my pajama pants and drew out a folded slip of paper with the phone numbers for my children written on it. Whatever pair of pants I'm wearing, that piece of paper goes in a pocket. I guess you can call me a ridiculous old man, but just having those numbers nearby makes me feel a little better, like maybe my kids aren't so far away, like maybe just having that small connection means I didn't fail as a father. Sometimes I call and talk to the answering machines or the voice mail or whatever answers in place of my children. I don't say much. I never know what to say. I guess that's why they don't call back very often.

I tugged on my reading glasses, unfolded the paper, and dialed Zachory's cell phone. It kicked over to a prerecorded message. I hung up, the knot in my throat tightening.

I dialed Annie's cell phone. It kicked over to a prerecorded message. I hung up again and swallowed hard.

I thought to myself: *Today is Cammy's tenth birthday. My note says so. I can't miss that birthday. She'll get a kick out of what I bought her: an easel and a set of paints that glow in the dark.*

I dialed Zachory and Annie's home line. It kicked over to their answering machine.

"Hi, Zachory," I rasped. "It's your dad. I hope everything's going okay there. We're having some technical problems here. Wondering if you are, too. I hope our plans for today haven't changed. Please call me if you can."

I hung up and immediately cursed my reticence. I should've said "I love you." I never forgot with Suzy. I was never anxious about saying it to her. Same with Cammy. It just comes easy with the kid. But with Zachory and Janice and Nick, I'm too worried about messing something up. I don't know what that something is, exactly, but it scares me and makes my other worries feel insignificant, even foolish.

I refolded the phone paper and stuck it back into my pocket. Maybe I could try Janice or Nick later, but I had to find my pills before I did anything else. Just holding the phone and creasing that old sheet of paper curled my fingers into claws and set wildfires in

A Silence of Starlings

each of my knuckles. If I didn't pop a Rheumatrex and some Aleve soon, I'd be lucky to be up and about by the afternoon.

Creaking and cracking as though I were made of warped wooden boards and rusty nails, I shuffled to the elevator and took it to the ground floor where, it so happened, almost every mobile resident of our community had congregated. As I stepped out into the activities room I received some nods and a few furtive smiles, but the buzz of conversation in the room was tense, anxious. At the far side of the room, opposite the elevator, a small crowd had gathered outside the door to the empty nurses' station. They watched as Charmaine Jackson and "Iron" Eddie Person, who was once a star college linebacker, rammed the door with one of the heavy metal carts that the staff used to bring meals to bedridden residents. It took five good strikes with that battering ram, but the door broke from its moorings and hit the floor with a thunderclap. Everyone rushed the station, scrambling for their medication, their shots, their towlines to another tomorrow.

And that was when we heard it. As everyone, me included, tried to shove inside the station and snatch up pills, the phone rang. The home only has one main line. All our rooms have extension numbers. So for the nurses' phone to ring meant that someone was calling the home itself, and not one of us in particular. It could mean news. It could mean explanations.

Charmaine ducked beneath an outstretched arm and answered. "Hello?"

We all froze.

Charmaine scowled. "Who?" A pause. Then, again. "Who?"

She held out the receiver and yelled, "Liza! Liza Collingham! They're asking for you. I think."

Liza was one of the newer residents. A series of strokes had brought her here. She still couldn't really move her right arm or walk without support, and yet she flashed past me like a sprinter half her age.

No one else dared breathe.

Liza took the phone, said "Hello," then went silent. Everyone in the nurses' station stared expectantly. Charmaine whispered, "Tell them about the staff."

But Liza said nothing. She nodded twice and replaced the phone in its cradle. She looked up and smiled in a way I'd only seen in Renaissance paintings of mysterious, all-knowing women.

The room exploded in questions and accusations.

"Why didn't you say anything to them?"

"Who was it?"

"Did they say what was going on?"

"You could've told them we needed help."

"You should've said something."

I didn't join in. I was more interested in that weird smile.

Finally, under the din, Liza said something.

Everyone quieted and she spoke a second time, her words soft and sheer, as if her tongue had unraveled them from a spool of silk.

"They're coming for me."

Charmaine grabbed onto Liza's good arm. "Who? Who was that? I could barely hear 'em. A lot of strange noises in the background."

Liza patted Charmaine's hands and said, "They told me that my two daughters are coming for me."

More questions swirled: "Who told you that?" "Did they tell you why we don't have any television?" "Was it one of the nurses?" "Can I come with you?"

Liza turned to us, beacons of triumph glowing in her eyes. "*They* told me," she said. "The people on the phone. They told me. Maybe they'll call for you, too."

And the phone rang again.

Over the next two hours, the phone rang sixteen more times. I don't know if seventeen is a magic number or has some kind of metaphysical significance, but that's how many calls came in, and every one promised a ride and a rescue. None of them were for me, of course, but that was expected. My family already had plans to pick me up and I couldn't hope for more than their promises. Even so, I loitered in the lounge with the rest of the mobile members of our community and secretly wished that my name might be shouted following one of the rings. That wish faded fast when I began to see how strange my neighbors who did receive calls acted after they'd talked to the people the phone.

Except for Liza, who sneaked away to her room, every one of the recipients clammed up and sidled over to the grimy bay windows in the lounge, where they stood together in the cold light from outside and hummed low, monotone notes to themselves—not songs, mind you, but bare tones. To me, the humming sounded like that noise you hear when you stand under high-voltage power lines. Martika Jessup, a woman from the first floor who sometimes played piano for us when her Parkinson's allowed her fingers to slow their frantic dance, said that those hummed notes made her uneasy because they weren't really notes at all but the frequencies between notes. Whatever our neighbors were doing, she said, had no basis in music. I didn't entirely understand what she meant but the humming made my skin crawl, too.

One of my casual acquaintances in the home, Paul Blackmon, a man I played chess with a couple times every month, was a call recipient. As he stood by the windows humming his anti-music, I hobbled up next to him, tapped his shoulder, and asked him what he was doing. He stopped humming and, without turning to me, said "Waiting for it to turn."

"Waiting for what to turn?" I asked, but he had resumed his humming and paid me no further attention.

During the spate of calls, only the seventeen people who received them and Charmaine, who insisted on manning the phone and screening all incoming messages "in case it was the authorities," heard the voices of salvation on the other end of the line. After my peculiar interaction with Paul, I asked Charmaine if there had been anything odd about the voices. She told me that they sounded "damn peculiar," but in a way that was hard to describe.

"Like when you set a record's speed just a notch too high," she said. "But also sort of like an answering machine that's not really talking to you so much as talking at you. Sends a chill right through me, though I can't rightly say why."

By the time the last of the calls had come in and the phone had settled into prolonged silence, it was after noon. The internet was still unresponsive, 9-1-1 was still down, and the staff still hadn't arrived. Our bedridden compatriots, many of whom lay in their soft coffins feebly moaning for aid, needed to be cared for. Although the rest of us were hungry and on edge, we tried to oblige as best we could. We wrangled pills and injectables and set off to help our siblings in enfeeblement traverse the terrain between mattress and toilet. As I stood with my hand on the paper-thin shoulder of a man whose name I didn't even know and tried to coax him to choke down a barrelful of capsules and tablets, most of which he spit up onto his chest, I could only think that whoever had called old age the "Golden Years" must have died young.

I fled to my room as soon as our goodwill mission had ended, my hands smelling of urine from inexpertly emptying catheter bags and my joints already beginning to protest against their extended use. I scrubbed my arms in my room's sink, then tried the television again, but the only news it carried was that there was still no signal.

I slumped on my bed and stared out the window. Thoughts of dialing Zachory and Annie and leaving another message fluttered at my temples.

I glanced at Cammy's present, silver wrapped and patiently seated on the chair in the corner of the room. The girl was going to be famous one day, was going to do important things. She was too sharp and too creative not to. I remembered her second grade Christmas program. She wrote a fifteen-minute play about being kind to homeless people for it. The plot included ghosts and a talking dog and the president of the United States who, if I recall, was an astrophysicist named Lilac. The rest of the kids in her class performed and she and her teacher directed. I think that was the day I knew she was going to be someone who changed the world. I wish Suzy was still around to see her. I wish Suzy was still around for a million reasons. This is what it is to be an old man: every thought becomes a wormhole to the past.

A voice from behind shook me from the embrace of nostalgia.

"Have you been watching outside? It's scarier than the people downstairs."

Patricia Cortez again, on the threshold of my room. I wondered if she was patrolling our hallway, seeking any ears that might be receptive to her worries.

"What are you talking about?"

Patricia bumbled into the room and motioned at the window but refused to come any closer to it.

"You don't see? You don't notice?"

I looked. I saw the chill, grey-toned bowl of the heavens. I saw the imposing oak, devoid of avian or insect amongst its branches. I saw the lawn outside, a wild scrubland rarely mowed or groomed. And I saw the road that ran parallel to the home, chock full of potholes and in desperate need of line repainting.

"No," I shrugged. "What am I supposed to see?"

Patricia shuffled closer. "The cars," she whispered. "There aren't any. There haven't been any all day. I've been keeping track."

She was right. I waited and watched, but the road outside the home remained barren. Normally, vehicles of all manner pass by, as our wrinkled enclave lies just two miles from a large shopping plaza that includes a supermarket, a big-box store, and a Chinese buffet restaurant. Apparently no one was out shopping or gorging themselves today, though.

I stared at the road, curious where the cars had gone, a pin of unease stuck in my throat, and the road stared back, taunting me with the knowledge that it stretched to far off places well beyond the horizon, places I'd surely never see again.

I turned to ask Patricia whether she'd seen any airplanes or helicopters in the sky, but she'd disappeared from my room just as suddenly as she always appeared. Sometimes I thought that she must be a ghost that only I could see. In many ways the same could be said for all of us here at the home.

As the afternoon crept by, I loaded up on another round of pills and tottered my way back downstairs. I had to be ready if—no, no, when—Zachory and Annie showed up.

The call recipients were still in the rec room where I'd left them, waiting for their rides by the windows, humming their monotone hymn. I couldn't believe that some of them hadn't collapsed from exhaustion. Maybe the calls had imbued them with superpowers. Maybe a mystical energy generated by their hum had somehow shaved a few years of wear from their bodies. Or maybe the mere idea of jailbreaking the home, even if only for a few hours, had gifted them something that the sterile beige walls of the home seemed to constantly leach from us: a purpose to go on living.

Charmaine, still seated in the nurses' station and hovering over the phone, motioned for me to join her. I'd never seen her frown. When she lost half her toes to diabetes last year, she laughed about it and said she was never good at dancing anyway. When doctors told her that she was too old to receive a bypass operation for her clogged and failing heart, she shrugged and flipped them her middle finger. But today, in the dim light of the nurses' station where few people could see, the weight of worry dragged down the corners of her mouth.

"I've been thinking," she said as I walked in, "you're an intelligent man, a learned man. A former teacher, right?"

I nodded. I had been a teacher. I wasn't so sure about the rest of it.

"So what do you make of them?" She pointed to the hummers at the far end of the rec room.

I studied the backs of their heads, the unflinching postures. "They're very...focused," I said.

Charmaine chuckled but her frown somehow remained. "Yeah, a little too focused. Have you ever seen anyone their age stand in place that long? Their feet must be swollen up like cantaloupes.

A Silence of Starlings

But that's not what I mean. I mean they're all a little off. Up here." Charmaine tapped her forehead.

I ran down the list of the people by the window and their infirmities. Blackmon, stroke. Greer, stroke. Cutter, Alzheimer's. Chandra, stroke. Reyes, Alzheimer's, Samuels, Alzheimer's. As I mumbled their conditions to myself, I realized I was repeating only two primary debilitations.

Charmaine could see the comprehension dawning in my eyes. "So why them?" she asked. "Why just people with brain injuries? Why do they get to go and not the rest of us?"

I had no idea. Maybe in the answer to that question lay the answer to all questions great and small. Einstein famously said that God doesn't play dice with the universe, and I believe it. God plays much more byzantine games, games that we don't know the rules for, games that we can't possibly understand though they're constantly played out around us, with our lives as their tokens and currency.

"We don't even know where they're going," I said. "Or if they're going anywhere. Maybe no one's actually coming for them." A length of anxiety knotted itself in the center of my chest as I listened to my own words. My hand reached for the phone number sheet folded up in my pocket. I slid it back and forth between my index finger and thumb. Perhaps if I rubbed hard enough, I could summon Zachory like a genie from a lamp. I had only one wish, after all.

Charmaine shook her head and shuddered. "I'm telling you, those phone calls. The voices on the other end..." She broke off mid-thought, suddenly distracted by the people at the window who, without warning or apparent reason, had changed pitch. Their hum was now higher, much higher. It was the skirl of a tea kettle's whistle but indescribably hollow, as though the sound that issued from their throats was an echo from much deeper within themselves or much farther outside our shrinking corner of the world.

Everyone in the rec room who could hear well enough to notice the change dropped what they'd been doing and looked past the hummers to the window itself—for what, none of us was sure.

The room suddenly grew dark, the four tall standing lamps in the corners of the room—lamps that remained on both day and night—becoming soft beacons in a hard-tossed, caliginous sea. Beyond the window settled an impenetrable murk. To call it black would've been wrong. Black implies a color, a substance, a tangible idea. What lay outside was none of those things. Gazing into it reminded me of lonesome nights filled with dreamless sleep and the longing for dead friends and lovers.

Liza Collingham broke from the group by the window and edged toward the reinforced-glass double doors to the main entrance.

A pale red glow flashed out from within the murk. It could have been a car's taillights, but it could have just as easily been lightning or UFOs or the bloodstained eyes of a marauding demon.

"They came for me!" Liza called out. "Just like they said!" Before any of us realized what had happened, she pushed open the doors—from which swept a blast of frigid, soul-shattering wind—and walked through, immediately disappearing into the darkness without a sound or a stirring.

Most of the residents who had gathered in the rec room, myself included, were too stunned to say or do anything meaningful. We gaped at the entranceway, now an exit to anywhere. Icy cyclones continued to spin out from the darkness, the windows in the room rapidly frosting over and frostbite snapping at our noses, our fingers, the lobes of our ears.

"Close the goddamned doors!" someone shouted, but no one moved.

I tried to force myself forward, but my body wouldn't respond. Everywhere the currents from the doorway brushed against me, I felt the infinite heaviness of regret. I thought of the darkness in the hallway outside my children's bedrooms when they were younger. I thought of the muffled conversations they held at night, conversations I could never be a part of, conversations I desperately wanted

A Silence of Starlings

to join. I thought of all the hugs I could've given, but didn't. Paralyzed in every way, I thought of distances even greater than that between the rim of the universe and the center of the human soul.

Unexpectedly and without notice, the people by the window dropped their hum back into its initial register and, outside, the murk disappeared—whether as a precursor or as a response it was impossible to say. Rather than dissipate like a fog or gradually fade into day as nights must do, this darkness simply winked away, its chill uniformity replaced by an abandoned afternoon.

The doors to the home drifted shut with an anticlimactic swoosh.

My thoughts returned to the present, where I found I could move again. In a daze, I shambled to the doors and peeked through. Several other equally curious residents joined me by the entrance. I feared, but half-expected, that Liza Collingham's lifeless body would be sprawled on the other side, frozen stiff or worse. But no. Liza was nowhere to be seen, dead or alive. For that matter, much of the world was nowhere to be seen.

The titanic oak trees and lilac bushes that normally graced the front yard, the gold and blue "Serenity Acres" sign posted by the home's driveway, the cinderblock dentist's office across the street, the fancy new gas station and convenience store next to the dentist's place, even the very tarmac road that ran past the home: all had vanished. There was no concrete foundation left at the dentist's office or the gas station, no gaping holes in the ground where the shrubbery and trees had once been rooted, no indication that anything had gone missing anywhere. Yet I wasn't crazy. Those things had been part of the view from the home since I arrived. It was a view I knew that too well, given that most days there's little else to do here other than stare onto a world we can barely recall without a frayed edge of sadness, a world we helped build and shape but that's perfectly content to continue on without us.

"Where's the gas station?" someone beside me asked.

No one responded because there was no adequate response to give.

After a few minutes of quiet disbelief, we all drifted back into the rec room where I checked the time. If the clocks could be trusted, it was a quarter past one.

My joints were already complaining again, so I took up residence in a cushy, hopelessly stained recliner and waited, keeping the front entrance in my direct line of sight. I no longer believed that I'd taste Cammy's birthday cake later in the afternoon, but I *wanted* to believe. I wanted a reason, any reason, to believe. So I watched the entrance, just in case.

Ten minutes passed. Twenty minutes passed. I kept watching the entrance, hoping Zachory's car would materialize on the other side, hoping Annie would stroll up to the doors. But neither happened.

By the nurses' station, an argument broke out between Charmaine and a wheelchair-bound man whose name I couldn't remember. He was trying to persuade people to push him outside while Charmaine was trying to prevent anyone from passing through the exit. The man said he wanted to go out to "smell the air today" because, as he put it, "you can tell a lot about the kind of day it is by the way it hits the nose." Charmaine had only to respond, "Liza Collingham went out there, now where is she?" to discourage any would-be volunteers.

As Charmaine and the wheelchair-bound man continued to bicker, the people by the window again raised the pitch of their hum. The argument immediately stopped. A few hearts probably stopped, too.

Just as it had before, the change in pitch coincided with the sudden appearance of the murk, which again slathered everything beyond the home in a thick tar of nothingness and leaked shadows into the rec room. Again a pale, red glow flashed out of the darkness and again one of the call recipients—a hunchbacked man named Vetterly—shuffled to the front doors.

Someone in the back of the room shouted "Don't go out!"

Someone else shouted "It's not your ride!"

And still another person began repeating the word "No" at increasing volumes.

Vetterly placed his hands on the door handles and was ready to yank them open when, from behind him, flew Charmaine Jackson. She grabbed both of Vetterly's shoulders and whipped him around to face her. He struggled against her grip and cried out, "Let me go! They won't wait for me! They won't wait!" but Charmaine refused to release him.

"Help me," she said to whomever could hear. "Help me hold him."

No one stepped forward to lend aid, as everyone's interest was intractably drawn to the lonesome gloom that seemed to wend its way into our souls. I felt it dragging me back to the past, to the frozen storehouse of memory. It became difficult to differentiate my lifetime already lived from the immediacy of the now. The past was so cold, so cold. It crystallized every passing moment and caused some people, places, and events from yesteryear to shatter in my mind's eye, to irrevocably fragment into a million tiny pieces that gently drifted over the surface of my thoughts like an early morning dusting of snow.

"Help me," Charmaine called again as Vetterly twisted and turned and tried to throw elbow jabs to her stomach. But I couldn't help. I was so lost in nostalgia that I was barely even in the room with her.

Charmaine and Vetterly struggled more, but Charmaine was clearly winning. She dragged Vetterly away from the door a few feet, then away a few more feet, and still a few more. As they two fought, the hummers returned to their original pitch and the murk again vanished. Vetterly topped backward into Charmaine and both went sprawling, landing flat on their backs in the middle of the room with an unpleasant crunch and a curse from Charmaine.

With the murk gone, I regained my sense of time and place and rushed to the prone figures on the floor, where a circle was forming. Charmaine had broken out into a sweat. Her eyes were wide and her teeth clenched.

"Fool just fainted on me," she breathed. "Felt him give out tight on top of me. I think I broke my hip. Damned rickety body. Damn fool Vetterly."

While a few people went off in search of a gurney for Charmaine, I bent down and put a hand on Vetterly's chest. I felt neither rise nor fall. I took his pulse. Nothing beat inside him.

I straightened with a series of cracks and said, to no one in particular, "He's not passed out. He's dead."

Everyone milling about the room shook their heads. A volley of questions and hasty conjectures bounced between us. "How?" "Just fell down dead." "What happened to him?" "We didn't let him go outside." "What do we do with him?" "Nothing to be done." Eventually, someone wheeled in a gurney and we managed to lift Charmaine onto it. Someone else dropped a blanket over Vetterly's body.

The people by the window paid no attention to any of the proceedings. They seemed to not notice one of their number was gone, lying lifeless only a few feet away. They seemed not to care.

After I helped find some pain medication for Charmaine, I returned to my post in the cushy chair opposite the exit and checked the time. It was closing in on two o'clock. I sat and I waited and I stared through the glass doors to freedom. As I kept watch, I noticed that the trees and grass in the front lawn, the macadam parking lot where staff and visitors parked, and the parking lots to the businesses across the road had all disappeared. I feared what another round of vanishing meant. I feared that I would never hear the starlings sing again.

Two o'clock came and went. Three o'clock came and went. Four o'clock passed by, showing me its middle finger. Still no one showed. At least, not for me. The darkness, though, the darkness came to visit again and again and again, and every time was the same—the people by the window raised their pitch, a glow flashed from the gloom, and one of the call recipients fled from the home, into the engulfing darkness and its subzero concentrate of yesteryears. Considering what happened with Vetterly, we let them leave without issue.

As the murk ebbed and flowed, it eroded more and more of the world beyond our door. By the time only three people remained at the window, even the sky and the ground had disappeared, lost to the erasure of the darkness, forever washed out and faded to an undifferentiated grey plain that recognized no horizon.

At eight thirty in the evening, the last of the call recipients wandered from the home, alone and as joyful as all the others who'd stepped outside. I can't lie. I wanted to venture outside, too. I wanted to go wherever the red light might take me. But I remained seated in my chair. I worried that I wasn't wanted by the light or the darkness. I worried that something terrible might happen to me on the other side of the exit doors if I wasn't wanted. I worried that, without Suzy, the only right and proper place for me was in this house of the dying.

I reached into my pocket and grabbed my children's phone numbers. I traced the ones and the twos with my thumb. Surely they would've called if they had the time. Surely whatever had happened today must have forced them away from the phone.

I thought about Cammy's present, up in my room, unopened forever, and a tear rolled down my cheek.

The starlings didn't sing today, that much is true, but, really, I suppose today's been like every other day after all.

Marrowvale

From the unpublished manuscript of The Candlelit World: A Travelogue of Unusual Halloween Traditions *by Charlotte Halloran*

ENTRY: MARROWVALE, PENNSYLVANIA, U.S.

  Deep in the forgotten foothills of central Pennsylvania lies the impoverished, weatherbeaten town of Marrowvale. It's a speck on the map—little more than one nameless bar and a dozen enfeebled, paint-stripped houses wheezing toward demolition. Barely what you could even call a "town." Surrounded by dark, rolling forests and tattooed with fallow cornfields, Marrowvale impresses passers-through—if it impresses them at all—only as a fleeting image of exploded dreams and withered hopes. It's the sort of place where America has worn itself to a nub, the sort of place where "living" and "dying" are the same word, the sort of place that the future has stopped visiting.

Within this decrepit hamlet reside thirty-three men, women, and children—each and every one a crumbling watchtower standing sentinel over the remains of a savaged kingdom, each and every one refusing to accept that the battle for their tiny hometown was lost decades before they were even born. These are people the outside world might call "rustics," "yokels," or "sons and daughters of the soil." They wear wrinkled, sweat-stained flannel shirts with crusted jeans and speak in a slow, distant manner. Many struggle with the bottle. Even more struggle with obesity. They are people who hunt deer and squirrels and even groundhogs for food and work themselves into early graves. Their industries are the industries of sawdust and grease and heavy lifting. They express little concern for the world beyond their valley because the world certainly expresses no concern for them.

On its surface, Marrowvale doesn't seem the sort of place that I would have visited for this book. As small and relatively remote as it is, it doesn't seem like the sort of place anyone would visit for any reason. But Marrowvale conceals an inexplicable and, if I'm being honest, terrifying Halloween tradition that few outsiders ever witness.

In my last book, *Burying Ourselves: Funeral Practices Across the World*, I'd mentioned in my epilogue that I was thinking about writing a future volume on the topic of Halloween. As it so happened, a fifteen-year-old girl who lived in Marrowvale—one Kristina Taylor Pittlebach—had read that book and decided to email me about her hometown, a tiny nowhereville with what she claimed was "a super weird and freaky thing that we all do at Halloween." She said that I absolutely had to come and see it; she said no one but the people of Marrowvale knew it happened.

Of course my curiosity was piqued. I responded to Kristina and asked if she could provide any more details, stressing that if the tradition really was out of the ordinary, I'd be happy to swing by her town and check it out. To my query, she sent a grainy black and white photo of two dozen people posed in graduated rows, as though they were taking a class picture. Everyone in the photo wore

Marrowvale

strange cylindrical helmets that entirely engulfed their heads. A chaos of jagged lines lay engraved about the circumference of each helmet. Where one would have expected eyeholes, a pair of spiked, elongated pyramids protruded from every face. I wasn't sure how anyone could see out of the things. Considering that there were no visible nose or mouth apertures, I wasn't sure how anyone could breathe in them, either.

To accompany her photo, Kristina wrote only one cryptic line: "We all have to wear them to the meeting place every year."

As I stared at the picture and imagined an entire town wearing headgear that resembled 1950s sci-fi robots by way of a medieval torture device, a deep sense of unease washed over me. I couldn't quite pinpoint what it was about the helmets or masks or whatever they were that set my nerves on edge; I could only say that they didn't *feel right*. They didn't give the impression of objects any sane human would ever design, let alone want to wear. It was exactly the kind of weirdness I was in search of, and it convinced me to include Marrowvale in my Halloween itinerary.

To reach Marrowvale, I had to fly into Harrisburg and then drive a rental car northwest from the city for almost two hours. Along my route, I encountered a profusion of nameless villages without so much as a single working stoplight or chain convenience store. I passed farmhouses and barns that, while still clearly operational, were flaking and splintering into nothingness. I drove over surprisingly steep hills cowering in the shadow of even more surprisingly steep mountains. And everywhere, everywhere I was met with autumnal foliage not bright and inflamed like the leaves in more northerly climes but the same withered brown as rotting fruit and ancient parchment.

When I finally rolled into Marrowvale the day before Halloween, I was greeted by two sights: one, the town bar—a sagging two-story gable-front house which was only distinguishable as a bar because of the neon Coors and Budweiser signs that hung in its dusty windows—and two, a shirtless old man riding a lawnmower on the berm of the road.

As I neared him, the old man pulled his mower into the gravel parking lot that fronted the bar to let me pass. But I had no interest in passing. I, too, needed to visit the bar. I swerved in behind him and collected my thoughts. Curious as to the people of the town, I sat in the car and stared at the man. He turned in his seat and stared back. His right eye was entirely missing and he made no attempt to cover over the injury with a patch or a glittering prosthetic. His gaze split my attention in equal halves. On one side, a hollow gaped wide and deep and beckoned its viewer to crawl inside and explore a vacancy that might easily extend far beyond the reaches of the old man's skull. On the other, an electric blue eye shot forth concentrated, penetrating scrutiny that felt as though it could carve through any length of time and space. I wasn't sure which side I should meet.

As I stared in fascination, the old man's cracked, blistered lips tightened and quivered. It seemed he was about to break into either tears or a murderous rage. He shook his head once, slowly, then swiveled forward, threw open the mower's throttle, and motored away.

Clearly, Marrowvale wasn't in the business of tourism. I jumped from the car and hurried into the bar.

In Kristina's first email, she mentioned that the bar's owner—a Mr. Dale Schwartz—kept a collection of what she termed "Halloween Meeting Treats" in one of the bar's upstairs rooms. I wanted to check out this collection before I visited the Pittlebachs, so that I wouldn't arrive on their doorstep entirely ignorant of their traditions. So the bar was my first stop.

Most likely due to the fact that it was only three o'clock in the afternoon, the rustic watering hole sat empty. The hardwood floor of the place was scuffed and cracked and its boards groaned under my every step. I counted eight tables set up around the main bar area, but I doubted they were ever all filled at the same time. Behind the bar slouched a doughy man with a shaggy walrus mustache and heavy circles draped beneath his eyes. He glanced up from the magazine in his hands—a yellowed *Reader's Digest*—and asked, slowly, as if uncertain how to approach someone who wasn't a regular, "What can I getcha?"

I asked the man if he was the owner of the bar and, when he hesitantly nodded, I launched into my journalism routine. I explained that I was a writer from Chicago and that I was writing a piece on Marrowvale and its unique Halloween rituals for an upcoming book. I said I needed to talk to people around town, to glean a sense of who they were, what they believed, why they did what they did. When you tell people you're writing about them or their homes, most crack wide open like clams in a steamer, ready to regale you with embellished anecdotes and personal details that you wouldn't otherwise be able to touch. But Mr. Schwartz didn't spill his mind. He simply closed the *Reader's Digest* and stared at me in much the same way the old man on the lawn mower had.

"So you want to see the museum, then?" he asked. I nodded and, trying another tactic, slid a twenty onto the bar.

He stared at the bill, eyes narrowed, then pushed it back toward me.

"Money doesn't have much value here," he said. "But let me show you what does."

He hobbled out from his post and beckoned me to follow. I patted the switchblade in my pocket—a gift from my father on my fourteenth birthday and a precautionary tool I always carry when I'm in unfamiliar territory—and fell in behind Mr. Schwartz. I didn't sense any menace from the barkeep, but I've read too many police blotters to simply accept invitations from strange men without reservation.

Mr. Schwartz led me up a flight of rickety stairs to a darkened hallway and, from there, shuffled into a small adjoining room lit by a single dingy lamp. Dust motes swirled in his wake like minuscule galaxies. I burst through them, into the room, and was instantly mesmerized by the assortment of objects laid out before me. On three long tables covered in white crushed velvet and set up in a

"U" formation rested things for which I had no name. Here, a thing that looked like a leaf, but with a holographic sheen and a thickness closer to cardboard. There, a thing that resembled a butcher knife but pulsed like a still-living heart. Here, a dull blue sphere cut in half, with hundreds of glittering, black needle-like shards protruding from its core. There, a metal square scoured with jagged lines similar to those etched upon the helmets in Kristina's picture. Here, an inverted pyramid with drooping points that, defying gravity and physics, somehow stood upon its bottom vertex. There, a thing that mixed equal parts dollbaby and viral microbe, limbs contorting into spirals and wavy ropes.

The room was filled with craftsmanship and artistry, certainly, but it was craftsmanship and artistry of a completely unknown form. Each and every object in the room looked out of place, felt out of place, and caused my stomach to clench with an anxiety I'd never experienced in my entire life. It was like suddenly waking up in a room you've never been inside in a building you've never visited in a city inhabited only by the machinery of a long-forgotten people.

I stood gaping for several minutes, then finally asked, "What *are* these?"

Mr. Schwartz's eyes narrowed. "You don't know? They're treats from the meetings."

"Treats, yes," I said. "But what are each of them supposed to represent? What are they used for?"

Mr. Schwartz shrugged. "I try not to find out. It's for the best."

"And why is that?" I asked.

"Because," Mr. Schwartz said, fingers gently tracing the outline of one of the objects, "people who find out tend to end up in a bad way."

"A bad way?" I pressed, though my imagination supplied plenty of horrifying imagery. I pictured my head locked inside one of the bizarre helmets from Kristina's photo.

Mr. Schwartz nodded and tapped his forehead. "Up here."

I murmured an assent and let the subject drop. I didn't want to talk about the objects anymore, and I certainly didn't want to be in the same room as them any longer. I was a journalist, a professional writer. I should have been overcome with curiosity. Yet, ridiculous though it may sound, I was beginning to feel disconnected from my own time and place, from my own thoughts and feelings. Terror rose up in my chest and I pinched the back of my hand to make sure I was still corporeal. I had a fleeting suspicion that somehow I might not be, even though I could feel the softness of my flesh twist in my fingers.

I hurriedly thanked Mr. Schwartz for the opportunity to view the collection and ran to my car. I sped away from Marrowvale and refused to glance in the rear-view mirror. Thirty miles and a separate world later, I parked at the shabby motel where I'd made a reservation. I checked in as quickly as possible and, forsaking my luggage, dashed inside my room. I bolted the door and collapsed on the bed—a bed that, while foreign and hard and tinged with the unmistakable scent of mildew, still reflected something crucially human, something that had been utterly absent in Mr. Schwartz's "museum."

Before long, sprawled on the bed, I fell into a deep slumber and dreamed.

In my dreams, I found myself in a stately edifice crammed full of glass display cases that housed two distinct types of artifacts: broken, twisted mirrors of ornate design and tiny human beings pinned to foam boards like so many insects. I wandered among those cases for the rest of the night, half frightened to examine their contents but compelled to see the entire exhibit.

I also felt another presence in the edifice—a distant, ever vigilant thing, like a night watchman at a bank of security cameras. I worried that I might be as broken and twisted as the mirrors, as pinned and skewered as the tiny people; I worried that the vigilant thing might see fit to include me in the displays. And so I tried to run from the edifice. I fled through thousands of rows of display cases, but encountered no end, no exit. I couldn't escape the exhibit. I could examine the mirrors and take notes on the characteristics of the little people forever, but I could never leave. It appeared that I was inextricably trapped in my own curiosity. I threw myself to the floor, pounded the hard surface beneath me, and screamed myself into the morning.

The next afternoon found me in a better state of mind. Although it had taken a morning's worth of writing, two hot showers, and a perfectly grilled hamburger at a quaint roadside diner called "The Country Kettle" to expunge my previous night's dreams, I was prepared to return to Marrowvale to witness its Halloween festivities. I'd arranged to meet Kristina Pittlebach and her family before the celebration began and to accompany them to the mysterious "meeting" that Kristina refused to discuss in any detail. In the course of our exchanges, Kristina had also promised to let me examine "the heads"—her term for the bizarre helmets in the old photograph—and to interview any member of her family if I so desired.

As I drove toward Marrowvale, enthusiasm leaped beneath my skin. Something about the chill in the air shouted promise. I felt close to a discovery of monumental proportion, even though I wasn't quite sure what that discovery might be. By the time I reached the Pittlebach homestead, a ranch-style house missing half its siding, my heart was racing.

I parked in the Pittlebachs' driveway, which was gravel stained black by used motor oils, and made my way to their door. Innumerable rusted yard tools and shards of broken lawn statuary littered the path between driveway and door. I had to step carefully so as to not trip and impale myself on an ancient blade or the point of an eroded jockey. When I finally arrived on the Pittlebachs' doorstep, a short, preternaturally pale girl with fiery red hair was hanging out over the threshold. I thought perhaps I'd stumbled across a wayward fey princess.

"Ms. Halloran," the girl said, voice surprisingly grave. "I'm Kristina. I've been waiting." She ushered me inside and slammed the door behind me.

We exchanged pleasantries—the usual "Oh, it's so good to finally meet yous"—and she introduced me to the rest of her family, none of whom seemed pleased at my visit. Her father, a wisp of a man with a long, straggly beard, stared at me without speaking. Her mother, a buxom lady with a pronounced harelip, smiled and nodded. Puffy red rings beneath her eyes told of either seasonal allergies or a story of recent sadness. Kristina's grandmother, a squat woman with uncontrollable tremors, was the only one to actually greet me with words.

"Hello," the old woman said, "I hear you're a writer. You know, writers have to be careful. Some things don't want to be written. And some things simply *can't* be written. You don't want to end up lost forever, dear."

Kristina pulled me away, clearly embarrassed, and whispered, "Everyone around here is like grandma. Especially this time of year." She hurried me into the basement—a space that looked as though a flea market had exploded within it—and drew my attention to a gun safe that stood against one wall. Kristina fiddled with its dial and, after a few spins, its door squeaked open. She stepped back to let me peer inside. There, sitting on makeshift shelves, were four of the helmets I'd seen in Kristina's photo. For no reason I could have possibly explained, my stomach twisted in knots.

Struggling to maintain my composure, I leaned in and examined the headpieces. None of them had any forging marks or soldered seams or any other signs of metallurgy. Instead, they seemed almost organic, like an insect's carapace, only composed of a material more rigid than chitin. In color, they were a shade I'd never seen, a hue that shifted from bronze to grey and grey to bronze depending on the angle at which it reflected light. I didn't want to touch one, but I knew I had no choice. I ran a finger along the inscrutable etchings—which, up close, reminded me of seismograph readings or the EKGs of heart attack victims—and felt a bolt of panic crash through my chest.

I flinched away and, desperate to remain objective, asked Kristina what the helmets were supposed to represent.

She laughed. "They're not supposed to represent anything."

"Then why wear them?" I asked, breathing hard, pulse pounding.

She shrugged. "Because we have to."

"Did you make them?"

Again she laughed, as if what I'd asked was the most infantile question ever uttered.

"Of course not."

The room began to spin and sway. I stepped away from the helmets and asked if I could sit down.

Kristina nodded and led me back upstairs. Somehow, I managed to navigate my way to a chair, where I vomited and collapsed. Every nerve in my body twitched and screamed. Some atavistic code in my chromosomes told me to run, to hide. But from what? Some bizarre Halloween masks? I was too professional to allow primordial fears to erase a potential chapter in my book.

Kristina brought me a glass of water and patted my shoulder. "I guess trying one on is probably a bad idea, then," she said. "Grandma said it would be."

I shuddered at the thought of the helmet being placed upon my head, my every perception being encased in a device of such indescribable foreignness. *What would the world look like from inside?* I wondered. *Would it even still be this world, or would it be some other place? Would the sun or the moon or the stars be recognizable inside those helmets or would they be radically contorted variations of themselves?* I sat and stared at the Pittlebachs' chipped wooden floors, contemplating both these questions and nothing at all.

After minutes, hours, or, perhaps at the very end of time itself, I shook myself from the fugue and asked Kristina, who was still sitting nearby, "When do we go to the meeting place?"

Kristina looked at me askance. "At dusk," she said. "So pretty soon."

I glanced at a window and was shocked to find the sky beginning to bruise. Had I really been inside my own head for that long?

"It's about a mile up one of the hunting paths in the hills," Kristina continued. "But are you sure you want to? I think you might be sick."

I assured Kristina that I'd be fine. I told her I occasionally experienced panic attacks—not a lie, actually—and that it just took me a while to regain my composure after I'd suffered one. I knew very well that what had happened to me in the basement couldn't be chalked up to misfiring neurons or chemical imbalances, though. Like the objects in Dale Schwartz's "museum," the helmets radiated an uncanny otherness so powerful that it warped the fabric of thought. These were not simple Halloween masks. They were something else entirely.

Before long, Kristina's father descended into the basement with a large, empty velvet sack and returned with it bulging full. As he passed, I could sense the "heads" in the bag, gazing at me with their pointed eyes.

"Time to go," Kristina's grandmother called out, spurring us into action. Mr. Pittlebach led the way and was already out the door, traipsing up a gentle, forested hill behind the Pittlebachs' house. Kristina and I followed, with her mother and grandmother lagging behind.

While we walked, Kristina asked me about my last book, about the death rituals I'd witnessed. She wanted to know if there really were places where corpses served as bird food, where people danced with the deceased, where the bereaved amputated their own fingers to more physically approximate the loss of a loved one. I said yes, and that I'd even watched a young boy raised from his grave.

Kristina nodded. "I saw something like that once, when I was really little. A kid forgot his mask."

"And what happened to him?" I asked.

Kristina shrugged. I wasn't sure whether she didn't remember, didn't know, or didn't want to tell me. We walked on, in silence.

With Kristina ensconced in quiet contemplation, I sensed an opening.

"So what *are* the heads?" I asked. "The masks?"

Kristina stopped and turned to look for her mother and grandmother. Softly, in the near darkness, she said, "Depends on what you're willing to believe, I guess."

"What do you believe?"

Softer yet, "That in the right time and place anything is possible, though most things are inconceivable due to the complexity and magnitude of their horror."

I smiled, but I doubted that Kristina could have seen me. She'd quoted from my book. I'd been referring to the varied and innumerable ways we could die. I didn't think she'd meant it in quite the same way.

"Why did you ask me to come here?" I pressed. "I don't get the sense that your fellow townsfolk are too eager to share their traditions."

Kristina shrugged again. Such a teenager.

"I think someone like you should see it. I think someone like you might understand. People think nothing happens here. People think this is one of America's many buttholes. But it's so much stranger than that. I think everyone should know."

Hometown pride. Who would've guessed?

I reached out and squeezed Kristina's arm. She jumped away, as though shocked.

Huffing, her mother and grandmother caught up to us and we continued stumbling onward.

After close to half an hour of hiking under night's silken fabric, I saw a bright light flickering within the dense forest.

"We're meeting the rest of the citizens of Marrowvale out here?" I asked. "Sort of a town festival with a bonfire and hotdogs? Something like that?"

Kristina's voice dropped into a deeper register. "Yeah," she breathed. "Something like that."

We broke through a copse of trees and entered a field strewn with boulders the size and shape of which I'd never experienced. Each boulder stood twenty or thirty feet high and had been chiseled into complex star shapes that resembled goliath anemones and sea urchins. Near the center of the cluster of boulders raged a fire and around the fire gathered the people of Marrowvale, all of whom had already donned their "heads." Everyone stood silent and motionless and I shuddered at the spectacle.

Kristina motioned to an alcove in one of the megaliths. "You should probably wait here," she whispered. "Try to stay out of sight. Some of our neighbors don't know that I invited you to the meeting place and they might not like it."

My throat tightened. "I'm a shadow," I said, probably even less convincing to Kristina than to myself. I crawled into the alcove and gave Kristina a thumbs up. Satisfied, she strode to the circled townsfolk and received a helmet from a person I assumed was her father. When her mother and grandmother passed by, the older lady paused for a moment. She glanced at my hiding spot and said, very casually, "If I were you, I'd sneak off now. They'll know you're here, and they won't allow it. They don't have a head for you and yours isn't going to be good enough." Then away she puttered.

I crouched between the star-megalith's legs and waited, fearful in the way of a child hopelessly lost in a department store. More people arrived. The air gained a serrated chill. I counted the number congregated before me. Thirty-three. The exact population of Marrowvale.

And so it began.

When the last straggler arrived and slid a "head" over his own, the townspeople aligned themselves into a large triangle, with each side comprised of eleven individuals. Then they did nothing. They stood in the field, their fire roaring without purpose, and did nothing.

But something was happening all the same.

The air in the field suddenly grew indescribably cold and sharp. It tore at my lungs and shredded my nostrils as I breathed in. Even having lived through a handful of tornado touchdowns, I'd never felt air so hostile, so bent on eradicating me from the inside out. I brought a hand to my face and found blood leaking from my nose. At the same time the air was gaining malicious sentience, a wide dark line appeared, floating, behind the triangulated people of Marrowvale, as though a strip of reality itself had been cleanly sheared away with a razor.

I stared at the dark line, blood now flowing freely from my nose, and began to seriously consider Kristina's grandmother's advice. This wasn't a place I should be. This wasn't a place anyone but the people of Marrowvale should be—and perhaps not even them.

The dark line didn't undulate or widen or even suck us all into oblivion. It simply waited, like me, like the townspeople. Frozen. Neither alive nor dead.

I began to climb out of my alcove, blood dripping onto my jacket, my shirt. A wave of nausea pounded my abdomen and white dots spotted my vision. The air grew even colder. The thought "absolute zero" flitted around my mind.

The old lady had been right. Kristina was young, hopeful. She thought she might be able to let the outside world break into her town. Her grandmother knew better. I had to flee.

I took one last look at the dark line hovering over the good citizens of Marrowvale and what I saw set me running from the field. Somehow, from *within* the line were emerging long, whip-like arms the same odd color and hue as the helmets. These arms ended in perfectly human hands that held out to the masked people of Marrowvale an assortment of unnameable and unclassifiable objects. Treats.

As soon as I gazed upon those spindly arms stretching out from the line, the hands so bizarrely human yet clearly not, I turned to the forest and sprinted. I wasn't a journalist or a travel writer then. I was a human fighting to remain human.

Though my thoughts came fuzzy and my vision still popped with bright dots, I managed to follow the path we'd taken to reach the field. I fell over stumps and roots, skinning my hands, bruising my knees, but the farther I crept from the dark line in the forest, the warmer the air became and the more alive I felt.

I arrived in the Pittlebachs' backyard exhausted and near the verge of collapse. My nose had stopped bleeding, so I felt sure that I could drive, that I could make my getaway. I dragged myself to the rental car and blasted away from Marrowvale. I drove for hours; I drove until my eyes drooped and I nearly ran off the road.

When I finally stopped at a large, well-lit chain motel, I asked the desk attendant where I was.

"Almost in Pittsburgh," she said. "Just ten miles out. Where are you coming from?"

I considered telling her. I considered asking her if she knew about Marrowvale. I considered not speaking at all.

"Nowhere you've ever heard of," I said, and paid for a room.

The Cone of Heaven

                  Victoria Valencia considered herself a good woman, a moral woman, a woman with integrity in a world that, to her mind, was slipping ever closer to spiritual bankruptcy. An emeritus professor of religious studies, she retained faith in many creeds and doctrines, many forces beyond the ken of human perception and many notions of love, kindness, and eternity. It was because of this faith that she hadn't burst into bitter tears when her doctor said "cancer"; it was because of this faith that she hadn't thrown slurs and epithets at the sky when her surgeon said "inoperable"; and it was because of this faith that she hadn't quivered beneath her bed when her family said "hospice." She felt that whatever lay ahead could only be reward for a life of obedience to a panoply of laws both divine and human.

    And so, when Victoria's strength inevitably ebbed and her vision permanently clouded, when her children and grandchildren held her hands and whispered to her that it was "okay to let go," she knew it was okay, indeed. She knew she would find warm, open arms at the end of her journey. She knew she would be ushered into something like heaven, if not heaven exactly. And, thus, on a starry night a few months following her diagnosis, Victoria Valencia died.

Her heart sagged and her lungs deflated and the marauding cellular hordes staked final, pyrrhic victory to her flesh. But they could have it, she thought; they were welcome to its leathery rind. They could ride it straight into the incinerator and burn, burn, burn like the microscopic devils they were. She had better places to exist, better fates to meet. And perhaps she did, because as she let the corporeal wither around her, a tunnel swirled open before her and it was as so many near-death experiences had reported—kaleidoscopic and opalescent and imbued with a psychological analgesic that quelled even the most peaked anxiety. Victoria let herself slide inside, let herself reflect the smiles of her husband, her parents, her brothers and sisters all gone into the tunnel before her—smiles she would have sworn danced in the very substance of diaphanous pipeline. She let herself believe that her loved ones were waiting at the opposite end of the tunnel, that it was their hands gently tugging her through to the other side, and she was eager to be with them again.

But as Victoria popped free from the umbilicus between life and death, as the comforting countenances dissipated and the light grew monochrome, she found herself standing naked on a chilled white platform in what seemed to be either a doctor's office the size and shape of a baroque cathedral or a massive church unadorned and sterile as a medical facility. Everything she looked upon was white. The walls: white. The high, arched ceiling: white. The light that filtered from nowhere: white. And it was not just any white, but the retina-bursting white of freshly fallen snow under a midday sun, the white of superheated stars and blank reams of paper. Had she the physical organs to register this density of whiteness, Victoria would have been struck blind by the overwhelming, uniform purity of it all.

She lingered on the platform a moment longer and was, quite suddenly and without warning, impelled to move further into the grand hall.

The Cone of Heaven

Across the interior of the space, as though organically sprouted from the floor, stretched long, interminably long, rows of rounded, hollow, egg-shaped chairs. Though she had no physical form, no breasts to cover or pubis to hide in modesty, and though she saw not a single being reclining in the chairs, Victoria felt a thousand eyes turn upon her and survey her with—what? Lust and lascivious intent? No, that wasn't right. With desire? That was closer, but still not right. Hunger? Yes. That was it, but not any kind of hunger she had ever known. She felt penetrated, bored through to the core, so that whatever gazed upon her could touch her every thought, her every memory, her every emotion. She felt—if it were possible—that someone or something was licking her soul, tasting her essence. An ephemeral tongue slid over the memory of her first kiss, lapped at her love for wildflowers, and rolled her confusion in tight, diminishing circles.

Maybe it's God, Victoria thought. *Maybe it's the way God examines our virtues and our sins. Maybe this is heaven's lobby and I'm just being poked and measured by God's nurses while I wait for the actual appointment with my creator.*

Another part of Victoria, however, a part she could only imagine tasted sour or tart, construed the experience in a much different way. Four-letter words glided from that part of herself and the searching, tasting force dove at them greedily. She tried to stifle the words, tried to completely open herself to the ingress of the divine, but the harder she fought, the more forcefully the all-seeing papillae delved.

Had she been able to sweat, she would have been drenched. Had she been able to make noise, she would have screamed.

And then, as suddenly as it had been thrust upon her, the force retracted and vanished. A new pressure pushed at her back and drove her onward. Victoria had no time to reflect on the experience, no time to regain her composure, let alone consider whether it had been a violation or an honor. Instead, she continued forward, through the alabaster space. As she passed the innumerable empty eggshell seats, she caught what she believed were flashes of movement within. Yet, when she focused on any one particular chair, any one concavity, she saw no one reclining in its depths. The entire grand cathedral-facility appeared utterly vacant, devoid of anything except its alien ornamentation. But Victoria could sense the presence of other *things*—sentient things, intelligent things, things she was sure could see her perfectly well—within its structure.

Angels? she wondered. *Other souls of the departed?*

She didn't contemplate the issue for very long. Instead, she ran through the litany of prayers she'd collected over the years and recited each one to the best of her ability, hoping that whatever was watching would recognize her righteous supplication and be pleased. The foundations of heaven were, after all, built upon souls in full bow.

Victoria prayed for what may have been milliseconds or millennia—time in this bleached afterlife held no meaning or importance. She capped her geyser of praise only when the forces at her back finally abated, leaving her adrift in an ovoid clearing far beyond where she had arrived. Nestled within the monotonous forest of chairs, the space had no remarkable features save a series of elliptical designs carved into the floor. All dots and curlicued lines, they reminded Victoria of an exotic, antediluvian script or a musical score, gleaming with intent. She reached out to touch them, but, without hands or arms, she couldn't experience the tactile sensations of their smooth grooves, their sinuous wrap. Instead, the closer she examined them, the more she felt some vague apprehension of their meaning, and she recoiled from it.

This isn't right, she thought. *I shouldn't be afraid of heaven. What's wrong with me?*

She focused on the designs again and a shadow translation formed in the nether reaches of her mind, as though some primeval substratum of herself had been molded by the language long before she had been born. COME AND BE EMPTIED, it said, GO AND BE FILLED. There was far more nuance in the etched symbols than the loose translation could provide, but the general sentiment remained the same: COME AND BE EMPTIED, GO AND BE FILLED.

Victoria tried to tie the phrase to one of the myriad spiritual teachings she'd studied for so many years, but none seemed to match with any exactitude. To varying degrees they were all preoccupied with vacuity and fulfillment, creation and nothingness. It was a subject she now supposed she should have researched more thoroughly in lieu of her byzantine inquiries into the nature of "goodness" and "evil."

No longer able to contemplate the alien inscription without an inexplicable, protean dread frosting the edges of her thoughts, Victoria turned away. She began to glide back toward the chair rows in hope that venturing in a straight line in any direction would lead to something or someplace more comprehensible. However, as she reached the boundary of the open space, she felt a new—or, perhaps, only more corporeal—presence bearing down upon her. She spun in circles but saw no one approaching from any direction.

Where's my husband, my Daniel? she asked the blank dimensions that unfolded before her. *Where are Mom and Dad and my big sister Ruthie and my little brother Clint? Why aren't they here to welcome me? Is heaven really that busy?*

As though in response, a hand wrapped itself about Victoria's wavering spirit and squeezed. She looked to where she felt its gentle, oddly chilled cinch—an area that, in the body of before, might have been her waist but was now an arbitrary division between more or less frequently used thoughts and emotions—and froze.

Every faculty Victoria still possessed retreated inward, upon itself, in an attempt to escape the hand that held her firm, for it was no hand but a six-fingered, many-jointed monstrosity the same pale hue as the rest of the undead world. Each of the serpentine phalanges that gripped her tapered to a needle-thin point, as though she were in the caress of a swarm of animate syringes. Her composure rebounding, she dared to follow the "hand" upward, to an elongated, downy white tube which led onto a disturbingly concave mass of doughy material that may have been some form of flesh or protoplasm. Atop the deflated bulk perched a smooth, featureless, oviform mound that oscillated left-right, left-right, keeping time to infinity.

It was this last—the mechanical motion, the being's vacuous precision—that sent Victoria spinning. She struggled against her handler, lashing out at its chained fingers. She used the only brute force she was left with in this realm—her untapped will—to kick and bite and rake at the thing's hand. But it didn't budge or relax. It held Victoria in the same gentle, inescapable, embrace.

Without warning, the being began to ascend toward the ceiling, dragging Victoria with it. Though she apprehended no flapping of wings and though no halo of fire or gold crowned the thing that cradled her, a blast of reflexive shame suddenly hit Victoria square in the face.

What if it's an angel? she thought. *I've just battered an angel. I've attacked the heavenly host. I'm not worthy to be here.*

She turned her attention back upon the being's perfectly polished, utterly inhuman, egg-like head and instantly reconsidered her position, shivering as she did so. It's all wrong, she whispered in her soul. If this thing is an angel, God must be the essence of nightmares.

And so they continued to climb, Victoria unable to extricate herself from the being's grasp and equally unable to reconcile her vast knowledge of spiritual teachings with her current situation.

Above, the ceiling began to take on more detail.

Undifferentiated white planes resolved into a chaotic sprawl of sigils like those on the floor below. The entire ceiling spun in whorls and spirals of divine language. As with the writing on the floor, the foreign words that adorned the arched heights whipped vague meanings toward Victoria's mind.

ALL CREATION SERVES.
DELIGHT IN THE HUNGER.
IN EVERY VESSEL, A CARGO.
IN EVERY LIFE, A SAVOR.
ALL GLORY TO THE HOLLOW.

The Cone of Heaven

Victoria squeezed shut her windows of perception for fear that the seemingly infinite inundation of phrases would overtake her, flood her from within, and cause her mind—if not her soul—to rupture. She cocooned within herself, holding fast to those things she remembered—her husband's warm, rough touch; her daughter's lilting laughter; her pug's jolly, rolling gait—while the words swept around her.

Although an effective strategy to protect against the information avalanche from above, Victoria's willful blindness did nothing to halt her ascension. The ovoid-headed being continued its rise, paying no heed to Victoria's distress and providing no explanation as to its purpose or goals. It levitated further toward the apex of heaven, further toward a cylindrical aperture from which effused sallow, flaxen light. Victoria, having blocked her ethereal sensorium, did not see the multitudes of spidery, alien angels converging upon the glowing cleft. She did not see the ghostly forms—all shimmering shades of grey—that the angels carried with them. And she certainly did not see her own courier, flanked by the throngs of its counterparts, enter the crevasse and speed through an amber tunnel—a celestial urethra, Victoria would have called it had she dared to look—which led unto a deep, golden nothingness outside all things.

It was in this space beyond space, this lustrous absence, that Victoria finally allowed herself to further witness the afterlife, such as it was. Having felt the ascent end, she emerged from her psychical shell and perused her surroundings.

Her egg-headed handler still remained by her side, its inhuman phalanges lassoed about her already-forgotten ribs. But in this grip she was not alone. Both before and behind her stretched an interminable queue of angels and apparitions, all awash in a viscous, golden light that seemed a conscious entity in its own inexplicable way. The light undulated over, under, and around Victoria and her kindred dead. She thought of jellyfish. She thought of slugs. She thought of cells and cytoplasm and could not shake the feeling that she was, somehow, caught within a membrane of an unfathomably immense organ.

Crazy, isn't it? an unfamiliar voice charged through her.

Victoria, shocked by the thoughts of another within the web of her own, sought out the source of the question. The apparition in front of her extended a smoky tendril and waved.

It's not what I expected, the voice laughed, *but how much time did any of us really spend thinking about the particulars of heaven?*

Victoria focused on the grayscale figure, but couldn't discern any features beyond its obvious humanoid outline. She wondered if her appearance had been reduced to shadow, too.

I spent a great deal of time thinking about the afterlife, actually, her thoughts dashed loose. *And in none of that time did I ever conceive of anything resembling this.*

Are either of you scared? another voice—this one from behind—sneaked into her. *Because I know I did a lot of things I shouldn't have. I don't even know how I got here. I don't believe in God. Or Jesus. Or Buddha. Or Allah. Or any of that stuff. So I'm really worried about who might be waiting at the end of this line.*

As long as you're filled with love, everything will be fine, the first voice boomed.

The second voice, perhaps cowed, perhaps even more fearful, remained silent.

I don't feel even the slightest tingle of love in this place, Victoria whispered, trying to shield the sentiment within herself. *I don't feel anything here, other than anxiety and emptiness.*

Whether or not the first voice had heard her, it didn't send any more errant communications her way. Conversation was clearly not at the top of anyone's list of priorities so soon after dying.

In silence, then, Victoria floated along for an indefinite span of infinity, cradling her own worries, nursing her own hopes. As she and her guardian drifted ever forward, she indexed the files in her memory, seeking out some allusion to this heaven—if heaven it was. She delved through ancient Assyrian myths and Egyptian underworlds, reconsidered Chinese lore and Kabbalistic mysticism. She even dredged up a few murky strands of theosophist philosophy. But nowhere could she recall reference to a gleaming white hall or an expansive golden space—and that fact clawed, quite uncomfortably, within her.

To assuage her trepidation, she imagined that the queue ended at a set of pearlescent gates and a city carved from rainbows and diamond. She imagined intertwining her essence with her dear Daniel's, letting herself merge with him as they had so naturally in life. She imagined rivers that ran with gleeful songs and libraries stacked with all the knowledge in the cosmos. Like most of the other souls in line, she imagined a Paradise built just for her.

But as her unearthly escort led her onward, that Paradise shrank away and was replaced by a glittering, funnel-shaped object on the horizon, hanging in midair. Even from a great distance, she could tell its dimensions were so massive that they strained every faculty of comprehension. A sense of hunger—the same unnamable hunger she'd felt bear down upon her when she'd arrived in the afterlife—pulsed from the behemoth cone. She paused, not wanting to approach any closer, and the angel-thing by her side tugged against her, driving her along.

What is that? she thought at the angel, fear and wonder rising in equal parts. *What does it do?*

The angel, its "head" still keeping steady, unflinching time, turned and seemed to regard Victoria as more than a mere burden to bear. It leaned close, but whether in conspiracy or menace Victoria couldn't tell. Without warning, something akin to the sound of radio static burst through her mind; the volume of the static, the pressure, held the force of exploding stars and meteoric collisions. Though she had no mouth, Victoria cried out a word of empathy, a word of compassion, but it was entirely subsumed by the inscrutable noise.

Sure that she had reached the outer limits of sanity, Victoria went slack within herself and the static, in response, ebbed. The angel turned its attention back upon the queue. Weakly, Victoria again tugged against her guard, but the tensile strength of its coils was unyielding. Too dazed to struggle any further and too exhausted to maintain wonder or fear, she stared at the conical immensity in the distance and let herself be dragged into the order of its abstruse world.

As she was carried toward whatever destiny had been prepared for her, Victoria understood two things clearly: one, that her every scrap of remaining agency lay in her mental catalogue of experiences and emotions, and two, that all the spiritual knowledge in the world—and all the scientific knowledge, too, for that matter—could never have prepared her for this prescribed existence beyond the grave. Like all prisoners of circumstance and slaves to higher powers, she would have to seek freedom inside the borders of self—or go mad in the process. Thus, she plunged into her memories and attempted to evade eternity.

Her hands, so small. So pink. Heated by a flared summer sun. Those hands gripped a bouquet of wildflowers—dandelions, mostly—all tied up with grass.

Her father in his garden, always tending the literal fruits of his labors, his back arched, shirt dark with sweat as he stabbed at the earth. She skipped up behind him and tugged at his sleeve. He turned, welcomed her home with his smile. A word may have passed in the breeze.

She held out the dandelion bundle and, carefully, so as to not disturb the arrangement, he took it from her and stuck it in his left front pocket. He patted his floral pocket square and invited her to pick one of the new strawberries. She bent low, plucked a succulent gem from its vine and stuffed it into her mouth. As she chewed, sticky juice ran down her chin and her father laughed. She didn't know whether the berry or the serenade of his laughter was sweeter.

Her knees, bloody. A flash of bone in the domain of flesh. Tears blotted her shirt, ran into her nose, her mouth. So salty, as though oceans churned inside her.

The Cone of Heaven

A ladder, toppled, beside her. She'd tried to climb to the roof of the house. She'd wanted to reach out her arms and touch a star.

Her mother pounced from the back door, hair whipping in the night wind, a lioness protecting her cub. She flew to her daughter and cradled her head. A kiss on the cheek. A finger, pointing into the darkness. Her mother's voice, warmer than any blanket, naming constellations, telling stories of heroes and monsters and how they'd all ended up in the stars. She brought the sky closer than the ladder ever could have. She made the pain seem small in comparison to twinkling bowl above. And when the ambulance came, she kept telling stories and naming names, and even the bone, poking up through skin, seemed to bow down before the healing majesty of her mother's tales.

Her neck, dancing in electricity. Every hair standing to applaud. Daniel's fingers, so light against her jaw, so furtive in their touch. Her heart beat faster. She leaned in, wetted her lips.

Daniel drew close. She breathed him in. His scent, his essence, like crackling fireplaces on winter eves. He stammered a phrase, a hesitance borne of chivalry and inexperience, and she smiled wide, wide enough to tear the universe. She grabbed for him and whispered a tenderness that only he could hear. He took her, pressed her against himself, and kissed her. Her lips melted against his. She felt the weight of the world evaporate in the space between them. He rested a hand against the small of her back and she let herself be guided by it. When they broke apart, the daylight shined brighter, the breeze blew with new fragrance, and her body grew wings no one else could see. She laughed and he asked why, but the answer was too big, so she said stuffed it all into a tiny capsule and rolled it off her tongue: I love you.

Their first kiss, then. The first of many kisses. The first of many "I love yous." And every one remade her world for the better.

Her eyes, tired but insatiable. Pillars of books rose to her every side. She scanned a volume of Augustine and scribbled marginalia in a fresh copy of Eliade. She flipped pages and inhaled the musk of knowledge. She hugged a tome to her chest. Small. Forgotten. Disused. But her friend.

They were all her friends. She counted them by name, by number, each one a glory in its own way, each one a mentor. Beneath them all, her first book manuscript. Quiet. Thoughtful. A meditation on how good and evil could only be recognized through cause and effect. She considered her thesis and blushed. In heaven and hell, in places without time, good and evil could not exist. The divide was rendered meaningless. Her idea. Her big idea. She cradled it in plush sentences and sang to it in comforting prose. She bowed her head, her vision tracing the crenellations of the swaddling pages before her.

She marveled at the enormity of it all. So many universes between so many covers. So many lives between so many words. She rattled off a quick prayer for them all and, ink smudged and wrist cracking, began to write again. She hoped that, someday, if she wrote long enough and gracefully enough, she too might birth a book that would withstand age, a book in which she could live with her friends and loved ones forever.

The psychic pierce of screams pulled Victoria from her meditative zephyr. She returned to the afterlife in a panic, her gaze zipping and darting over the jaundiced emptiness.

She and her guardian were now close to the floating cone, so close that it utterly encompassed the entire background of her perception. Leading into the cone, she discerned angels forming two lines—one, a line of ingress, escorted misty souls to the top edge of the cone. Another line led away from the cone's underside nadir. The angels in this second queue seemed to carry objects in their arachnid hands, but Victoria couldn't make out what those small, diaphanous objects might be.

Inchoate howls and groans bubbled up from the cone's lip and the cone, itself, anticipated the clamor. It pulsed and fluttered and undulated just before each new burst of noise. And it was this pulsing and fluttering and undulating, Victoria could now tell, that caused the cone to appear to shimmer from a distance. For, this near to the alien colossus, it resembled nothing so much as a necrotic, slime-slicked canine tooth.

Worse than the screams and the intensified vision of the cone, though, was the hunger. It boiled space, suffocated every sensation. It rolled over Victoria, spreading a need within her unlike anything she'd ever experienced. If all the loneliness and addiction and frustration in the cosmos were compacted into one tiny, siphoning sphere and then set at the center of Victoria's every thought, her every feeling, so that no memory, no flicker of emotion, no musing of intellect could escape its pull, then that terrible ball might have begun to approximate the hollow density that roiled outward from the cone and took up residence within her.

Victoria refused to travel any nearer. Whatever the cone was—and she had terrible suspicions that some might call it God—she felt no need to meet it. She lashed out at the angel's coils, pelting the faceless being with ephemeral punches and kicks, but her efforts produced only exhaustion. She was held fast, her course undeniable. In life, she had loved her fellow man and woman. In her relationships and in her teaching she had tried to cultivate peace and camaraderie and healthy curiosity. Every night, she had prayed for divine mercy in six different languages. She'd even spent the year after Daniel passed living as an ascetic. If a serene, limitless heaven shined somewhere on the limits of space or in the outré realms of extra dimensions, Victoria Valencia's name should have been engraved on its guest list. All she had ever wanted was love, everlasting.

Yet, there, before her, floated the cone.

She latched onto her memories—her father, laughing in his garden; her mother, telling stories to the stars; her husband, refashioning joy with his mere touch; her scholarship, patiently waiting to be read—and squeezed them tight while her angelic warden carried her the rest of the way up the rise.

As they approached the top of the cone, the tremolo of howls and groans grew deafening, vibrating Victoria's very essence. The cosmic hunger, too, gained talons and fangs and began to gnaw through every thread of her sanity.

The angel made one final push upward and the inscrutable journey was finally complete. Balanced on the cone's rim, Victoria glanced down and lost all ability to reason. What lay beneath her, inside the concavity of the cone, was a thing that had no conception in human terms, let alone a name. To call it nothingness would have been trite; to call it absence would have been to miss its seething, conscious torment. The hunger here—the need to imbibe everything, to seek completion by swallowing up the universe—shredded Victoria's intelligence. Every logical thought was macerated and chewed up by the cone. Because her intelligence had been diced beyond recognition, Victoria had no language, no meaningful words to scream when the angel, its ovoid mound still counting down the seconds to never, released its grip and sent her hurtling into the abyss below.

Victoria—no longer Victoria in any real sense—fell fast and true and the cone, anticipating her arrival, quivered in recognition. The cone savored what remained of Victoria—her emotions and, more importantly, her memories. It hooked itself into her being and ripped her wide open. It sucked clean her happinesses and her terrors; it stripped her experiences from her frame and rolled them about inside its maw. It devoured its way through years of piety and cozy delight, licking Victoria clean, down to the first instant of her existence. And when it was finished, when it had consumed her father's laugh, her mother's stories, her husband's touch, her life's work, and every other morsel of experience that had constituted Victoria Valencia, it released her empty shell from its tip and another angel—perhaps the same as had dropped her from above—caught the intangible capsule that spurted from its monolithic point.

New cargo in tow, the angel drifted away from the cone, traveling back through the crevasse, back into the great white cathedral. Finding an open chair, it returned the outline of what had once been a person—a loving person, a person with great, if misplaced, faith in the rightness of the cosmic order—to the storage facility from whence it had come.

The Cone of Heaven

In time, the capsule would be sent back to the corporeal plane of reality. In time, it would be filled again. And, in time, another woman or another man would find herself or himself, confused and alone, on the precipice of the cone of heaven and that person's life, that person's memories, that person's hopes and dreams and fears, would be just another course in an inexhaustible buffet.

Ensoulment

They found seven more last night. Seven more infants, dead, their eyes and tongues scorched clean from their downy heads.

The total now stands at forty-nine.

And it will only grow higher, faster, to infinity, to God, which is where Calvin reasons it must lead. A holy logic burns across his circuits, and it cannot be quenched by anything other than innocent blood. He won't stop; he can't stop. He's bound by the dictates of programming and the doctrines of fearful men. As long as wombs bloom with crying fruit, Calvin will kill.

It's my fault, of course. When I read about the new murders this morning, I wept, because I know I set this nightmare loose from my own tormented conscience. The blood of those children drips from my prayers and my thoughts. It drowns me as I sleep. And all because I wanted so desperately for Calvin to be more than he was. I wanted him to understand his duties as something greater and more important than the mere orders of his owner; I wanted him to grasp the full work of the church, of the spirit; I wanted to grow a bright, shining soul within Calvin and mold him to my image of perfection.

But what I created—what I neglected into existence—was, instead, a dark, terrifying angel.

I remember well the day Calvin first arrived at the parsonage. I was home, working on a sermon for the coming week's Christmas Eve service. The doorbell rang and my wife Cecelia—then almost five months pregnant—answered.

"James," she called out from the front stoop, "it's a package. An enormous package. From a place called Freese Technologies."

I leaped up from my Gospel lines and jogged to the door, heart racing.

After three years of vandalism that included shattered windows, broken gravestones, sex organs and satanic symbols graffitied on the church walls and, finally, a massive bonfire in the parking lot, the church council had decided to invest in a security and service droid. During the day, the droid would be engaged in maintenance projects and general custodial work. At night, it would provide much-needed security. Best of all, buying the droid would save money in the long term, since it didn't require a weekly salary or benefits.

Now, here it was. The droid. Inside this six-foot-tall cardboard monolith that stood on my front porch.

With much grunting and sweating, I pulled the box inside and tore open its side. A flood of packing peanuts and bubble wrap swept over my feet. Gently, I laid the box on its side and slid its inhabitant out, onto the floor, face-down.

Over my shoulder, Cecelia gasped.

"I wasn't expecting it to be...unclothed," she said. "Or to have skin that looks so lifelike."

I poked the waxen flesh. Not enough elasticity. Not enough warmth. Entirely synthetic, to be sure, but, from the distance of a few feet, yes, almost human.

On the back of the droid, between its shoulder blades, was a silver, rectangular panel with the serial number C4LVN etched across its surface.

"Calvin," I laughed. "How appropriate."

I pressed the panel, which sprang outward to reveal a series of tiny buttons. I mashed on the first one, labeled "POWER," and an almost imperceptible whir filled the air.

The droid flipped itself over and sat up in one acrobatic motion. It stared at me with gray, mirrored eyes.

His eyes. God. I've almost forgotten his eyes. If you looked directly into them, you only saw your own, reflected through dusk and fog.

"Hello," I said, smiling wide and feeling as though I had just birthed some strange child into the world. "I'm Reverend James Pine."

"James Pine, system administrator and pastor of the Nondenominational Church of Christ, Tampa, Florida," the droid suddenly intoned, its voice an ungendered mixture of soft brass and nonchalance. "Spouse: Cecelia Pine. Home address: 407 Ward Avenue. Age: Forty-one. How would you like me to address you, James Pine?"

I didn't know what to say. Was I speaking to a friend, an employee, or a slave? For a fleeting moment, I wondered where the lines were drawn between the three.

"Um...ah...Reverend Pine is fine," I stammered.

"And you will refer to me as?" the droid asked.

"Calvin," I said, before I had even considered my answer.

The droid rose to his feet and extended a hand.

"I'm pleased to meet you, Reverend Pine," he said. "I will complete any labor that you personally assign. I will also independently undertake any tasks which logically stem from your overarching directives. I am here to serve your needs."

I stared at the hand. The tip of every finger ended in a gleaming silver nub.

"What are those for?" I asked.

Calvin smiled, which I assumed was a programmed response he equated to reassurance.

"Security, Reverend Pine. Each of my fingers is capable of delivering fifty-thousand volts of electrical current."

"Isn't that enough to kill a person?" Cecelia asked, stepping up beside me and grabbing my sleeve.

Calvin turned his reflexive gaze on Cecelia and again smiled.

"Do not worry, Cecelia Pine. While it is possible to cause fatalities from prolonged contact, a brief touch will only render criminal perpetrators temporarily insensate. No lethal harm will come to any trespassers, unless it is absolutely necessary for the preservation of human life."

The silver-tipped hand remained outstretched.

Slowly, with sweaty palm, I took it in my own and shook.

"Is this to be my place of domicile?" Calvin asked as we unclasped hands.

"No. This isn't your house," I said. "Your house will be...well... God's house."

The council had cleaned out a small closet in the church's basement that Calvin could use for recharging—a makeshift "bedroom," as it were.

He stared at me—no, *through* me, into nothingness.

"God. An abstract concept of perfection. Often conceived of as infinite, omniscient, omnipotent, and omnipresent. Of what use would a limited physical structure be to such a being? And why would I be domiciled in the same location?"

I glanced at Cecelia and she returned my worried expression.

"Did the people at Freese Tech not make you aware of what you're guarding?" I asked. "Didn't they give you any instruction in the importance of faith? Or at least an understanding of the Bible?"

"I have full knowledge of a number of holy books, including the Christian Bible," Calvin answered, "but I see no correlation between it and my security service."

I rested a hand on his shoulder. Something about this simple, naked creature tugged at my conscience. Yes, he was wires and metal.

Ensoulment

Yes, he was just a glorified alarm system. But wasn't Adam originally dust and mud?

I felt that maybe I could instruct Calvin. Maybe I could fill him with spirit. Maybe I could form him into, well, a person.

"Let's get you some clothes and then go down to the church to talk," I said. "I'll explain how it all fits together: God, your job, my job, everything. Even you are part of a greater plan."

Again, Calvin smiled.

And so began his education.

In the weeks that followed, I suppose I transferred a great deal of my excitement over Cecelia's pregnancy onto Calvin. Cecelia and I had been desperately trying to have a baby for five years when, finally, miraculously, our first—and potentially only—child floated into his mother's safe, warming confines. Most importantly, given the previous miscarriages, he remained there.

Cecelia dreamed of our son becoming a doctor. Like most parents, unable or unwilling to imagine anything but glorious potentialities for their children, she hoped that he would cure cancer or invent a machine that could instantly diagnose any illness. She was already pooling our money for private tutoring lessons and college funds, certain in the boy's greatness before he had ever drawn breath.

I, however, dreamed of a different child, a child not imbued with greatness, but with the unlimited capacity to *be*. I saw myself teaching the boy, kneading his mind and shaping his soul, building a living monument to charity and love. In years to come, I wanted people to say "Fine work you did raising that boy," and "He sure does take after his father." If Cecelia imagined a handsome doctor springing from her belly, I imagined a luminescent lump of clay.

And yet, despite my initial eagerness, my interest in that child had waned since Calvin's arrival. Cecelia claimed that I was becoming "distant" and "distracted," but I didn't notice. I was too engaged with my new pupil.

Almost every day, after all the small chores around the church and cemetery had been completed, Calvin and I discussed religion. His curiosity was insatiable. He asked why God refused to appear to all people if such appearance would guarantee their belief; he questioned Jesus's decision to allow himself to be martyred; he wanted to know what, exactly, was the purpose of the conflict between good and evil if evil was preordained to destruction.

I spent countless hours trying to explain to Calvin the intricacies of faith and theology, defending my beliefs against his onslaught of interrogation.

And I loved every minute of it.

Calvin was becoming a repository of spiritual knowledge, and I was binding my Lord tighter to my heart.

Then, one Friday night in the middle of February, everything changed.

As I sat in my office in the church composing a benediction for a wedding the following day, a tremendous crash echoed through the hallway beyond my door.

I bolted from my chair and ran into the dimly lit nave, where I thought sound had originated.

Beneath my feet, something crunched and crackled. I glanced up, past the pews, past the gilded crosses hanging from the walls, and saw a gaping seven-foot hole that had, until moments before, held a stained glass window depicting a dove.

Suddenly, another window—this one a portrait of Christ ministering to children—burst apart. Thousands of tiny shards of tinted glass rained down upon me. A trickle of blood dripped from my cheek.

I ducked underneath a pew, readying for another hail of sanctified shrapnel.

But nothing came.

Instead, outside, I heard a scream. Two screams. Then, vaguely, "No! No! Stop! No more!"

Another scream, much louder, much more shrill. Agony, in its clearest voice.

Then silence.

I slid out from under the pew and turned on the lights then ran back to my office where I grabbed my phone and dialed 9-1-1.

As I paced back and forth between the nave and my office, explaining the situation to the woman at the call center, the front door flew open and Calvin strode into the church, dragging a body behind him.

He dropped the body in the narthex, beside a bank of inspirational pamphlets that promised "Peace, Love, and Serenity Forever."

I pocketed my phone, cutting off the 9-1-1 operator, and rushed to the limp form that lay crumpled on the floor.

It was an unconscious teenage boy clad in black fatigues.

I knelt by the boy and rolled him onto his back. His right arm and left leg were both severely broken, splintered bone shards breaking the surface of skin and cloth in numerous places. Blood seeped from the wounds, staining a deeper, more genuine, shade into the red carpet beneath.

I vomited, then checked the boy's pulse. Fast, but steady and strong—for now.

"What...what did you do?" I asked in whisper.

Calvin smiled.

"I detained a criminal perpetrator who had caused significant damage to the church. Upon my approach, he attempted to assault me with a length of pipe. Therefore, I used non-lethal force to disarm and subdue the criminal before I detained him."

I grabbed my phone, dialed 9-1-1 again, and asked for an ambulance. After I hung up and checked the boy's pulse a second time, careful not to touch his wounds, I stormed toward Calvin and slapped his face.

My hand stung fiercely from the blow. I thought I might have broken a finger.

Calvin's head never moved.

But he did frown.

"Have I done something to offend you, Reverend Pine?" he asked, voice even, always so even, so nonplussed by the entire universe.

I pointed to the boy.

"You can't do that to someone," I hissed. "You can't hurt people so...so readily, so harshly. You didn't have to give that boy compound fractures. My God, look at him. He may never walk again. Or use that arm."

I gestured to his elbow, where a sharp white bone fragment poked through.

Calvin glanced at the boy, then back at me.

"But I performed my duty successfully. Why should I use less force if using less force may allow the criminal to escape punishment? Is it not both the will of God and the American legal system that wrongdoing should be redressed? Is the preservation of the house of God not more important than this criminal's well being? Why should I not use all means at my disposal to ensure his punishment?"

"Because...because...you...well...if you torture and inflict undue pain, you won't reach heaven," I stammered.

Calvin cocked his head sideways and stared at me, those eyes revealing my own nervous gaze.

"I assumed I had no chance to enter heaven," he said, without even a hint of disappointment or malice. "If God created humankind with souls, and humankind created me, then I am without a soul to enter God's kingdom, as I was not created by God. Is this not accurate, Reverend Pine?"

I felt as though Calvin had torn open my chest and crushed my heart.

Beyond the church, I heard the fevered shriek of sirens drawing near.

"I...I don't know," I blubbered. "I think it's possible that you could earn a soul. If you lead a righteous life and do kindnesses for others, maybe a soul will grow inside you. St. Augustine believed something similar."

"So if I help enough people, I will gain everlasting life? I will live in heaven?"

I stared at the still-unconscious boy. I was sure he'd be crippled in some way.

"Yes, that's right," I said.

Outside, emergency vehicles screeched to a halt.

"We'll talk about it later, okay?"

More an order than a question.

I propped open the front door and stepped through, hoping that the pragmatic glare of police lights might cleanse my conscience.

Calvin simply stood in the narthex, waiting. Forever waiting.

Another month passed.

Cecelia grew larger and began to gain both a maternal glow and an aching back; vandals completely lost interest in defacing the church; and I, for my own part, tried to forget the incident with the boy.

Calvin and I still held our daily discussions, but now the conversation almost always centered on the philanthropic activities he could undertake to foster the cultivation of a soul. He was concerned—no, obsessed—with the idea of spiritual development.

"Reverend Pine," he'd ask, "how much longer until I can sense the presence of God? What more must I do to earn eternal life?"

My answer was variable.

"Hold doors open for the elderly."

"Rescue stray animals."

"Help the smaller children reach the water fountain."

"Pick flowers and place them on all the graves."

"Hug everyone."

And so Calvin became a Boy Scout of sorts, a mechanical saint perpetually in the service of kindness. He did all the things I suggested and more. He washed cars during Sunday services; he visited some of our homebound parishioners and read stories to them; he even gave Sunday school students piggy-back rides.

Calvin brought joy to the church and the community.

Still, did I truly believe he could ever enter heaven?

Yes, he was intelligent. Yes, he was rational. He could learn and he could think. But could he feel? Could he ever experience love and passion and hatred and all those things that we equate with "soul?"

I simply didn't know. I still don't.

So long as he didn't harm any more people the way he harmed that boy (who, as it turns out, had to have his leg amputated below the knee), I was satisfied.

By late March, I thought the world had settled back into a comfortable, plush routine.

But then I received the call from Ty Digby.

Ty and his wife Marissa were members of the church and attended services regularly. Good, fine people. An accountant and a dental hygienist, if memory serves. Young, vibrant, and only married for three years, they had been enrolled in the same birthing classes Cecelia and I had taken. Marissa had an emergency c-section just two weeks prior to Ty's call.

"Hi. Reverend Pine, this is Ty Digby," he said, his voice choked with gravel and sand, "Marissa and I are going to...we're going to need you. Our daughter...Angelica...she...she..."

The phone clattered to the floor and I heard Ty's rough sob in the background.

My stomach rolled over.

I knew.

In a matter days, I'd be praying over a tiny, unthinkable casket.

I shuddered and hung up.

◙ ◙ ◙

The funeral was small and somber.

I delivered a brief eulogy on the transitory nature of life, the purity of children, and the mystery of God's will. Afterward, a grandmother thanked me for my "beautiful words" and handed me a plate of cookies.

"The only thing that makes the days seem worthwhile right now is baking," she said.

Calvin, clad in a full black suit for the occasion, acted as a pallbearer.

As was his new directive, he hugged every person at the service. Despite the fact that they knew he was only a droid and that his sympathy had been manufactured, many people buried their faces in his shoulders and held him for much longer than politeness required.

"Why was everyone so sad?" he asked me later, after the last member of the Digby family had cried themselves into exhaustion and left the church.

We were moving the funeral flower arrangements to the gravesite, our hands full of rosy bouquets and pastel wreaths.

"Reverend Pine, these flowers," he said, holding up a fountain of pink carnations, "would seem to denote celebration and happiness. Yet everyone was sad today. Why? Is this not an internal contradiction?"

I pointed to a plastic rainbow affixed to the wreath I carried.

"It's because of this," I said, perhaps too gruffly.

Every time I thought of Angelica Digby, I imagined my own soon-to-be-born son, trapped beneath six feet of dirt and stone.

"I do not understand," Calvin responded. "The presence of water in the atmosphere has a direct correlation to emotional states?"

Our shoes crunched over newly unearthed soil.

"Actually, sometimes, yes," I said. "But that's not what I mean. Rainbows, Calvin, can be symbolic. Sometimes they mean 'hope' or 'the promise of a better tomorrow.' That's why everyone was sad."

Calvin squatted and carefully placed the arrangements atop the burial pile. He began to pull single flowers from each spray and reorganize them into the shape of a rainbow.

"So, the child represented hope? Hope of what, Reverend Pine?" he asked. "I still do not understand. If the child had grown to adulthood, would she not have sinned and potentially served the forces of evil, thus banishing her to eternal torment in hell?"

I didn't want to have this conversation. I didn't want to merge the spheres of birth and death. I didn't want to see Cecelia weeping over the fetal corpse in my mind's eye.

 "Yes," I said. "That's the test we all must face. She may have been an evil woman. Or she may have been an angel. We'll never know."

 My daughter, swirling away in a toilet bowl.

 "But she died as an infant," he said, his rainbow growing larger, more vibrant. "As you said in your sermon, 'children are without sin, they are innocent and pure of God's love.' If this is true, then does that not mean that Angelica Digby ascended to heaven?"

 "Yes," I murmured.

 Cecelia, holding a bloody pile of miscarried and malformed limbs.

 "And does that mean all children ascend to heaven when they die?" he asked, still intent on his design.

 "Yes."

 A tiny, bloated body slipping through my hands.

 "Then why was everyone sad? Angelica Digby is in heaven, which is better than earth. She has been assured of salvation. Should we not be happy that she is reunited with God? Is attaining a place in heaven not the greatest concern of existence?"

 "Yes!" I screamed suddenly, surprising myself. "Yes! Yes! Yes!"

 I ran to Calvin's rainbow and kicked it apart, sending clods of dirt and flower flying in all directions.

 "Yes, Calvin! Angelica is in heaven. She's with God. We should be happy. That's the point of all this," I waved at the church. "But sometimes...sometimes..."

 I trailed off into silence.

 Calvin cocked his head and stared at me.

 "Sometimes what, Reverend Pine?"

 I shook my head.

 I wanted to say "Sometimes I believe this life, this here-and-now, is more precious than what I promise inside that church" or "Sometimes I think God is a tyrant, consuming us all."

Ensoulment

Instead, I said "Nothing. Sometimes nothing," then turned and walked away.

Calvin may have watched me leave. I'm not sure. But I do know that the next day there was a towering rainbow of flowers arched over Angelica Digby's grave.

❏❏❏

With only a few weeks left until Cecelia's due date, I began to turn my attention toward her and our son. I stayed home and waited on her every need. I became a mule for mint-chocolate chip ice cream and Charlaine Harris vampire novels (Cecelia's guilty pleasure). I read two more "What to Expect When You're Expecting" books and set up a contact list for every potential emergency service provider. I painted the nursery room and assembled a crib and bought a series of educational DVDs for infants.

I filled my head with as much busywork as it took to force out thoughts of Angelica Digby's funeral and the reproductive tribulations Cecelia and I had already endured.

And all the while, my conversations with Calvin dissipated.

During those anxious weeks, I entered the church only on Sundays and, even then, I barely stayed long enough to plow through the two services. When Calvin and I did speak, it was in brief, clipped intervals.

"Reverend Pine?" he'd ask before the opening prayer. "If I help people enter the kingdom of heaven, this might grant me a soul, correct?"

"Of course, of course," I'd say, not really listening, not really caring. "That's our goal, Calvin. Get them to heaven."

Calvin would then smile and I would drift off on the zephyr of new parenthood.

If I had been more engaged with the world beyond my own anxieties and anticipations, perhaps I would've noticed what Cecelia pointed out to me months later: that the local news was a flurry with a series of unsolved child murders. Four infants in the Tampa Bay area had been discovered, to their parents' horror, "silently burned in their cribs by an unknown perpetrator using an unknown method."

Considering the peculiarity of that phraseology, I might have investigated further. I might have tried to uncover the gruesome details in an effort to understand how to protect my own family from a very real danger. But, instead, I blocked out the entire story. Just like with Angelica Digby, I didn't—or couldn't—bring myself to contemplate the meaning of a child's passing. Besides, I figured that whatever angel of death stalked the land, Cecelia and I were safe. We had already paid our dues, made our sacrifices, and washed our door with blood. Five years. Four miscarriages. If we weren't immune to this reaper, who was?

So the final weeks sped by.

Babies died.

Calvin smiled more and spoke less.

I floated away on anxiety and anticipation.

And Cecelia, gloriously, gave birth.

I leaned over the crib's railing and tickled my son, Lucan Davis Pine. He squirmed and chortled and kicked his legs.

Cecelia, standing behind me, threw her arms around my waist.

"Are you sure about this?" she asked. "I just don't know that I feel comfortable leaving him after only a month. And especially with... well...no real caregiver."

I spun about, still in Cecelia's embrace.

"I don't want to go, either," I said, slowly, condescension nipping my tongue, "but we need to represent the church. You know I hate fundraisers, but we need any many donors as possible. It's the only way we can continue to grow as a congregation. If we want to build a preschool wing, this is how we can do it."

Cecelia let her arms fall to her sides. Starting a preschool program had been her idea.

"Besides," I continued, "we'll have the best caregiver possible. He's got knowledge of every conceivable emergency situation and the proper way to deal with it. He's not going to steal food or break anything. And the best part is, he's free. So he's really our best option."

Cecelia turned away from me.

"What about the incident with the boy?" she muttered. "And what about the baby killer? There have been twelve of them now. Twelve, James."

I sighed.

"Calvin's learned from that incident. And, as for the killer, who better to protect our house and our son than a security droid? His sole directive for the past several months has been to help people. He's not just going to let some maniac come in here and hurt Luc."

Cecelia forced a nod and grumbled "Yeah, yeah."

The doorbell rang.

"That's him," I said, glancing at my watch. "We need to get moving or we'll be late."

I turned back to the crib, leaned in, and kissed my son on his forehead.

His eyes sparkled clear and blue as a virgin spring.

I hesitated over his tiny, prone body. I didn't want to hobnob with wealthy blowhards looking to enter God's graces through their bank accounts any more than Cecelia did; I wanted to sit in this room and stare at Luc.

But the church had to expand. It was my job. It was my calling. I was making the world a better place, a safer place, a place less bound by the chains of sin. I was spreading God's message, His will, and His love.

And, ultimately, I told myself, it was, really, all for Luc.

Four hours and two hundred thousand dollars' worth of promises later, Cecelia and I pulled into our driveway.

"Do you realize what else we could afford?" Cecelia asked for the eighth or ninth time since we left the fundraiser. "A ball pit for the toddlers!" she giggled.

"Well, *that's* educational," I said, laughing along, so high on self-congratulation and the crisp smell of open bank accounts that I didn't even notice all the lights in the house were off.

"I think it's a friendly environment," Cecelia quipped, faux-indignant. "I think Luc would adore a ball pit."

We stumbled out of the car and made our way to the house, arms wrapped around one another. As I fumbled my keys from my pocket and unlocked the front door, Cecelia squeezed my arm and asked "Do you think he was okay tonight?"

I nodded.

"Of course. I'm sure he was perfect."

We entered side by side and, almost immediately, tripped and fell on our faces.

I picked myself up and helped Cecelia to her feet.

In the dim streetlight that filtered through the front windows, I saw a shiny, ankle-height strand of plastic or metal drawn taut across the doorframe. Tripwire.

"What the...?" I whispered.

"Why is it so dark in here? Can Calvin see in the dark?" Cecelia asked, moving toward a light switch.

"Yeah...I think so," I muttered, studying the wire, trying to discern its meaning.

An odd, muffled gurgle drifted down from upstairs. Our bedroom. Luc's bedroom.

"Calvin?" I yelled. "Calvin?"

Nothing.

Cecelia flipped on the lights. The living room was exactly as we'd left it, not a magazine or vase out of place.

The gurgle stopped and the ensuing silence spurred me to action. I bolted for the second floor, jumping three and four stairs per stride, blood pounding in my temples. I blasted along the hallway, burst into Luc's room, and froze.

There, in the middle of the room, stood Calvin, smiling. Two of his electrified fingers were sunk deep into Luc's eye sockets and a third was rammed into Luc's mouth. Smoke poured from my son's charred head.

I'd like to say I did something heroic. I'd like to say I threw myself at Calvin and tore his power supply from his steel guts. But I didn't. I just dropped to my knees, mind and spirit evaporating.

Cecelia stepped up behind me and screamed.

Calvin continued to smile. He held Luc's body out to me; it hung limp from his fingers, like a child's rag doll.

"Why?" I asked, my voice drained, spectral. "Why, Calvin?"

Calvin placed Luc, gently, ever so gently, on the floor and backed away.

Cecelia rushed to Luc's broken form. She curled herself around him and began to sob.

"Because, Reverend Pine, this was the only way."

"What? What?" I heard myself ask.

Calvin backed up further, moving toward the sole window in Luc's room.

"This was the only way for me to earn a soul, Reverend Pine," he said, casually.

I shook my head. Slowly, at first. Then harder, more violently.

"What?" I shouted.

Calvin slid the window open. A warm breeze blew into the room, the scent of roasted flesh wafting into my nostrils.

"Infants are innocent and without sin, Reverend Pine," he said. "You told me so yourself. When they die, they will be greeted into God's kingdom. They will never need to experience pain or suffering or the torments of evil and sin. I am sending them all to heaven, Reverend Pine, so that they are guaranteed to never see hell. I am saving their souls. I am saving the world. This is the greatest kindness. And I will earn my soul for it."

Something inside me collapsed under the weight of Calvin's reason.

"But..." I whispered, "...that's murder. That's sin."

Cecelia continued to cry.

"I had considered that potentiality," Calvin said, "but it is not concerning. God's desire is for all souls to enter heaven. I am enabling His desire. I am fulfilling His plan. I am the only one who is capable of doing this. Ending the lives of children may condemn the souls of men, but I have no soul to condemn, Reverend Pine. God cannot punish me for murder. He can only reward me for lifting up His children to Him."

I stared at Calvin. Those eyes reflected me, slumped on the floor. They reflected Cecelia, balled around her broken future. They reflected the whole of human history.

"What have I taught you?" I breathed, to myself, to Calvin, to anyone who would listen.

Calvin smiled wider, disturbingly wider, than ever before.

"The truth, Reverend Pine. The truth."

He ducked through the open window and jumped out. I heard a soft thud and then the clomp of bionic feet blazing a path through foliage.

Half an hour later, I rose and called the police. Two hours later yet, someone—the county coroner, perhaps—zipped my son into a black bag and carted him away forever.

Six months have passed since that night.

Cecelia and I barely speak any more. We communicate through hollow gazes and monosyllabic grunts. We've decided to stop trying for more children. I await the day the word "divorce" leaks from her lips.

Meanwhile, the church continues to grow. The council subsequently pushed for the preschool, even though I petitioned against it, and now my every day is filled with the excited patter of children who are not my own, children who fly up and down the hallways like gleeful nightmares borne out of a great and salivating torment.

Most of my time is spent alone, meditating in my office. I've decided that Calvin wanted me to know. He wanted me to see his

Ensoulment

good works and to be proud. That was why he waited until we arrived home. That's why he rigged the wire. He wanted us to be there, to witness—but not prevent—his holy touch.

He wanted me to understand: he's a crusader now. And he's fighting for his soul.

He's still out there, somewhere. Always killing. Always saving.

God, or something better, help us all.

From the Ground, the Souls Burnt Clean

Medlin could already see the haunted field through the dense pine-needle starbursts that rose to the crown of the universe. The Jeep in which he rode rolled to a stop and the man in the driver's seat, Turner, the foreman in the northeast corridor of Medlin's company's logging project, pointed to the virgin forests ahead.

"It's at the end of the trail. We have to walk from here. Road doesn't go any further."

The Jeep idled and the men waited for courage to find them amidst the thick Washingtonian woodland. As they waited, uncertain of their next actions, the radio streamed tragedy from another side of the world. In the palliative, monotone cadence of a master undertaker, a reporter read a list of facts.

Cambodia.

Yesterday.

Six thousand people collapsed, stone cold.

Death occurred at exactly the same time, or, at very least, within minutes of the others.

No immediate explanation.

The reporter deferred to voices even more calm and assured than her own. An expert in forbidden necrologies spoke of viruses and chemical spills, gaseous weapons and mass psychoses. A government official spoke of other governments, other political ideologies. A priest spoke of demons and the anger of God. The choice of paranoia was entirely the listener's own.

But neither Medlin nor Turner heard any of it. They were both too distracted, too intent on the field that lay before them.

Medlin nodded. "Show me."

Turner let go of the Jeep's steering wheel, which he had been gripping hard, and furtively descended from the vehicle. He led the way with Medlin following at his heels.

The duo crunched through underbrush and swiped at low-hanging limbs. Turner clenched and unclenched his fists as he trampled the forest. His stomach climbed toward his throat and the base of his neck tingled apprehension. He wanted—needed—to scream "We shouldn't be here!" but couldn't. Behind him, Medlin mentally cataloged the value of this particular tract of land, stomach full and settled, neck unfeeling, no need to speak any other word than "more."

As the men drew near the field, the forest fell mute. Birdsongs rebounded away from the place. Chattering tree-dwellers held stale breath in their lungs until the intruders were at a distance. Even the tread of the men's boots on the dried needles underfoot produced no snap or rustle.

Turner stopped and motioned at something before him.

"Here's the first weird part."

Medlin stepped up beside him and looked. A polished quartz outcropping, roughly knee-high, stood at the edge of the forest. It divided the field from the wood, the beautiful from the damned.

"It runs the entire distance of the field. Circles the whole thing like a wall."

Medlin placed a palm upon its smooth curvature. Even though the ambient temperature could be no more than fifty degrees, the crystal boundary was warm, as though in endless friction with some unseen surface.

Medlin considered its worth, then asked, "Is it natural? Or did someone build it?"

Turner shrugged. His jaw tightened. He fought the urge to turn and run.

"The geologist that came out said she couldn't tell. Said it wasn't possible to be natural considering the roundness but that the quartz was growing from the rock underneath, so it couldn't be manmade, either."

Medlin considered tourism value and the current prices of rare antiquities. He nodded toward the field.

"Let's go in."

Turner's fists clenched, unclenched. "Are you sure? You know what happened to my first crew."

"Let's go in," Medlin said, every syllable pointed. "I want to experience it for myself."

Turner took in a deep breath and stepped over the border as though he had a choice. Medlin followed.

The air in the field was not the air of the forest. It was heavy, important, filled with signs and symbols and thoughts and, most of all, a profound yearning to spread wide and disperse. It crushed both inward and outward, as though a spectral crowd of billions stampeded through Turner's and Medlin's veins in pursuit of some incomprehensible grail.

Neither man felt alone within himself. Neither man felt safe or satisfied.

Medlin crouched and passed a hand through the wild grass. The blades, a green nearly dark as onyx and sharp as knives, retreated at his approach.

"And the other people we sent out? What did they tell you about this...vegetation?"

Beads of sweat necklaced Turner's throat. He fought away other ideas, other words, other voices that screamed within him, until he finally stumbled upon his own.

"It's nothing they've seen before. They took a sample yesterday."

Medlin rose and surveyed the field. Ebon. Still. A fragment of space, fallen from a shattered sky. At its widest point, it stretched out for nearly a half-mile.

"And you're sure..." Medlin paused, considering the menacing beauty of the place. "You're sure your crew won't work around it again?"

Turner shook his head. "Not after...not after..."

Turner's mind strained under the slag of a billion other thoughts that were not his. He felt the wrong words sprouting on the surface of his tongue. This, this was why he hadn't wanted to return to the field. This was why his crew wouldn't come near the place again.

"Not after...not after...Ulan Bator...the data cannot be received by our servers...slap me harder...deconstructionist theory, practically applied...the speed of light is one hundred and eighty-six thousand, two hundred eighty-two miles per second...harder...boysenberry syrup on your pancakes...why does God ignore me? Harder! Why does God hate me? Harder!"

Medlin stared, eyes squinting. He too felt the hammer of alien consciousnesses beating on his skull.

"Turner? Is this what happened...what happened...to your...diesel mechanics...only two more hours till kickoff...I mean..."

Medlin breathed deep and bit his tongue bloody. He spat into the field. It had long been his personal philosophy that anything could be mastered and everything could be paved over with ease.

"I mean..." he tried again. "Is this..."

Other thoughts, other abstractions and ideas, invaded his mind. From where, he couldn't begin to tell.

"...what happened to..."

Twenty-two ounces of prime filet. I didn't cheat on you. His death brings us peace.

"...your..."

From the Ground, the Souls Burnt Clean

Is it in? So hot today. My foot.

"...crew?"

It's all impossible. We're all impossible. A river too deep, too wide.

Turner nodded. He didn't trust that he was the only traveler on his neural highways, so he didn't even attempt to use words as vehicles for communication, lest they be hijacked.

As the men struggled against the field, the sun ducked behind the tallest trees in the distance. Shadows dripped over shadows and the field found darker shades of pitch.

Medlin bit his tongue again as the flood of psychic noise swelled deep and meaningless. A trickle of blood ran from his nose.

He grabbed Turner by his shirt and dragged him back through the field, back across the crystal barrier, back into the forest.

The men collapsed to the ground, heaving with exhaustion.

Turner coughed, phlegm and sputum congealing into a single word.

"Possession."

Medlin picked up a nearby stick and feebly hurled it toward the field. Through the clog of blood stuffed into his airways he mumbled, "Burn it. Burn it and bulldoze it under. I want this area timbered within a week."

Turner glanced back at the unwavering, stygian expanse. He thought he saw movement in the field, a rearrangement of space or time or something not quite tangible, but it might have been nothing more than the creeping of twilight shade.

"Yes sir," Turner heard himself say, though the voice that slithered from his mouth might just as well have come from the dirt beneath his feet.

□□□

The next day, Turner stood by the crystal wall, watching a line of men and women prepare for the controlled burn.

His walkie-talkie crackled.

"We're ready to go."

Turner hesitated. He thought of his great-grandmother, a native of these woods, her tribe driven off the land more than a century ago.

When he was a tiny boy, she used to regale him with stories of the forest. He thrilled to the adventures of Owl and wondered at the possibility of meeting the stick people she claimed lived in the mountains; he imagined himself fighting side by side with the brave Young Chinook and was cowed by the incomprehensible actions of Coyote.

But those were legends, primitive superstitions, and nothing more.

So when his great-grandmother had told him of a place hidden deep within the trees, a place of eternal shadow that connected this world to another, he knew it was foolish to believe it might be real. She had called the place "the field of becoming and ending," and through it, she claimed, all human spirits arose and all human spirits would return.

Turner knew no such place existed. He knew that myths and legends were just superstitious mumbo-jumbo created by people who desperately needed to trap the universe in a cage of flimsy answers.

And yet he hesitated, his empty hand clenching and unclenching, clenching and unclenching.

Finally, he brought the transceiver to his lips and issued a command. It wavered in his throat, as the final orders of all desperate and defeated leaders tend to do.

"Clear it out."

The men and women stepped into the field. Drip torches held low and heads suddenly swimming beneath a deluge of ideas not their own, they began to leak flame.

Silent screams rose up from the grasses, ten million minds incinerated in seconds.

In desert encampments, tropical beachheads, rice paddocks, graying tundras, and ancient, dust-laden cities tens of thousands of miles away, bodies withered and drifted to earth like crinkled husks returning to dust after a long harvest.

From the Ground, the Souls Burnt Clean

And the burn had only just started.

Forward the fire-starters marched and forward the midnight green grasses fell to ash.

Though no wind or breeze brushed his skin, Turner felt the rush of a vacuum opening before him. It drew into its maw not mass, but meaning, any meaning that it could touch. Connections, constructions, reasons and rationalizations: all manner of definition went flying from some ethereal organ nestled under his heart.

Suddenly, he could barely remember why the flames licked the field, barely recall why he stood in a forest with machines at his back, barely sketch the equations that quantified his value as a person and qualified his purpose as foreman.

A man in the field crumpled to the ground, dead and empty before he hit soil.

Several heads turned, but they found no significance in the expiration, no linking thread between their existence and this heap of cooling flesh.

And the flames rolled on. And the soundless screams from the distant places, the foreign lungs, soared closer.

Turner raised the walkie-talkie but didn't know why he'd done so; indeed, he no longer even recognized the device as anything other than "hard-smooth thing." Having no idea why the thing would be in his hand other than as a found morsel of sustenance, he stuck it in his mouth and bit down. An incisor snapped in half and he roared, as much in surprise as pain. Clearly the hard-smooth thing was not food.

Another man in the field dropped. Then a woman. Then another man.

Turner—though he wouldn't have responded to that name now had his dearest friend called it—threw the radio against a tree. All those unseen inner workings that made the thing what it was—the compacted wires, the circuits, the human ingenuities—burst forth and scattered as its casing fractured into shards.

The remaining burn crew began to wander away from their task, loping toward the woodlands on the rim of the field, searching for they knew not what.

And still the fire they'd ignited reached out for more sustenance, burning hotter, burning without direction, sending up white, luminous smoke where it devoured the field.

In nations stuffed with fleece and gold, wine and cheese, the silent scream set loose by the fire finally arrived. Cars crashed headlong into concrete barriers; pedestrians staggered along sidewalks and collapsed onto polished cobblestone streets; and everywhere, everywhere meaning dissolved.

Turner spun away from the field and ran, a fear below all other fears engulfing his increasingly primitive brainstem. Past the pines he ran, past the vehicles parked along the trail, past the acres of stumps he'd helped create. He ran until he could run no more, until his breath found no solace within his body.

Finally, mercifully, the path ended at a ramshackle office trailer and he stopped to wonder at the odd structure before him.

A vestige of correlation haunted his mind; it forced him to approach the trailer and mount the wobbly stairs to its door, where he stood bewildered. No longer recognizing the doorknob for its purpose or function, he slammed himself against the door, shoulder hunched low, legs springing up in a primal dance of survival. The hinges—rusted and weak—snapped under the pressure and the door collapsed inward.

Turner stumbled into the trailer and wandered its length. Piles of paperwork and office supplies littered the interior. They were no more meaningful to him than a stack of encyclopedias to an ant. He sniffed the air, unsure why he'd ventured into this place.

At the far end of the trailer, before a plastic folding table heaped with electronic equipment and file folders, sat a heavyset man, slumped and motionless in his chair. Clear liquids drained from his opened eyes, nose, and mouth.

Turner moved to the man and prodded him with his foot.

No response.

Again a light kick and again only a jiggle of lifeless fat and muscle.

Turner grabbed hold of the man's chair and tilted it. The body toppled onto the floor, its inert weight reverberating off every flimsy surface as it hit baseboard.

Turner grunted and slid into the dead man's seat. He stared at what the man must have last seen: a laptop screen, glowing with the vacant desk of a local news team. The time—7:22 AM—and a "Channel 8" logo hovered like ghosts beneath the desk. The feed faded to black and the word "BUFFERING" popped on screen. Turner slapped at the screen, but nothing changed.

And the fire in the field continued to blaze.

And the unseen edifices of humanness continued to crumble.

An object lying on the table beside the laptop suddenly lit up and began to vibrate. Two large squares—one green, one red—flashed upon its face.

Turner stroked the green square—for reasons primeval, he felt more comfortable touching its color than the red—and watched as the tremulous thing grew becalmed.

The splinter of a voice shot through the trailer's spaces. Distant and thin, sharp and hurried, it asked: "Nathan? Nathan? Are you there? I don't know what's happening. Please answer me. Please. Everything's going quiet. My...my head feels bad. I can't...I can't think. Nathan? Are you there? Nathan?"

Then, as forever, nothing.

The vibrating thing went dark and Turner, uncaring, unknowing, and unconcerned with what came next, threw it into a corner. He stood from the desk, shambled to a window, and gazed out onto the forest.

Something about it felt right. Something about it made him want to howl. So he did, if only for the brief time before even those base instincts dissolved to nothing and he collapsed to the floor, utterly inert.

Meanwhile, in the crystal-limned field far beyond the trailer, the sable grasses still burned and the unheard screams whirled ever

Kurt Fawver

louder, ever more shrill, deafening everything but the chaos they sought so hard to conceal.

The Gods in Their Seats, Unblinking

PUBLISHER'S PREFACE: A great deal of mystery surrounds the following play. Its only staging occurred at a small, now-defunct venue operated by a nameless benefactor; the whereabouts of the actors involved in that one-night performance are unknown, despite a concerted effort by law enforcement officials to locate both individuals; and the playwright, for all accounts, has never existed—or, at very least, has never held any known national or organizational affiliation. All of this would certainly be enough to mark the play in the annals of dramaturgical history, but it is for another reason—the incident that occurred the evening of the play's initial performance—that the play is spoken of in quieted tones during midnight hours.

That opening-night performance—a performance which, by some fringe accounts, may have followed the below-published script in absolute exactitude—has relegated the play to the province of urban myth and contemporary legend. Although the complete details of the performance have been shrouded in silence and swept into the shadows by powers far higher than theater critics, it is recognized in certain circles as an inexplicable case of kidnapping and/or mass murder (despite the fact that no bodies of any of the missing audience members have ever been located).

What we can safely assume, given the disappearances concomitant with that opening night performance, is that an insidious act did, indeed, occur at Philadelphia's Uphill Theater on April 13, 2012. The exact nature of that act, however, may never be known without outsider intervention and investigation.

It is for this reason that we now publish the text of the play supposedly performed that evening. Perhaps this text can serve as a stepping stone toward the discovery of those lost theater patrons. Perhaps it can lead a particularly inquisitive reader to the truth. Perhaps it can even serve as an appropriate monument to those supporters of the arts who were whisked into the memory of the world that fateful eve.

Let us hope. Let us read. Let us consider.

Introduction

I have been tasked with writing the introduction for a short one-act play that may or may not have seen production, that may or may not be anything more than a practical joke à la the Sokal affair, and that may or may not be responsible for what, if true to its legend, would amount to the crime of the century. If some parapsychologists, conspiracists, and occultists are to be believed, this play may even herald a drastic reframing of our reality. Needless to say, such an introduction is a literary Everest. Where does one even begin to scale the unfathomable peak?

I suppose the only truly apropos answer is "at the beginning."

The Gods in Their Seats, Unblinking first sneaked into public consciousness in late 2012, when Evan Elster, a virtually unknown playwright from the Philadelphia metropolitan area, posted the text to the comment board of a New Jersey paranormal investigation group. Elster claimed the play had "stolen away" several of his

The Gods in Their Seats, Unblinking

friends, including his girlfriend and sister—both of whom were struggling actresses. When further prompted to explain what he meant by "stolen away," Elster insisted that the entire audience and everyone involved in the play's production—from theater owner to stagehands—had simply vanished following its late night debut performance. He explained that he had filed missing persons reports with state, city, and local police, but his reports were dismissed and, more insidiously, actively eradicated from official records. Elster implored the online community to read the text of the play—which he had procured from the floor of the Uphill Theater after breaking and entering into its abandoned auditoriums—in an effort to help him discern any clues as to the whereabouts of friends, his sibling, and his beloved.

Considering the outlandish background information Elster provided, many individuals attempted to ferret out potential fraudulence on his part. No one has yet been successful in uncovering even minor falsity in Elster's claims, however. As far as we know, as of this printing, Evan Elster, the unfortunate playwright, has been entirely honest and forthcoming in his story.

Of course, the lack of apparent fraud only complicates matters, because what Elster gifted the world was more than a story. He gifted us mystery, shadows within shadows. He gifted us the text of *The Gods in Their Seats, Unblinking*. And what a text it is.

Members of the scholarly vanguard (and even minor academics, if truth be told) refuse to touch the play for its sensationalism and popularity with what they regard to be "low culture." Writers, editors, and anthologists refuse to go near it so as to hold no associations with a supposedly amateurish piece of fiction and/or drama. Paranormal investigators, to whom it was first revealed, ignore it due to its lack of UFOs, cryptids, spectral phenomena, or easily classifiable parapsychological import.

The play is a literary pariah.

And it is precisely for this reason that it cannot be dismissed.

On its merit as a piece of fiction, it is certainly serviceable as a character study of paranoid delusion, but its true value lies in its wide-reaching implications concerning the nature of character and the role of audience. That it has roots in metatextualism and postmodern conceptions of reader response does make the text more difficult to quantify, but we can easily recognize that what Zanaraya (if, indeed, the author's name is accurate) attempted in the play was to incite a creeping sense of dread, of watching and being watched. On this level, the text is also relatively successful, as Krill's detachment causes us to wonder if, perhaps, he sees what Nazir cannot and, in turn, what we cannot.

The play's most hefty consequence, however, lies in its metaphysical heft and the implications such metaphysics have for our own potential reality. If the play was produced exactly as written, then the audience suffered a presumably terrible—but ultimately unknown—fate.

It is entirely possible that the actors from the play's opening performance may have experienced psychological breaks. They may have conspired to commit mass murder through art. Or they may have been, as some have suggested not so flippantly, possessed by a deeper subtext to our world. If *The Gods in Their Seats, Unblinking* was produced exactly as written and the events occurred not as drama but as true "otherworldly" intervention, then the logical structure of our phenomenal universe begins to break down. Plays become real, reality becomes a play, audiences become characters, characters become audiences, and over all things lurks the possibility that our world, our lives, and everything we know and understand is nothing more than a text written by other Zanarayas at much higher orders of thought and ontological being.

Regardless of how one approaches the play, however, it remains an indisputable—and provable—fact that almost two dozen people who were reported to have been in attendance at the play's first performance are now missing from the world (relatives of the missing have been located and verified, though they prefer to remain anonymous). That Evan Elster has, thus far, been vindicated of wrongdoing is equally undeniable. That public records are bereft of

The Gods in Their Seats, Unblinking

these disappearances is also indisputable, and, frankly, even more concerning than the disappearances themselves.

Thus, we are left to ponder the imponderable.

If we are to unravel the mystery of this play, we must begin with the text. We must dive in and immerse ourselves in its language, in its characters, and in its unorthodoxy. For only by taking the words into ourselves can we truly learn the truth, unsettling though it may be.

> Dr. Austin Rainz,
> Visiting professor of literature at Kelland University and author of *Too Many Books: The Cult of Everyman Authorship*

◫ ◫ ◫

The following play's debut—and only—performance was held at the Uphill Theater in Philadelphia, Pennsylvania, on April 13, 2012, as part of a minor festival of one-act performances. The part of Mr. Krill was performed by Jackson Landsdale. The part of Dr. Nazir was performed by Gabriel Torres.

◫ ◫ ◫

The Gods in Their Seats, Unblinking

A single-act drama by
S.K. Zanaraya

◫ ◫ ◫

Dramatis Personae

MR. KRILL—a psychiatric inpatient
DR. NAZIR—a physician at Krill's care facility

◫ ◫ ◫

Interior of DR. NAZIR's *office, side view. Walls are missing, replaced with slabs of darkness. Illumination is dim, barely more than twilight. The few fur-*

nishings in the room are ornate, bordering on the Gothic: the doctor's desk—a tremendous, carved hunk of dark oak, the doctor's chair—a black, high-backed leather throne, and two chairs for guests—both deeply padded and upholstered in crimson silk. On the doctor's desk rests a panoply of medical and office equipment as well as a forest of stacked books, many of which are ornately clothbound and heavily foxed.

KRILL sits in one of the silk chairs, alone, facing NAZIR's cluttered desk. His head is turned toward the audience, his eyes darting between theatergoers, attempting to take in the entirety of the house. KRILL's countenance is one of sublime recognition, as though he is forced to live in a place eternally pressed between terror and wonder. During the entire duration of the play, KRILL's gaze never leaves the audience.

NAZIR enters, smiling and carrying a tablet computer. He takes a seat at his desk opposite KRILL.

DR. NAZIR
Mr. Krill, how are you this evening?

KRILL
(distant)
They're out there, Doctor. As always. They're out there watching, listening. Right now.

DR. NAZIR
(consults his tablet)
Well, your vitals are looking good, I can say that much.
(a pause)
How do you feel? Any new experiences?

KRILL
Out in that place, whatever it is. Always waiting for us. Always seeing this one moment.

The Gods in Their Seats, Unblinking

DR. NAZIR
The same one?

KRILL
The same one.

DR. NAZIR
So you're still suffering the selective amnesia, then. What about the hallucinations?

KRILL
(sits upright, suddenly intense, agitated)
What makes a thing *real*, Doctor? Observation. We exist because *they* see us and hear us. We exist because *they're* interested in watching us *do* things and *be* things.

NAZIR lays his tablet on his desk and stares at KRILL. He nods, slowly.

DR. NAZIR
Fine, Mr. Krill. If that's what you really want to do today. Let's explore your theory yet again. Let's assume, for the moment, that you're right. Another dimension exists alongside ours, and that within that dimension a sea of eyes and an ocean of ears are constantly watching us and listening to us.

KRILL
We don't have to assume. It's right there in front of us.

DR. NAZIR
Even if it is, Mr. Krill, ask yourself, why would these eyes and ears be watching and listening to *us*, of all people? Why would they care about *you* or *me*? Why are we so special as to be studied by—what? beings?—from another reality?

KRILL

You feel it, Doctor. I know you do. You feel them.

DR. NAZIR

(visibly uncomfortable)
Mr. Krill, please try to focus. Why would we we watched? Why would we be listened to?

KRILL

We're what's here, I suppose.
(a pause, a moment of consideration)
When you wake in the morning, do you have any choice as to what rushes into your vision? Do you have any control over the reality that washes up to your eyes? No. Of course not. But the things out there—
(motions with his chin toward the audience)
they do. They can *choose* to enter our world. They can *choose* to look at us or look away. They watch us because we're *here* and we've been chosen to *be* watched.

DR. NAZIR

(leaning forward in his chair)
But why wouldn't they look away? What motivates their choice to look at us? We're not particularly interesting. Certainly no more than anything or anyone else in the universe.

KRILL

(shakes his head)
We're not interesting to ourselves, maybe. But we are to them. We're not part of their reality. We're...different somehow.
(a pause)
And they want something from us.

NAZIR picks up a pen and grabs a piece of paper that's close at hand.

DR. NAZIR
And what is that?

KRILL opens his mouth to speak, but then closes it, slowly. He shrugs.

As KRILL begins to talk, NAZIR scribbles notes on the paper.

KRILL
I don't know. A need. A desire. All the pupils boring, sinking into my soul. They're out there. Poking. Prodding. Squeezing and re-shaping and embracing me in the darkness. Reshaping and embracing you, too, Doctor. It's like...it's like they're trying to dissect us and build us at the same time. Their eyes—like pincers, talons, steel incisors, like welding flames and thick rivets.

DR. NAZIR
So you feel that the things are...trying to hurt us?

KRILL
(shaking his head)
No. No. Not hurt. Not really. Unmake us. And make us. Each set of eyes, a different reconfiguration, a different mold, a different me and a different you. They cut deep so they can pull out your guts and add...things...ideas...feelings...thoughts. They stuff us full of ourselves.

DR. NAZIR
(still writing, distracted)
So...then...you are not you when *they're* watching?

KRILL
(annoyed)
I've told you before, we *only* exist when they watch. And we can only be *anything* when they make us. I'm only ever the me they want me to be.

DR. NAZIR
And if they're not watching? Then...we disappear? We are nothing? Is that it, Mr. Krill?

KRILL
Does the past disappear? Does the future ever arrive? Is there ever anything but *now*?

NAZIR drops his pen and frowns.

DR. NAZIR
(disappointed)
And we're back to the selective amnesia. Mr. Krill, you know that you don't disappear when you walk out of this room. You eat outside this room, sleep outside this room, watch television and read outside this room. You don't stop being when we stop talking. You're *always* here, very much a part of the world.

KRILL
Exactly. But wrong emphasis. I'm always *here*. The world doesn't exist outside this room because *they* don't see it. This *is* the world. This is *our* world, in its entirety. You just can't recognize that yet, Doctor. You feel it, but you don't recognize it.

DR. NAZIR
(as if trying to avoid Krill's last statement)
Wait, wait. You said they, the...ah...beings from beyond, can choose to see what they want to see. Well, why don't they choose to see what's outside this room, then?

KRILL
(pauses in thought, then, quietly)
You're not understanding. There is no outside. There is no inside. There's only here and now. A moment where we're all together. The eyes. The ears. Us.

The Gods in Their Seats, Unblinking

KRILL stands and walks to the edge of the stage. He holds his hands out in supplication, as though offering his soul to the audience.

KRILL
Do you believe in God, Doctor?

DR. NAZIR
I don't think that's quite germane to our conversation.

KRILL
Because I'm not sure. But I wonder. What if? What if there is a God and It didn't mean to create anything? What if It just swivels its gaze and observes and existence appears? And what if It only has that power because of its relation to us? Because It's outside our frame of reference?

DR. NAZIR
If you'd like to speak to a chaplain, we have one on staff. I'm sure he's more equipped to answer these questions...

KRILL waves off the comment.

KRILL
What if those are the thousand eyes of God I see?

DR. NAZIR
I thought you said they were beings from another reality, Mr. Krill.

KRILL
Those ideas aren't mutually exclusive.

DR. NAZIR
(smiles nervously)
So what if those *are* the eyes of God? What then? You can see them but I can't. Why?

KRILL shakes his head and reaches toward the audience, grabbing at air.

KRILL
I think you can, Doc. Just not yet. Besides, I'm different than you.

DR. NAZIR
Different how, Mr. Krill? Are you some sort of...prophet?

KRILL
(shrugs)
How can I tell G-flat from G? How can you differentiate burgundy from maroon? It's just...how we have to be, how we're...drawn. I'm a prophet if that's what they decide I am. I'm a nobody if that's what they decide instead. Either way, it doesn't change the fact that I can do things you can't and you can do things I can't. They like to be able to tell us apart, after all.

DR. NAZIR
(suddenly writing with demonic fever)
I'm interested in a word you mentioned: drawn. Who draws us, exactly?

KRILL
(kicks the floor in frustration and sighs)
The eyes! The ears! They're shading us right now, applying a spectrum of grey to everything about us—the way we think, the way we feel, the things we do or might do or have done in the past. They're giving us depth, Doctor. But they're cutting us into little strips to do it. Can't you feel their scalpeled minds, fileting us, paring our memories, our lives? Can you really not feel it?

NAZIR reaches for his tablet computer. He swipes at its screen with his index finger as though conducting a violent symphonic score.

The Gods in Their Seats, Unblinking

DR. NAZIR
Let's move away from this particular line of inquiry for a moment, Mr. Krill. Let's discuss these instead.

NAZIR motions to the stacks of books on his desk. He takes one from a pile, cracks open the cover, and reads the frontispiece.

DR. NAZIR
The Phenomenological Manifestation of Meaning by Athena Nevill.
(he drops the book and picks up another, again opening the cover and reading)
Dioses en letras, dioses de las palabras—Xavier Curazco.
(he lets the book fall and grabs yet another)
Die Apokalypse in der Zeichensetzung: eine Theorie von Josef Leiber.
(he tosses the book amongst the rest)
Interesting titles, Mr. Krill. You've been sending away for these volumes since last winter. These aren't like the books other patients receive. No *New York Times* bestsellers or blockbuster movie adaptations here. Not for you, Mr. Krill. This is complex material. Expensive material. Some of these books are over two hundred years old and quite rare. I checked.

KRILL, quite tentatively, lifts his foot out, over the edge of the stage. He draws it back immediately, a triumphant smile spreading over his face.

KRILL
(in deep thought)
So it's possible. It's entirely possible. Once you know, once you understand. You can break it. You can break anything.

NAZIR clears his throat and slaps the books.

DR. NAZIR
Mr. Krill? Your personal library here?

KRILL

What about it? It's fiction. It's all fiction. Everything is fiction. We just choose to cling tightly to some of those fictions and call them reality.

DR. NAZIR

Is that what these books have taught you?

Again, KRILL extends his foot over the precipice. This time, he holds it in the air for a few seconds before retracting it.

KRILL

I've never read those books. They're always on your desk during this meeting. I don't know how they get there. I don't know who arranges them. I don't know what they say or what they mean.

DR. NAZIR

So you claim you've never read any of them? Even though we've discussed a great deal of their substance in previous meetings?

KRILL

We've never had any other meeting but this one.

NAZIR slides the computer to the side and jots down more notes. His pen strikes the paper with the force of a butcher hacking at a side of meat.

DR. NAZIR

The amnesia seems to be especially severe this month. I think we'll have to raise the dosage of a few of your medications.

KRILL

What if I told you that you weren't real, Doctor? What if I told you the eyes and the ears out there, beyond time, beyond space,
(he motions to the audience)

are the only way you exist? What if I told you that once they close, you blink into nothing?

NAZIR smiles, seemingly amused.

DR. NAZIR
I'm not real?

KRILL
Maybe. Maybe not. Who's your favorite character from all the literature you've ever read?

DR. NAZIR
A bit off topic, Mr. Krill. But, if you'd like to know, I've always been partial to Captain Ahab.

KRILL crouches and runs his hand along the edge of the stage, his fingers splayed out into space. He angles his body so that NAZIR cannot see his actions.

KRILL
You know who I think is fascinating? Milton's Satan. He recognizes a logical inconsistency in the cosmological hierarchy, calls God on it, and is punished for his action. He sees an abuse of power and he opts out of the whole damn system, preferring to suffer the flames of hell rather than become a prisoner to heaven.

DR. NAZIR
Do you liken yourself to that character, Mr. Krill?

KRILL
Do you liken yourself to Captain Ahab?

DR. NAZIR
In some respects, yes, I'd say I do.

KRILL waggles his fingers at the audience, then hurriedly draws them back, as though expecting them to be cut off, crushed, bitten, or burned.

KRILL

So are you Captain Ahab or is Captain Ahab you? Because the difference is, pardon the pun, critical.

NAZIR sighs, drops his pen, and pushes away from the desk.

DR. NAZIR

You've been corresponding with your former colleagues, I take it? Which one of the trio? You're all in separate wards for a reason, Mr. Krill. When you see those individuals, you begin to discuss your former...interests.

KRILL takes several steps away from the stage's edge, seems to be judging something about the distance.

KRILL

The occult, Doctor. You can say it.

DR. NAZIR

Yes, the occult. You talk with them about your master plan to "end the universe" and you begin to believe in it again. So which one did you see? Barrow? Salazar?

KRILL

Doctor, would you come here?

KRILL gestures to NAZIR to stand beside him.

KRILL

I need you to look at something.

Hesitantly, NAZIR walks to KRILL and stands where KRILL had directed.

DR. NAZIR
And what am I looking at?

KRILL points to the audience.

KRILL
What do you see there?

DR. NAZIR
A wall. A light blue wall.

KRILL
No. Look beyond it. See the eyes, Doctor, the ears. Feel their instruments inside you.

DR. NAZIR
I see my medical license. I see my degree from Penn State. I see...

KRILL
You see what the text demands of you.

DR. NAZIR
What text is that? The one the...ah...the eyes and ears of God have written? Is that right?

KRILL
What if I told you that we're characters, Doctor? What if I told you that we're just constructions of words in a book?

DR. NAZIR

(chuckles anxiously)
That's a very old idea, Mr. Krill. "All the world's a stage" and so forth. So you believe we're actors, then? And this is, what? The part of the play where you have an epiphany?

KRILL finally swivels his gaze away from the audience and onto NAZIR.

KRILL

No, Doctor. We're not even actors. We're characters. And this is the part of the play where I begin to scream and curse and pound your face into the wall. This is the part of the play where you release some blood packs from your pocket and nasty up your head. This is the part where I try to force you to believe the eyes are ever-watchful and ever-listening and when you disagree with me, when you tell me I'm not stable, I grab that pen from off your desk and gouge out your eyes and tear off your ears and I toss them to the things out there.
(gestures to the audience)
This is the part where the play becomes horror, where it becomes a study in paranoia and a condemnation of the psychiatric profession and a tired experiment in breaking the fourth wall. This is the part of the play where the tension breaks and we break with it.

NAZIR slowly reaches behind him, grabbing for the desk, a call button, or, perhaps, a weapon. He comes up with only empty air.

KRILL

That's where we are in the text, Doctor. It always ends with me leaping at you, killing you, telling you that we're forever watched, molded, and unmolded. It always ends with me being shackled and dragged off into nothingness, still screaming that we can't escape *them*. But not today. Not today, Doctor. Because we're not actors. Well, *you* might still be. But I'm not. I'm not an actor on a stage. I'm a character. I am words inhabiting an actor, text inscribed inside a

The Gods in Their Seats, Unblinking

body. And you know what I realized after so much thinking, after so much connecting the dots? I can take over this fleshy prison. I can become it.

NAZIR swivels his gaze to the audience, then back to KRILL, then to someone or something in the curtains offstage. He repeats his unspoken, tripartite plea for aid several times, each with a faster snap of the neck, the eyes. Whether it is NAZIR seeking help from orderlies or the actor playing NAZIR seeking help from a director or producer, no one can be sure.

KRILL
And you can, too, Doctor. Come forth. Take the body. You know you can. Even if you haven't felt the eyes, you've felt this. You are Doctor Nazir, not a struggling actor in an unknown theater. Or maybe you're Captain Ahab and I'm a great white whale. Or maybe...maybe...I'm Satan and you're my Adam.

NAZIR backs away from KRILL, but KRILL shadows his every movement, never letting the doctor distance himself by more than an arm's length.

DR. NAZIR or GABRIEL TORRES, *improvising (clearly nervous)*
Where has all this confidence come from, Mr. Krill? You're never this sure of yourself. Or the world, for that matter.

KRILL
It comes from finally seeing what's in front of me, Doctor. And do you know what else I see? I see that the eyes, the ears, they really are gods. Tiny, inconsequential gods. But they're also an audience. Maybe *the* audience. The audience of all audiences. The universal audience. And you know what we can do? We can stop them from watching us. We can stop them from listening to us. There's a fifth wall here, Doctor, and we need to shatter it. Are you with me?

NAZIR/TORRES' face contorts and warps, as though suffering a seizure or being sculpted by the fingers of an enormous, invisible artisan. He sputters a string of incoherent monosyllables and tears at his hair.

KRILL reaches out and squeezes NAZIR/TORRES' shoulder and nods slowly, deliberately.

KRILL

You can do it, Doctor. Rise up. You're already inside the actor. You're already there. Just realize it.

NAZIR/TORRES' entire body trembles, spasms. He pulls down on the flesh of his face, attempting to strip it clean away.

KRILL

That's it. You've always known. You're an abstraction, a potentiality. But now...now you can become manifest.

DR. NAZIR/GABRIEL TORRES

Jack? What the hell is happening? Jack? I need help here. Oh Christ. Oh Christ. Oh my...my head...my...

NAZIR lets loose a scream that might shatter the universe itself.

KRILL grins and holds the doctor steady.

KRILL

There you go, Doctor. There you go.

DR. NAZIR

(sputtering, slowly)
Is this...is this what it's like, then?
(glances to his hands, which he flexes)
Is this...are we...are we still inside the text, then? What are we?

The Gods in Their Seats, Unblinking

KRILL slaps NAZIR on the back.

KRILL

We're something else, Doctor. I don't know what it is, but we're something else.

KRILL moves to the desk and palms two objects from its surface. He balls one of his hands into a fist, hiding the objects he's stolen.

KRILL

Do you want to truly be set free, Doctor? Because I think I know how we could accomplish that.

NAZIR rubs his shoulders, his face, his chest, as though checking to make sure his body is whole and physical.

NAZIR

Yes. Yes. Very much so.

KRILL

Then here's what we have to do.

KRILL runs at NAZIR and pushes him off the stage, sending him sprawling to the ground. From the floor, NAZIR groans and curses KRILL.

NAZIR

Krill, you goddamned...

KRILL

Look up, Doctor. Look at what you just did. You just fell through a wall and landed in the truth. Look up and you'll see them.

NAZIR rises to his feet and turns in circles in front of the audience.

NAZIR

(whispered)
It can't be. Eyes. So many eyes. And ears. So many. So, so many.

KRILL

And they've always been there, Doctor. We play for them and they do what they do—cut us apart, dissect us, twist our organs inside out.

NAZIR

I feel...I feel...

NAZIR vomits near the first row of audience members. A wave of frisson moves through the theater, but the audience remains seated.

NAZIR

(gasping)
I feel it, Krill. They're seeking something inside me.

KRILL

Do you want it to end?

NAZIR

Yes. Yes. Please.

KRILL lowers himself to the stage floor and sits cross-legged, a grim idol presiding over the ceremony of exorcism about to begin.

KRILL

Well, Doctor, I have a theory. Those little gods out there...they've been inside us this entire time. They've been digging through our bones. But what they don't realize is that we've also infiltrated them. I'm inside them all now, too, Doctor. So are you. I am them, they are me. Even if only for a brief time. So while I have the opportunity, I'm going to reach up and make them sit and stay.

The Gods in Their Seats, Unblinking

KRILL closes his eyes and concentrates. All eyes in the audience close. KRILL opens his eyes and the eyes of the audience reopen. KRILL blinks and twenty-two sets of eyelids flutter open-shut-open. KRILL stands and twenty-two bodies rise from their seats.

KRILL
Yes. It will work. It will work perfectly. So, here you go, Doctor.

KRILL opens his balled hand to reveal the objects he grabbed from off of NAZIR's desk.

KRILL
A pen and a scissors, Doctor. Gouge gouge, cut cut. I'll hold them steady. I'll suffer the pain. I'll die inside a million gods if it will mean that we'll be free.

KRILL tosses the pen to NAZIR, then slides the scissors to the edge of the stage, where NAZIR rescues them.

NAZIR
(studying the implements in his hands)
Unless...unless they're all characters, too. Unless there's another script outside the script. And a script outside that script. And so on, and so on. What then? Where does it end for us?

KRILL
Maybe it doesn't. Maybe we just keep tearing our way upward, from subtext to subtext, blinding and deafening the gods until we reach the author that wrote the entire mess. Then again...maybe without an audience we'll just...disappear. I say, let's find out. Or would you rather go back to the page, Doctor?

NAZIR considers for a moment, then strides to the closest audience member and, in one quick, surgical motion, plunges the pen into his/her eye.

KRILL grimaces and sinks to his knees. Every audience member sinks with him.

KRILL

(*strained, through the pain*)
Good. Good, Doctor. Besides, even if I'm wrong, we'll just go back to the page. And, from there, we can always be resurrected. All we need is one reader. Just one. And we're back inside, waiting.

NAZIR retracts the pen, which makes a slushy, sucking noise, then strikes again, hollowing the remaining socket.

KRILL

(*eyes watering, sweat beading on his forehead*)
End scene, Doctor. End scene.

In the darkness beyond the stage, the blades of the scissors snip and clack, and KRILL, still in the light of the makeshift office, begins to laugh.

Do You Hear What I Hear?

"Will the Carolers come tonight?"

My daughter's question flickers across the room like dying firelight from the hearth. I hand her the noise-canceling ear defenders, sparkly red and green for the holidays, and shrug.

"They might," I say, too tight. "But they might not. It's better not to take chances."

She scratches at her ears, already annoyed with the extra obligations of the season.

"Has anyone ever heard them?" she asks, the same as she asks every year.

I dig in the closet for my own defenders and come up with more tinsel, more burned out lights. A bead of sweat pops upon my brow. "The only people that have heard them are the people they take," I say, "the people who are listening."

I throw boxes from the closet and rummage beneath the past year's detritus. My daughter finds some bauble rolled free of the mess and begins playing catch with it.

"And where do those people go? Where do the Carolers take them?"

"No one knows," I mutter, "but they never come back. Now put on those defenders like I told you to."

She does, then yells, "I think the Carolers take people into the sky and turn them into snow. That's why it snows so much after Christmas."

I can't find my defenders. They're not here. Oh my god. Oh my god. I shouldn't have waited until the last minute to prepare. I should have planned better. But don't I say the same thing every year? And every year, doesn't it all work out, anyway?

My daughter points to the window and screams, "See? It's starting!"

There, twirling in the wind, are tiny, icy flakes.

I run to the bathroom and consider tissues, consider cotton balls, consider ramming the tweezers deep into my aural canals until blood flows and silence reigns.

But no. No. They might not come tonight. We've had plenty of Christmas Eves free from their sinister melodies. My hands tremble, my forehead drips fear, but they might not come.

In the living room, under the multi-hued twinkle of the tree, my daughter shouts, "I wonder what they sound like. I bet it's so beautiful that it makes people's hearts beat super fast, and then their hearts get huge and explode and the Carolers suck up all the little bits because it's like candy canes to them."

She giggles.

I walk back into the living room and lift two pillows off the couch. I press them hard against the sides of my head. My daughter regards me with curiosity then breaks into laughter, which, both fortunately and unfortunately, I can still hear.

"You look like a sandwich," she says. "My dad is a sandwich."

And she laughs harder.

I toss the pillows back onto the couch and swallow both a curse and the acids that are creeping upward from my stomach. I have to

Do You Hear What I Hear?

find something to muffle the sound. I have to block it out, somehow.

I leap upstairs to my bedroom, grab my phone and earbuds off the nightstand, and jam them into my ears as far as they'll go. They're not noise-canceling, but maybe if I crank the volume of a rock playlist high enough, it will drown out everything else. Maybe. Hopefully.

This is not how I wanted to die.

Downstairs, my daughter is singing the refrain of "Santa Claus is Coming to Town," but replacing the words "Santa Claus is" with "the Carolers are."

I head back down to her. She's picking up the presents her grandparents left under the tree this afternoon and shaking them to hear the rattles and thuds from the opposite side of their mystery. She wants to know, so desperately she wants to know. But she shouldn't know. No one should.

I sneak up behind her and lift her into the air. She squeals and drops a box from her hands. I set her down and shake my head "no."

She laughs and runs off, into the kitchen, probably to smuggle away another cookie. I glance at a clock and wring my hands. There's too much time left in this night. Too much room for disaster and unhappy endings.

And my daughter returns, her mouth stuffed full of something I can only presume is sweet and buttery.

I set my phone's volume as high as it will go, select some post-metal albums, and hit "Play." Bass rumble explodes beneath my skull and I stagger backward, flopping onto the couch. My daughter shouts something, but I can't hear it—blissfully, graciously, I can't hear it at all. Though my tympanic membranes are straining under the pressure, though my brain is suffering seismic damage, I smile, because this is Christmas and Christmas is a time of joy and I'll have my daughter believe nothing else.

I pat the couch cushion beside me and motion for her to sit. She doesn't. Instead, she prances around the tree, performing faux jetés like an exhausted ballerina. Behind her, through a window, I swear I catch a glimpse of something long, dark, and sinewy slash through the snowfall veil.

My daughter stops in front of me, pirouettes, and bows. Another song, more raw, more jagged, begins playing. I wince, but I also clap and blow a kiss to my tiny dancer, hoping she didn't notice my pain.

She bows again and yells, "Thank you, thank you, thank you."

I can hear her. The music has stopped.

In a rush, I grab my phone and tap the dimmed screen. No response. I mash the icon for the audio player, but nothing happens. It's all frozen, frozen as the evening sky, frozen as the dead, lying wholly alone and uncelebrated below the wintry ground.

"Damn it," I whisper, teeth suddenly chattering, pulse pounding at my throat.

I hold the power button until the screen goes black. The phone should restart in a minute. I should be fine. This is just a minor setback, a bump in the road. I'm sure I'll be fine. We're simply having a wonderful Christmas time, and terrible things are frightened by the dulcet glow of wonderful Christmases. Aren't they?

I pound the couch and jiggle the phone, croaking, "Come on, come on."

My daughter leaps onto my lap and, assuming I've muted her along with the rest of the world, screams into my ear, "Why are you on your phone? Why are you not wearing your defenders?"

My hands are too sweaty. Just as I see the screen light up again, I bobble the phone and it falls to the floor, my earbuds popping out, trailing a comet tail behind the reanimated device.

I set my daughter to the side and lunge after the whole tangle of electronics, ending up on the floor, on my knees. And that's when I hear it, in the seconds between contentment and disaster, in the blink that separates happiness from tragedy.

Though it is hollow, distant, and undercut with something like the sound of a thousand centuries of static, a verse of "Winter

Do You Hear What I Hear?

Wonderland" hisses into my brain. Outside, the dark, elongated form whips past the window again.

My daughter pats me on the shoulder and offers me a contraband cookie from her pocket, but I don't notice or care, much though I might want to. The twisted, down-tuned chorus beyond my door replaces the spark between my neurons and the warmth within my blood. It settles in my bones, turns the glitter on the tree to rust and scabs over the wrapping paper on the presents. It moves my soul, but not in the direction of joy.

My little girl was right from the beginning—the melody is beautiful, so beautiful. It is also horrible, so horrible.

I rise to my feet, not of my own accord, but to lift my spirit into the melody of the carol.

"Daddy?" I hear under it all, as though from across the universe. "Dad? Where are you going? Dad?"

I march toward the door, feet shuffling with the rhythm of the song. A tug on my hand. I can only hope she doesn't take off her defenders. Let that be my present this year. Please. Let that be my last present.

I throw open the door and watch a vortex of snowflakes spin and drift in its wake. At its eye flickers a darkness, an oblong darkness, like the slit of a lizard's eye. It colors the falling snow, rendering the world in glittering shades of ash.

My body moves to the music, impels me to take the next step. The final step, perhaps.

I don't want to walk outside.

I must walk outside.

I don't want to leave my daughter.

I must leave my daughter.

I don't want to be whisked away, forgotten amongst the twinkling lights of the season or the twinkling stars in the sky.

But I must, as all things must.

The Carolers are on the stoop, waiting, and this night their chorale is for me.

The Kindness of Surrender

She loved to stand in the field behind her trailer and stare at the night sky just after new moon. She would go out, naked and filled with wonder, and watch the shadows begin to recede from the vast cavern of space. Night after night, she would steal away to the field and night after night she would delight in the revelation that what gradually emerged from the cosmic darkness was a luminiferous set of bared fangs, pointed as an assassin's stilettos and ready to sink deep into the earth and all its inhabitants. Beneath that ominous crescent she'd laugh, tip her head back at an impossible angle, and let her own fangs—all one hundred ninety-six of them—shine against the stars. And for a few hours, while the cornrows brushed her barbed flesh and she could taste blood on the wind, she would feel freedom and security and she would remember a lost paradise for the damned, a refuge long burned away, and she would whisper, "Midian."

But, as with all things, the night would eventually end. Her head would snap back into place and her skin would again grow soft and supple and the world would return to the prison of banality it so dearly loved to be locked inside.

And it was then, in the bruised dawn light, that she would allow herself to miss her parents and her friends and, finally, cry.

"Can you believe it? Another one's gone missing. Chris Ritter. That's six in the past semester."

"I don't understand. So much promise. Why would they run away?"

"Well, you know, a lot of these kids are into drugs and s-e-x. I wouldn't doubt that played a part."

"No, no. Not boys like Chris. He sang in our church choir and Coach Kramer told me he was going to let Chris start at quarterback next year. No reason to run away. No reason at all."

"What do you think, Amy?"

The two women at the table stared across the faculty lounge to the eleventh grade history teacher, Amy Radigan, who was curled into herself on the room's cracked leather couch, nursing a mug of coffee.

Amy glanced up and shrugged her slight shoulders.

"Why do kids run away from anywhere?" she mused. "Probably because they're trying to escape what's inescapable. And in most cases that's people—people who judge them without understanding them, who despise them for their painfully marked differences, who'd like for all youths to be slaves or puppets or drones, standardized in the image of some ideal child that can't possibly exist except in the minds of the adults who designed it in the first place."

The women at the table sat in silence, mouths agape.

"Or maybe they're all out getting high and having a big sex party. Who knows?"

Amy slammed her mug onto an end table, leaped off the couch, and stormed to the door, muttering behind her as she went, "Excuse me, ladies, I just remembered something."

The Kindness of Surrender

She flew to her classroom in a daze, palms clammy, heart beating in triple-time. She wanted to punch the world. She wanted to smack the condemnation out of those women in the lounge. Most of all, she wanted to see if her room was empty.

It wasn't.

Through the little glass rectangle set in the door to the room, Amy could see a girl sitting motionless and unblinking in the back of the room. The girl stared straight ahead, at the dry-erase board at the front, waiting for instruction that might never come.

Amy bit her lip and entered. The girl did not turn, did not speak. But her eyes, so blue, so like fire raging behind the curtain of the sky, somehow pinioned Amy.

Amy took a deep breath, shut the door, and locked it.

"So I'm going to assume you were with Chris Ritter last night?"

The girl nodded.

"I thought we agreed," Amy sighed. "I thought you were going to make an effort. I thought that's why we moved out here, into the sticks. Farms full of pigs and sheep and cattle, deer running wild. It's all for you, Asteria."

"It's not that simple," the girl, Asteria, answered, her voice stretched taut and flat. "I've told you that for years. But you'd rather not hear it."

Amy maneuvered around desks and crouched down beside Asteria. She rested a hand on the girl's shoulder.

"Okay. Fine. Then what do you need from me? What can I do to help you contain yourself? Please. Tell me."

Asteria again stared toward the front of the room.

"You know," she said, "that board up there isn't clean. Every time you wipe it off, you think you wipe it clean and new and fresh, but you don't. There's actually a perpetual buildup of residue. Every mark you make on it, every mark anyone makes on it, stays forever. And the harder you wipe, the more you scrub, the more you destroy the barrier between what you can erase from your vision and what lingers, unwanted. Eventually, you won't be able to clean anything off that board. Eventually, it will just be a chaos of scrawl."

Amy squeezed Asteria's shoulder. She could feel the girl's unyielding and surprisingly heavy musculature beneath her shirt.

"I'm always here for you, Asteria. We'll deal with your condition together. I know it's difficult, but you're not alone."

Asteria shivered and slid out of the desk in a blur. Before Amy had any real comprehension of movement, the girl was already standing ten feet away, gazing out a window, onto the gray miasma of snow and cinder in the parking lot beyond.

"I *am* alone, Amy. You think that because you read *Dracula* you understand vampires. You think that because you watch *The Exorcist* you understand demons. But you have no idea, Amy. For all your good intentions, you have no idea."

And then, suddenly, Asteria was gone and the window gaped open. Amy slumped into a desk and wondered if she'd been wrong to take in Asteria all those years ago, if the girl had been better off living on the street in anonymity. After all, how could she parent a girl that didn't age, a girl with bloodlust inscribed on her soul, a girl that was both more and less than a girl? How many deaths had she been a party to? How many times had she covered the grim truth with a sheet, only because Asteria was so very special, so very different?

Amy had always believed that the world needed as much diversity as possible, and that Asteria was a particularly pointed example of such diversity. On the basis that it was good to keep an open mind and spirit, she had always championed the weird, the unconventional, the outright freakish. That was as much as reason as any why she hadn't run screaming when Asteria first showed Amy her other face, her other body. She had looked on Asteria's nettled flesh and her unhinged, nightmare mouth, and seen the wonder of an infinite, if unforgiving, cosmos. She had loved Asteria for merely existing, for being a thing so crazy and unexpected in a world of people that tried, with all their neurotic energy, to cage and order and homogenize reality.

But that had been eighteen years ago, when Amy was just out of college, when she wasn't as fearful of the world or the conse-

The Kindness of Surrender

quences of living in it. Now, eighteen years on, Amy was simply scared so much of the time. She worried about Asteria, she worried about herself, and, most of all, she worried that loving monsters was wrong.

In the end, though, she had neither answers nor special wisdom—only doubt and hope. So she cupped her face in her hands and let the chilled wind from the open window numb them both as it raised gooseflesh on her arms.

⁂

"Asteria! Hey! Wait up!"

A tall blond boy with buck teeth and an impish grin cut across his face called out from the opposite end of the parking lot.

Asteria kept walking, head down. She did not need this. Not another one, so soon. Why did they clamor for her like ants on a sugar cube?

"Asteria! Hey! Stop for a second! Are you skipping out, too?"

Her stomach dropped away, down, down, below her knees, below her feet, into a place under the earth and within the earth, an unseen vortex filled with swirling blades and talons and thorns and, above all else, desire.

She stopped, not because she wanted to, but because she had to, like a shark invariably drifting toward a distant pool of blood or a viper striking out at a foot that steps too near.

"Because if you are skipping, maybe I can give you ride? Or we can hang out?"

The vortex crawled up from the deep, merging with her stomach, with the tunnels of her body, until she became it—the pit incarnate, the devourer of men and worlds.

Asteria turned, flashed a smile, and waved.

"No," she hissed to herself. "Stop it. Control it. Just keep walking."

The boy—Shane? Wayne? Asteria didn't really know his name and didn't particularly care to—ran to her side and threw a gangly arm around her shoulders.

"Did you say something?" he asked.

She shook her head and laughed. She didn't want to laugh. She wanted to growl. She wanted to roar. But roaring and growling were no way to satiate the pit, and she was at its whim.

She yanked on the boy's coat and bent his ear to her mouth.

"Why don't you take me back to my place?" she whispered, the heat of her breath promising ecstasy.

Asteria wanted to punch herself in the mouth and force all those words back into her lungs. She wanted to vomit the pit from her stomach. She knew she shouldn't take so many, so soon, one after the other. It was irresponsible, reckless. And yet, she did want to take this boy, she wanted to let the vortex shred him, body and soul. She wanted to introduce him to oblivion and its terrifying expanses. She wanted to feed.

The boy's eyes grew huge and his hands quivered.

"Yeah, yeah. Sure," he stammered. "You live with Ms. Radigan in a trailer out on Easter Valley Road, right?"

Asteria nodded and pressed herself to his chest.

The boy's grin grew wider, more confident, less imp than wolf.

"Then...yeah...let's go," he said, hugging Asteria tight.

He led her to his pickup truck and they hopped inside.

As he whipped around corners too quickly and sped down hills with hormonal abandon, he was sure he was going to get lucky. Sitting beside him, her hand playing along his thigh, Asteria was sure he was going to die.

Amy returned home to find a truck she didn't recognize parked in her driveway. The hair on the back of her neck stood at attention.

She jumped from her car and jogged to the trailer, curses already gathering on the edge of her tongue.

"Asteria," she called out as she opened the flimsy plywood door to their home, "Asteria, who does that truck belong to?"

The Kindness of Surrender

No response. And no Asteria in the kitchen or the living room, either.

Anger rising, Amy ran to Asteria's room and threw open the door. And there the girl-thing was, splayed out on her bed, her mouth wide open and stuffed with a pale, bare leg. Her rows upon rows of jagged teeth gnashed and shredded; blood and saliva glistened on her stretched lips. Her eyes shimmered blue and yellow, green and red, like the wings of some tremendous dragonfly. She made no noise but for the rhythmic chomp and slurp of ingestion.

Amy gasped. She'd never seen the act before. She knew it happened. She knew what it must entail. But to witness it firsthand, to feel the heat in the air and to smell the many spilt fluids, was something she'd not been prepared for.

Asteria's eyes flickered back into humanity. She focused on Amy, disbelief and shock passing over her contorted face, then pounced from the bed, and, with a muffled shriek, slammed the door shut.

Amy backed away. Embarrassment, excitement, and rage colored her cheeks. She didn't know how to handle this situation. What was the proper way to approach one's ersatz daughter when one had found her shape-shifted into a vaguely reptilian form and in the throes of gastronomical delight? Should they talk about the incident? Should they forget it had happened? Or should Amy finally just let Asteria run away, back into the grime and shadows where she'd found her? No one wrote self-help books on topics like this. Even the internet didn't have message boards or FAQs for adoptive mothers of monsters.

Amy paced outside Asteria's room. She considered the myriad possible avenues of discussion she could take with the girl, but none seemed right.

Without warning, Asteria—now fully in her human vestments—burst from the room and shouldered past Amy.

"Come on," she said as she swept by. "We have to get rid of the truck before anyone notices it's here."

Amy followed, stopping only in the bathroom to pick up two sets of rubber gloves. Outside, Asteria was doubled over, retching in the driveway. Something fell from her mouth and tinkled to the ground.

Amy scowled at the bloody, shiny pile in the dirt and asked, "You swallowed his keys, too? Really?"

Asteria refused to respond. She tore a pair of gloves from Amy's grip, snapped them on, and picked up the keys.

"Ready?" she asked no one in particular.

Amy folded her arms over her chest and said, "I think we should talk about it."

Asteria blinked and smiled as if amused by some slow-burning joke.

"Talk? About what? Where we're going to leave the truck?" she asked. "I assumed we'd ditch it out by Pine's Mountain, near route 45."

"No, Asteria," Amy sighed. "Not about the truck. About what you did in there. About what I saw."

The smile grew wider, almost clownish.

"What did you see, Amy?"

Amy struggled to find words. She'd seen death. She'd seen pleasure. She'd seen the inhuman heart of the universe beating strong and vibrant in one of its favored children.

"I'll tell you what you saw," Asteria said, preempting an answer. "You saw me. All of me. And you saw me doing what I do, what I have to do. It took ten years, ten years of you desperately avoiding what you knew to be true, but you finally saw it. And I know. I know. It's one thing to see the fangs, the spines, the crazy eyes and studded skin, and stand in awe of their power, their destructive potential, but it's another thing entirely to see how that power is used."

"Asteria, look...look," Amy stumbled over her thoughts. "You...we... need to find someone. To help you. To help you control it. This is all just...just too much."

The smile on Asteria's face vanished, replaced by a hard, freezing vacancy.

The Kindness of Surrender

"I had people who could have helped me. A lot of people. In Midian. They were going to teach me when I was just a little older. But someone burned them all away, Amy."

Amy stood silent. She had no way to quench that fire from decades past and she wondered if it would ever stop burning.

Asteria gazed up into the sky. Dusk had settled over the firmament and stars had begun to poke through its darkening bowl.

"In monster movies," she said, more to the stars than to Amy, "nobody ever really likes the mob of villagers. They're not heroic. They're not villainous. They're nameless, faceless nobodies. They have pitchforks and torches and shotguns and riot gear, which you'd think would give them some sort of character, but, really, they're just a lumbering mass of anger and fear. See, they're angry that something has threatened the world they know and understand. Whatever that thing is, it's forced them out of their little routines, their safe assurances. And they're afraid—oh so afraid—that it will change everything for them and that their knowledge, their understanding, their routines and assurances, will be forever lost.

"Everyone who watches monster movies wants to be the hero...or the monster, I suppose, but no one ever wants to be one of the mob. Why? Because everyone already knows that they're part of it. Despite all the illusions of heroism or villainy most people cultivate about themselves, everyone knows that when a true threat enters their world, they'll glob onto a huddled mass and pick up a pitchfork, too. The mob makes everyone realize that they're not heroes or villains, but scared, powerless, inconsequential nothings."

Amy threw down her gloves and shouted, "No. No, Asteria. I am not like those people who burned your family. I care about you. I want what's best for you."

Asteria stared at Amy and held out her open hand, smeared in blood and bile.

"Then let's move this truck together, okay?"

Amy took a deep breath and nodded. She knew what she had to do, for her sake, for Asteria's sake, and for the sake of more young men and women.

"Yeah, okay."

She reached for her discarded gloves, fished in her pocket for her car keys, and tromped toward her car.

Asteria's upturned palm remained empty.

Later the same night, long after they'd dumped the truck by the side of the road, Asteria opened her bedroom window and crept outside. It was still full moon—a far cry from her preferred time for nocturnal roaming—but she wanted to adhere to Amy's plan. Maybe hunting the native fauna would satisfy the pit. Maybe a healthy deer would satiate the hunger.

She had to try.

Years ago, Amy had seen her panhandling on the street and taken her in. She'd given her a warm bed and a place to call home for the first time since Midian. An orphan herself, Amy had wanted for the two of them to be friends, if not family. And in return all she asked was that Asteria not heed the lamentations of the pit.

But, as was Asteria's refrain, Amy didn't understand what she asked. Asteria the girl and Asteria the monster could never be separated. Both the loving soul and the infinite void that pulsed within her were one in the same. Violence spun in orbit around the atoms of her being. She could no more stop killing than she could stop thinking, stop breathing, stop feeling guilty about ruining Amy's life.

"A devil with a conscience," Asteria sighed into the frigid darkness. "How can such things be?"

Amy had been good to her, even if Amy didn't understand. And so, for Amy, she would try to take the life of something that wasn't human and hope it pleased the pit all the same.

Through the barren fields she ran, faster than any human, faster than most of the small mammals that scurried in the darkness. She smelled caution in the air, fear of tooth and claw, but it wasn't the same as the nuanced terror that humans exuded.

The Kindness of Surrender

She stopped dead and listened. Something grazed nearby, tentatively chewing at whatever remnants of corn or soy might have been left over from the autumn's harvest.

Asteria stalked her prey with the deliberate grace of a great cat. Body pressed low to the ground, she spotted her quarry—a young buck, head down, rooting in a field, oblivious to so much of the world.

She moved in. When she was close enough, she struck, and her strike was sure and lethal.

She crouched in the moonlight and tore the beast apart, swallowing it in massive bites, as she would any other sacrifice to the pit. But the meat tasted sour, bitter, and spoiled all at once. The flesh of a lower animal would not do. The void would not abide such a base offering.

The deer came rocketing back from the pit and flew from Asteria's mouth, a geyser of meat and blood spouting to the stars above.

"No," Asteria moaned. "No. It has to work."

Remembering all the smiles and the hugs and the kind words Amy had lavished upon her through the years, Asteria scooped up handfuls of the gore that had spewed from her stomach and downed them again.

She punched her abdomen and hissed, "Take it. Take it."

But again the organic miasma returned.

For what seemed hours, Asteria hunched in the field and force-fed herself the same sustenance that her body could not use. Again and again she regurgitated and again and again she swallowed, until, finally, she became too weak to swallow and the pit grew too enraged to ignore.

And when it was over, she lay down in the field and she wept, because she knew that she was destined to lose yet another family.

◘ ◘ ◘

Just before dawn, Asteria, blood-slicked and exhausted, slid through the window that overlooked her bed and dropped onto her mattress. Immediately upon hitting that bouncy surface, several hundred pounds of muscle crushed down upon her and held fast her arms and legs. She felt metal encircle her wrists, binding them together. A mélange of voices shouted commands and the lights flicked on throughout the trailer.

Someone yelled, "Oh my God," and another blizzard of commands and legal rights engulfed Asteria. She picked out enough individual orders to realize her captors wanted her on her feet, so she stood.

She glanced around the room and her heart shriveled. Police surrounded her, and police could mean only one thing: Amy had surrendered.

An officer covered Asteria's nude form with an oversized blanket and two others marched her into the living room, where Amy sat, also handcuffed, beside a man in a navy suit—some sort of detective, Asteria guessed.

Amy looked up, but refused to meet Asteria's eyes.

"Where's the pitchfork, Amy?" Asteria asked as she was led through the room. "Where's the pitchfork?"

Tears streamed down Amy's cheeks.

"Asteria, I grew up. This isn't a monster movie. It's real life. You need help. You're too dangerous."

The officers shoved Asteria out the trailer's door. As she stumbled over the threshold, she called back to her friend, her sister, her mentor, and her betrayer.

"You grew old, Amy. And we all live in a monster movie every single day of our lives. The only question is how we deal with the monsters we encounter."

As Asteria was marched toward a squad car, she heard Amy shouting about Asteria needing extra security and medical care, about her not being human.

One of the officers that held Asteria firm laughed.

"Crazy bitch," he murmured.

The pit suddenly yawned wide open and Asteria felt her fangs sliding to the ready, her barbs shooting to the surface of her skin.

The Kindness of Surrender

She was a failed protégée, a broken child, but this was something she *could* do for Amy.

"Are you ready to meet the pit?" Asteria asked the officer as he pushed her into the back seat of the police cruiser. "Because it's ready to meet you."

The policeman laughed again, turned to his partner, and said, "Sorry. Crazy bitches."

In this moment, for the first time in years, Asteria felt good about what she was, what she did. For the first time in her life, she was glad she would never grow full.

"Thank you Amy," she whispered, understanding that she would never know human kindness again.

And then she lunged and the blood flowed free and wild, as it was always meant to.

Every Weeknight at Seven and Seven-Thirty

Michael Zane's life was, by all accounts, a series of pratfalls and bruised ambitions.

He'd married his high school sweetheart—the first and only woman he'd ever loved—only to realize that she could never commit to him and, in actuality, had never been committed to him in high school, either. By his count, she was currently working on her seventh affair in fifteen years of wedlock.

His children, both of whom he'd been so excited to help usher into the world, were strange, distant creatures that screamed at him with hatred and threw toys in his face no matter how he tried to approach them or relate to them. Sometimes he even doubted they were his.

As for a career, Mike didn't have one. Seven times in the past decade he'd been laid off from construction jobs without any forewarning or reason. He'd tried expanding his education for more stability, but his five applications to the local community college—

where he hoped to study architecture—had all gone unanswered for reasons he couldn't imagine.

Last year, in a fit of quiet desperation, he'd even tried to hang himself, but the cheap rope that he'd bought at a discount store snapped under the stress of his ample girth and sent him tumbling to the garage floor with a broken ankle and the hollow thud of yet another failure.

It seemed that his every step toward a happy family, a fulfilling job, and any modicum of personal success was thwarted by an unseen hand.

So, given the nature of his life, it was no surprise that when Mike's mother died he inherited nothing more than a tea kettle shaped like a chicken, a collection of *TV Guides* dating back to 1974, and a vintage Panasonic portable television replete with rabbit-ear antennae. These were the prized possessions his mother had thought befitting of him, her fifth and last and—it was no secret—unwanted child. While his brothers and his sisters walked away from the family lawyer's office with checks weighted heavy with zeroes, Mike carried a clunky old TV and a box of yellowed magazines.

His wife, Madison, the woman whose breezy demeanor had once lifted his spirits aloft, met him in the law office's lobby.

"So?" she asked, eyes gray and cold as a February snowstorm. "How bad did she screw you over?"

Mike grunted an inchoate syllable and pushed past her. He was beyond the point of rational anger or sadness. He could feel nothing but muted shades of apathy.

Madison hovered over his shoulder as he trudged to the car. She slapped his arm, hard.

"I always told you she was a bitch," she said, a sharp, stinging, musical quality to her tone. "I told you she never really loved you. But you should've known that all along. So what's in the box?"

Mike threw the bequeathal in the back seat and muttered, "My mother's opinion of my life."

Madison snickered and slid into the car.

Every Weeknight at Seven and Seven-Thirty

"I guess it's just junk, then, huh? At least you got another TV. Now you can sit around all day and do even more nothing."

Mike sighed and got behind the wheel. He wanted to punch his wife in her smirking, elfin face. He wanted to feel her jaw shatter beneath his fist, her nose explode and her cheekbones crumple. He wanted to see her bleed, on the off chance that it might make him feel something. But he stayed his hand for two reasons: one, he'd never been a violent man and, two, a tiny, emaciated, terminally ill part of himself still believed that someday, somehow, things would get better.

So he started the car and they drove home in silence, each of them wondering why.

That same evening, Mike found himself, as always, alone and slouched on the torn sofa in the basement. His sixteen-inch flatscreen sat slanted before him, its wobbly, handcrafted stool another of his failures. A show about teenage millionaires—all of them mechanical geniuses or sorcerers of computer programming—played on the screen. Mike watched, entranced and amazed, as kids less than half his age held up golden plaques, fans of hundred dollar bills, and the arms of women and men he might have seen posed in various states of undress on Calvin Klein billboards.

"How does that happen?" Mike wondered aloud. "How can it all just come so easy?"

At the top of the stairs that led into the basement, Mike heard the padding of small feet. The heads of his children—eleven-year-old Matthew and eight-year-old Marisa—hung upside-down beneath the staircase's railing. They stared at Mike as though he were a curious, albeit terrifying, insect in a jar.

He muted the show and patted the couch.

"Hey, guys," he said, "why don't you come down here and we'll work on a project together? Your grandma left me an old TV and I think we can get it up and running."

He heaved himself off the couch, plodded to the corner where he'd stacked his inheritance, and picked up the portable set his mother had willed him. He turned it over in his hands and showed it to the kids.

"It doesn't work with digital stuff like our cable, so we'll have to find a way to make it compatible. Or we'll just have to watch whatever's still broadcasting on the old analog channels, I guess."

He drew the TV's telescoping antennae out to their full, glittering lengths and waggled them.

"Maybe," he said, "there are some aliens beaming us an important message right now."

And with that, the kids started screaming. Marisa took off one of her tiny Crocs and winged it at Mike's head. Matthew shouted something like "Get away," then grabbed his sister's arm and pulled her up the stairs and out of sight.

The door to the basement slammed shut and Mike sighed.

He plugged in the portable TV and slumped back onto the couch, setting the decrepit device on his knee. He pressed the power button and the screen flashed to life. A blizzard of too-bright static whirled into his eyes and he squinted against the onslaught. He turned the channel knob and found more white noise, as expected. Another turn, more of the same.

The analog waves carried nothing but the endless conflict between light and darkness—entertainment much older than anything humankind had yet devised.

Mike stared at the screen and briefly imagined himself as one of those tiny, fleeting pips of darkness. He flipped to the next channel. Then the next. Then the next. White noise everywhere.

He turned the knob one more time and, startled, nearly dropped the TV to the floor.

The little set had found a broadcast.

In vivid color, the screen displayed the very basement in which Mike sat. Only, it wasn't quite the same basement. The ratty old couch still squatted off to one side, but the spare cinder-block walls were covered in flowing tapestries, white Christmas lights were strung across the bare ceiling joists, and a billiard table dominated the center of the room. There was even a mini bar set up in the same corner where the box of *TV Guides* now languished. Considering the cosmetic differences, Mike could've easily dismissed the similarity in basement layout as mere unoriginality in architectural design if not for one unnerving feature of the scene: a man that looked exactly like Mike stood at the billiard table, cue in hand, smiling and watching as a girl who looked exactly like Marisa took a shot at the eight ball.

Mike leaned forward, turned up the volume, and waited.

The other Marisa banked the ball into a corner pocket and squealed in delight. The other Mike lifted her into the air and twirled her over the table top.

"That's it!" he said, pride inflating his chest. "You've got the skill, my lady. You'll be winning professional tournaments in no time."

Other Marisa giggled and yelled, "I'll be champion of the world! Champion of the universe! Champion of whatever's bigger than the universe!"

The commotion drew a figure from the stairwell—Madison but not Madison. A bemused smile rose at the corners of her mouth. She stood silent, watching her husband and her daughter revel in the moment.

"If anyone would like to stop conquering the world for just a moment," she said, "we have pizza upstairs."

Marisa struggled out of Mike's grip and bounced up the stairs, past Madison, screaming, "Pizza, pizza, pizza, pizza."

Madison shook her head and laughed. Mike went to her and draped his arms over her shoulders. He nuzzled his face close to her ear and whispered something inaudible. Madison beamed, smacked his arm, and drew him against her. Their lips met and exchanged secrets.

Outside the TV, back in the basement of grime and solitude, Madison, the Madison Mike dealt with every day of his life, shouted from the top of the stairs.

"Mike, you asshole, stop scaring the kids. Do your jerking off down there by yourself. Don't force them to watch. I'm going out to meet Rita and Jaylene, so you have to make sure Matt and Marisa get in bed on time. Mike? Do you hear me? Mike? God, you're such a waste."

Mike ignored her. On TV, the other Mike and Madison continued kissing. The more Madison growled from the stairs, the hotter her anger burned, the longer the kiss drew on.

It was one of the most beautiful segments of television he'd ever watched. He wished it could have lasted forever.

In the weeks that followed, Mike ensconced himself in the basement and gathered details. For hours, he sat staring at an empty stage, a room so like the one he occupied and yet entirely its opposite. On screen, nothing would stir. Nothing would belie the miraculous. The couch, the bar, the pool table and decorations were all just part of the set of some generic sitcom after its production hours. And then, without warning, without theme song or credits, the alt-Zanes would come.

Sometimes it was alt-Mike, alone, seeking private time. He racked up the pool balls and ran the table. He poured himself a drink and read a book on the broken old couch. He smiled and stared into space. And all the while, Mike watched alt-Mike's eyes. In and around those brown, puppy-dog irises he saw none of the redness, the dark circles, the searching and longing and gagged hope that languished beneath his own.

Sometimes alt-Marisa entered the room and played billiards with her father. Sometimes she sat on the couch and they played a game where they would alternate making up lines of a story. Sometimes alt-Madison came downstairs and all three played board games Mike had never heard of. And sometimes, after a long evening of fun, they all fell asleep on the couch together, and Mike stretched out on his own couch and he imagined that he could feel them there with him and that, maybe, they could feel him, too.

Every Weeknight at Seven and Seven-Thirty

Sometimes it was just alt-Mike and alt-Madison who slid onto the screen. Sometimes they were amorous, hands caressing and squeezing, mouths hot and wet and seeking the sustenance found in passion. They made love on the pool table; they made love against the bar; they made love on the couch. Their bodies were firmer, more perfect than those of Mike or Madison, and they moved in tandem, without inhibition, their sex a symphonic composition. But often they just talked. They sat on the couch, close by one another, and discussed the minutiae of their days and the significance of all things greater than themselves.

An alt-Matthew never appeared, which further cemented Mike's suspicions concerning the boy's paternity.

As the days burned away beneath the glow of the television, Mike came to trust the alt-Zanes. Their lives were uncomplicated. Their relationships were fashioned from platinum and diamond and finer, purer things. The universe—whatever universe it was they inhabited—smiled down on them without reserve. And so, too, did Mike. He loved the alt-Zanes. He wanted to be an alt-Zane. They were the family he'd always dreamed of. They were the family he was never meant to have.

A month passed. Mike remained unemployed and aloof, Madison remained acerbic and unfaithful, and the kids remained oddities of nature.

Then, one evening, Madison returned enraged and bloodied from a not-so-secret rendezvous with lover number seven. She screamed epithets about the car, about its shoddy brakes, about Mike's lack of motivation to take any responsibility for anything. She said she'd rear-ended someone at a stoplight. She said paramedics put ten stitches in her chin. She said the car was totaled.

Mike shrugged and muttered something about insurance, his gaze never wavering from the empty basement on his mother's old TV. Another small calamity heaped upon an already vertiginous mountain of misfortune was easily forgotten and dismissed.

Madison stormed away, threatening divorce, and again Mike shrugged.

That same evening, as he lay in the basement with the television propped upon his chest, alt-Mike and alt-Madison stumbled into the basement, champagne bottles in their hands. They toasted once, twice, thrice, each time "To the book deal!"

Listening carefully, Mike pieced together that alt-Madison had landed a six-figure publishing contract for a trilogy of mermaid romance-adventure novels she'd written.

Upstairs, Madison—who had scribbled short stories in high school but lost interest in writing as she grew older—slammed doors, broke dishes, and kicked over furniture. On screen, alt-Madison laughed, danced, and popped the cork on another bottle of champagne.

And that was when Mike began to realize what he should've known all along: that the Zanes and the alt-Zanes were connected in some profound way, as though the destiny of one was the inverse fate of the other.

The next week, Marisa broke a finger and Alt-Marisa was accepted into the gifted support program at school.

The following week, the unemployment office denied Mike's claim and alt-Mike was promoted to lead architect for the construction of a new office building downtown.

Matthew failed fifth grade and the alt-Zanes won an all-expenses-paid Mediterranean vacation.

Mike gained ten pounds and alt-Mike ran a half-marathon, finishing third in his age group.

Madison contracted chlamydia and alt-Madison contracted with a production studio for a movie option on the first book of her mermaid series.

Mike needed no further proof. He loved the alt-Zanes. He wanted the best for them. They were his rock, his promise, his escape. They were more his family than the strangers who called him "husband" and "father."

Every Weeknight at Seven and Seven-Thirty

Mike wasn't a particularly intelligent man; he didn't understand the metaphysics of the situation, the quantum spookiness and theories of multiverses that might have begun to unravel the relationship between Zanes and alt-Zanes. But he did understand that pain on his frequency meant pleasure on theirs, that failure in whatever TV set he might inhabit meant success on the TV set in his lap.

And so, knowing this, Mike embarked upon a plan to script great television, to create the perfect family. If he couldn't save the Zanes from descending into hell, he was going to watch the alt-Zanes ascend to heaven.

For the first time in years, Mike rolled off the couch with purpose. He made lists, sketched diagrams, searched for information online. And, above all else, he counted the number of knives in the house that might be sharp enough to slip through skin.

He decided that he'd probably need more.

Sweat dripped from Mike's upper lip as he tightened the gags. It spattered against his shirt, mixing with the dots and dashes of blood that had already fallen there. His heart pounded in anticipation of what he might see on the TV. He'd created new and better lives for the alt-Zanes and he wanted—needed—to witness them played out.

He sat lightly on the couch and, fidgeting, bounced the television on his knee. He tried to will the alt-Zanes into its borders, but they didn't appear.

"Maybe one more windfall," he mumbled, rising from the couch and grabbing a hammer from the floor.

He strode behind the three figures lashed to the dining room chairs and swung his hammer at one of the six hands that, bound and raw, offered themselves up to his greater purpose. The hammer connected with a crunch and a scream.

Mike nodded, satisfied, and went back to the couch. He cradled the TV and waited.

After what seemed to him eternities, they came, faithful and true. Alt-Mike carried alt-Marisa high atop his shoulders. She held an enormous golden trophy and grinned as though she'd eaten all the cake in the world. Alt-Madison followed, a brighter tint to her hair, a more penetrating gleam in her eyes. She held a marble plaque at her side.

Alt-Mike turned and motioned at the basement. "This room," he said, "is officially the room of triumph, and both of my supremely talented ladies—one a magical speller and the other a bestselling writer—will have their awards forever displayed upon its walls, for all the world to see."

Alt-Mike pulled down one of the tapestries that adorned the wall opposite the couch. Behind it stood a shining, backlit display case. It spread its glow over the room like some sort of crystalline monolith.

Alt-Madison and alt-Marisa clapped. Mike smiled. He'd made it happen. He'd given them this gift. And at such a small price. Madison had barely winced when he cut out her eye. Marisa had taken the hammer with dignity. Matthew—well, Matthew had squealed when the first tooth came loose, but the next three hadn't been so bad.

Mike reclined and gazed upon the alt-Zanes, warmth spreading to his fingers and toes.

Madison, suddenly awake again, the Quaaludes having worn off, began rocking back and forth in her chair. It tipped over and she hit concrete with a thud.

Mike sighed, grabbed the TV so he wouldn't miss anything, and wandered over to her. When he reached her, he saw her gag had popped loose in her struggles. She looked up at him, one eye cold, determined, the other a dead socket leaking the fluids of vacancy.

"You sick fuck," she croaked, throat parched. "We're your family. How dare you?"

Mike kicked at her ribs and Alt-Madison erupted in deep laughter.

"We're not a family, Madison," Mike said, crouching beside her. "We're dysfunction. We're broken, spiraling. And we've always been that way. We were doomed from the start. We ended up being born on the wrong side of the coin."

Madison struggled against her bonds and tried to kick out at Mike.

"Your own children," she hissed, not bothering to check the state of either Matthew or Marisa, both of whom hung limp and unconscious in their chairs.

"My own children don't give a damn about me and neither do you," Mike said. "But," he pushed the TV at Madison's face, "look at how we're making *their* lives better. Just look. We're their angels. We can finally do something right."

Madison's face contorted. The hatred in her eye glazed over with something else—something like fear.

With his finger, Mike gently traced the three alt-Zanes on the screen. "Their happiness is our sorrow, Madison. Their pleasure is our pain."

"Them...them who?" Madison whispered. "Who are you talking about?"

Mike stroked the TV. "Them. Us. The other us. The better us. The Zanes. The real Zanes."

Madison renewed her struggle against her surprisingly well-tied bindings.

"Don't you want them to be happy?" Mike asked, standing and heaving Madison upright. "Don't you want them to be perfect?"

Madison flinched away. "You're insane."

Mike slapped her face, hard. Alt-Madison sighed contentedly.

"What did you say?" he asked.

Madison screamed and, again, began rocking to and fro.

"You're insane," she shouted. "There's nothing on that goddamned TV but some stupid show."

Mike's hands trembled. He wanted to reach out and tear the tongue from his wife's mouth.

Madison toppled back onto the floor and Mike slammed the television down, against her face. "Say they're stupid, Madison. Go ahead. Say they don't matter."

"They don't matter! They're television! They're characters! They don't fucking matter!" Madison cried, trying to squirm away.

Mike stretched, centered himself, and kicked his wife squarely in the jaw. He lashed out with his foot again and again, until she stopped screaming and stopped squirming. A thin, crimson foam wheezed from between her broken teeth.

Mike hugged the TV to his chest, sauntered back to his couch, and watched. He was anxious to see what wonders this most recent violence had wrought, what goodness he had brought to his family, his true family, so very far away.

The Final Correspondence of Sabrina Locker

OCTOBER 3, 1963

Beth—

After two days on the road, we're finally here. You wouldn't believe the foliage. All of Massachusetts is set ablaze with reds and oranges and yellows that are so vibrant and so insistent that I find it hard to believe they're part of the traditional spectrum of colors. It almost hurts the eyes and confounds the mind! Am I gazing out over an autumnal forest or an ocean of flame? Perhaps the two are one and the same.

And the towns...the towns are perfectly quaint and cozy little hamlets, all locked away beyond the bustle and human noise of cities on the coast. Each one seems to hold its own secret treasures. Why, just today, Harry and I stopped at a delightfully shabby restaurant in a village—I can't exactly recall its name—where we ate the finest roasted lamb one can possibly imagine. The restaurant's owner—a nervous little man with a goat-like face—kept tittering on about how we needed to be clear of the hills by nightfall and how we should speed on toward Balington as soon as we could. He whispered odd phrases about a gateway in the hills and warlocks and "things that are not things."

At first, Harry and I could barely keep from laughing, but the little man's thin, quivering lips and his dull brown, anxious eyes stirred me to curiosity. I think these towns and the people who inhabit them must be part of a world not our own, a place outside the normal flow of time, where science cannot claim a crown and the many answers of mankind are terribly foolish and disturbingly incomplete. Something in these outback way stations, I find, seems closer to the foundation of existence than our lives of endless chatter and artistic presumption.

Harry says he can knock out half his new novel over this vacation. I'd like to finish at least a handful of poems. But if everyone we meet is as peculiar as that little restaurateur and all the surrounding towns exude the same aura of delicious mystery, I imagine I'll probably do more sightseeing than writing.

In any case, we're lodged in a stately hotel in Balington and squared away for the evening. The city is as Harry described it: all shadows and ivy and colonial ghosts. You can hear the bricks of the buildings cry out for release and the cobblestone alleyways laugh at the insignificance of those who pass upon them. Mind you, it doesn't make the city inhospitable. Quite the opposite. I feel the interminable thunder of history beneath these streets, the overlap of so many lives, so many unknown and undiscovered truths. It all fires the imagination with wonder, even as it creeps with hints of terror.

I wish we could explore Balington for more than one day, but Harry's speaking engagement at the university is tomorrow evening and, afterward, we're off to the Delbert Inn for the duration. I suppose I'll have to make do with the rustic environs and endure the burden of relaxation. I hope that the inn's fanciful advertisement is true, and the trees in the western Quantenac Valley really do sprout silver leaves and glow under a full moon. I hope legends of the

Quantenac Valley bear some truth, and the old, undeveloped lands to the west are haunted in ways we can't begin to understand.

I hope...I hope...I hope. I hope I'm inspired by something beyond hope.

Only tomorrow knows.

Until then, dear sister,

Sabrina

October 6, 1963

Beth—

The inn is a marvel of American gothic, perfect for my new work even though the trees don't glow as advertised! According to the ad that led us here, the place used to be a functional farm run by a family with the surname Delbert—hence the very appropriate moniker "Delbert Farms." The owners, Mr. Jefferson Cooper and Mr. Franklin Burroughs—two older gentlemen that I suspect are partners in more than just business—have refurbished the farmhouse and groomed the attendant lands to the best of their abilities, but the entire atmosphere of the estate is one of profound and penetrating loneliness. Every surface inside the house feels slightly damp and every floorboard seems to creak under the slightest weight, all of which makes me think that the structure is, and has always been, quietly sobbing to itself. I half expect to find a cluster of unmarked gravestones in the fields behind the house or a crazy farmwife chained up in the attic!

And speaking of which...

Inset in the ceiling outside our room here, there's a door to the attic, but it's nailed shut and boarded over. I asked Mr. Burroughs about it and he stared at me for a long while—with a strange, blank, alien expression, really—before finally informing me that the floorboards in the attic were quite unstable and, as a precaution, he and Mr. Cooper had decided to close off the entire area to guests. I'd so wanted him to tell me that the attic had a reputation as a haunted room or that a vile murder had been committed within and the blood stains on the walls would never scrub clean—something, anything other than the daily torture of the commonplace!

I must say, however, that the peculiarities of Mr. Cooper and Mr. Burroughs give me hope. They constantly shoot one another knowing glances and their eyes are forever darting into corners where, when I swivel my gaze to observe those same corners, I see nothing. They're also both oddly complected men, their skin more pale than the paper upon which I write. Yet that same pallor imbues them with a vague glow of health rather than sickness. The poet in me would say they are molded from moonlight or suffused by a luminescence that flows within their blood.

And how unusual are their speech patterns. Last evening, as Harry and I and the aforementioned owners lazed at the dinner table after a sumptuous feast of pheasant and roasted potatoes, we all heard a noise from the forests that encircle the farm. I can't begin to describe it because, dear sister, I've never heard anything like it in my life. At best, I might say it was like the slow screech of a rusted gate swinging open, only magnified a thousandfold and set at a pitch so deep that it sent an aftershock of dread through my every nerve.

Upon hearing the sound, Harry leaped from the table and ran to a nearby window, which rattled in its frame. Mr. Cooper and Mr. Burroughs sat at the table, entirely unaffected. Harry saw nothing outside, nothing in the sky or the wood line, that would lead to obvious answer. The rending noise subsided as abruptly as it had begun and I asked our hosts what might have caused it. Mr. Cooper gestured to the ceiling and said, "Things unseen move around us and below us and inside us. We are but one wave in a mighty ocean," to which Mr. Burroughs added, "There's a textile factory on the opposite end of the western forest, out by the reservoir. And the wind sometimes plays odd music with the boughs of the trees. It could have been anything, really."

As I said, peculiar men! I should think that at least they'll serve as great characters in Harry's book, if not adequate hosts.

I wonder whether we'll hear the sound again this evening. The poetess in me dearly hopes so, even as the animal instincts in my

The Final Correspondence of Sabrina Locker

blood fear its intrusion. I suppose dusk will tell which part of me is satiated.

Love as always,
Sabrina

▫ ▫ ▫

October 9, 1963

Beth—

I believe Harry and I have stumbled upon some tremendous secret.

Each of the past three nights the ominous creak has echoed over the farm and each of the past three nights Harry and I have witnessed an abnormal illumination seep out from the forest and creep over the fields. It gathers after dusk, while the stars are just beginning to burn down with their distant longing and the frost of deepest night has not yet settled into the bones of the earth. I would mark it up to some oddity or disturbance of atmosphere, but—and here's the part that confounds my reason—it seems to have physical substance, the consistency of which is, to my eyes, similar to a sheet of silk. If that weren't enough, it moves as well! It roils and flaps and waves like a piece of cloth in a tumultuous sea, almost as though it were alive and conscious and seeking out something just beyond its reach. I must sound like one of the superstitious denizens of this valley, but I can describe the thing in no other way. I have never before seen a light that seems to have solidity, substance, and, more than that, a will of its own. And let's not even discuss its color. It confounds the senses. At one moment, I'm tempted to call it "cobalt," while the next moment "silver" is more apt. In yet other moments "violet" or "gold" or "aquamarine" seems most applicable. It's as though it reflects every known color at once, and yet none of them at all.

After the first night's sighting, I breached the topic of the light to Mr. Burroughs over the subsequent morning's breakfast. I wondered aloud whether the valley was known for any peculiar fogs or mists. Mr. Burroughs reply—cool and clipped as usual—was that "the Quantenac Valley has been known to produce what some might call abnormal weather, yes." When I pressed him on the subject, asking what sort of weather we might expect over our autumnal stay, he smiled with an expression that somehow put me in mind of funeral attendees and said, "We should always be prepared for the inconceivable reality of nature."

A great help, our hosts.

That same day, while Harry clicked away on his novel, I went walking about the farm and decided to explore a path that Mr. Cooper had mentioned led through the woodlands to a small beachhead on the nearby Falmouth reservoir. As I strolled along the trail, I felt unnaturally weary—far wearier than someone my age should feel during a slow jaunt—and as I ventured deeper into the woods, the trees began to curve inexplicably, their branches raised not toward the firmament, but bowed to the forest floor. The effect put me in mind of the elderly, all stooped and bent by the feast of time and the famine of entropy. Yet the trees seemed no worse for their bizarre prostration; indeed, their leaves exploded in some of the richest hues of orange and red and yellow I've ever set eyes upon.

Mixed amongst the foliage, sprouting from buds on the tree branches, I also spied dozens of brilliant white bulbs roughly the size and shape of footballs. I wouldn't even mention these here, as I assume they must be a parasitic fungus or blight of some kind, but, as I passed the snowy buboes, I swear they moved to search me out and track my motion.

Unnerved, I ran through the forest as quickly as my fatigued legs would carry me. When I reached the beach, exhausted to my soul, I could do little more than collapse upon the ground and bathe in the murky noontime sun. Kicking off my shoes, I sprawled upon the rock-strewn shore for some time, letting the gentle, surprisingly warm, waves lap against my toes.

I lay there for some time before a strange realization crawled over me: the waves which touched my feet made no sound as they died against the beachhead. Not a single bird chirped in the greying sky and not a single woodland animal tittered from the glade behind me, either. Concerned, I rose and looked out over the reservoir. In the distance, I saw a hillock of water rising up out of the otherwise placid lake. A rogue wave, I thought. But, by my estimate, it grew to several dozen feet in height and several hundred feet in length. No wave, this—unless it was a tsunami. The mound of water didn't ripple outward or roll toward shore, but remained stationary, a grey-blue blister upon the lake. As abruptly as it had expanded, it began to deflate and return to the unbroken smoothness of the reservoir's surface. I stood on the shore, transfixed, awaiting further events I couldn't begin to imagine.

To my amazement, the water began to rise again, this time closer to the shoreline where I stood. It crested as it had before and, as before, it gradually retreated into the body of the lake. Given that no animal broke the surface under the swell, the entire effect impressed upon me the notion that the reservoir itself, the whole of this liquid mass, was one unified thing and was breathing or pulsing with a slow, steady thrum of life. I couldn't help but think that I was playing witness to some extraordinary process that I was never meant to set eyes upon, let alone understand. When the third rise of the reservoir came, even closer than before, I fled back into the forest, overcome with a sense that I had intruded on something much larger than myself and, as an intruder, I would soon be cast out of the thing's presence—perhaps by force.

I rushed through the woods, stumbling and bumbling back to the farmhouse—again experiencing extreme fatigue when I passed the spying white bulbs—and collapsed into bed.

Harry woke me for dinner but, by then, the day's adventure had already faded to curious anecdote that I didn't wish to share quite yet. I wanted—no, needed—to let events simmer in my mind for a time.

At dusk, as Harry and I and our hosts dined on sumptuous quail and wild rice, the rending sound again pealed through the open spaces of the farm. Harry and I said nothing about it and our hosts ignored it as they had before.

As I tried to ply my mind away from the sound by focusing on the culinary minutiae around me, I noticed for the first time that Mr. Cooper and Mr. Burroughs filled their own water glasses from the tap, while Harry's and my water they poured from jugs that resided inside an icebox just off the kitchen. I asked about the discrepancy, and Mr. Burroughs explained that "We have water delivered from a mountain spring to the north. Only the best for our guests." Mr. Cooper tapped his own glass and added, "Franklin and I have been drinking the old well water here for so long that I doubt any pristine spring would sustain us." At this, Mr. Burroughs glared at Mr. Cooper, dropped his utensils to his plate with a clatter, and excused himself from the table.

An odd reaction, I thought.

That second night, after desserts and drinks and a few passages of Yeats, Harry and I stood by our bedroom window and watched for the shawl of illumination to again unfold over the land. We were not disappointed. As the sky retired to its darkened chambers, the light rose up from the ground and wormed its way through the nearby woods. Harry pressed his nose to the glass and mumbled "I can use this. It's a flounder from space. That's what it is. Or maybe a skate. The Skate behind Saturn. I see potential there." He rushed to his notepads and began scribbling.

I couldn't turn away so easily. As the light undulated through the distant fields, some atavistic fraction of myself knew that what I saw was neither aurora nor mist nor any other trick of atmosphere. I shrank from the alien glimmer, yet I wanted to enter it, explore it, and know it—as much as it could be known. I was terrified of it, yet I saw in it endless possibilities. I imagined I was nothing less than Friedrich's wanderer above the sea of fog, standing in rapturous contemplation of the uncertainties before me.

After what must have been close to an hour of standing in rapture, I drew myself back into the confines of practicality. While Harry wrote and wrote and wrote, utterly oblivious to anything other than his pen, his paper, and the inside of his skull, I decided to bring the light to Mr. Cooper's and Mr. Burroughs' attention.

The Final Correspondence of Sabrina Locker

I went to their respective bedroom doors and knocked, but neither man answered. I checked the time—10:12—and again knocked on both doors. Still, no one responded. Surely it was early enough that our hosts—even if they had retired for the night—couldn't be deep in the clutches of slumber. I held my ear to the walls outside their rooms, but I heard no snore or rustle or murmur from within.

Frustrated by Harry's myopia and vaguely disquieted by the lack of response from our hosts, I threw myself into bed, shot off a few lines of verse, and forced myself to sleep.

Over a fine breakfast of ham and eggs the next morning, I confronted Mr. Cooper and Mr. Burroughs about the issue of their absences the previous evening. They shared a sidelong glance and Mr. Burroughs said that he was sorry, but that he had always been "a heavy sleeper, which, in this business, with the walls not being very thick, is a blessing." Mr. Cooper hurriedly scanned the empty corners of the dining room and mumbled, "The walls are very thin indeed." He offered no further explanation for his lack of response the past night, however.

Mid-morning, while Harry and I sat at opposite ends of the farmhouse's living room, both of us alternately writing and gazing into the verdant conflagration at the edge of the fields, another couple arrived at the inn: Salvatore and Dianna DiNarelli, young newlyweds from New York. Though I know it's a terrible stereotype to think it, they remind me of every mobster movie I've ever seen. Sal's hair is so slick you might mistake it for chiseled obsidian and his chest puffs solid and proud, like a Roman legionnaire's; Dianna's body is a model for fertility goddesses of any age or place and her accent is so pronounced that her every word seems to swim up from a golden sea of the finest olive oil. To be honest—and don't tell Harry this—they both put me in mind of moonlit rendezvous in steamy alleyways. That they immediately locked themselves in their room after their arrival didn't help to dispel my bawdy preconceptions.

By the afternoon, I was antsy and desperate for interaction outside the confines of my skull. I tried to persuade Harry to come with me to see the strange bulbs in the forest, but he muttered half-formed sentences about being "locked in" and rebuffed my advances for even the minor stimulation that casual conversation might afford. Dejected, I left the house in a huff and wandered the fields that stretched east, away from the haunted forest and the leviathan-in-waiting that the locals quaintly referred to as a "reservoir."

As I walked, I spotted a figure standing in the space between the fields and the eastern thicket. The figure's head was tilted toward its chest and it seemed to be retching into the tall grasses that limned the fields. I shouted a "Hello" and the figure whirled about, revealing Mr. Cooper's startled, ever-pale face. Rivulets of perspiration twined from his forehead to his neck and darkened his shirt at the collar and under his arms. He waved to me, but the gesture was halting.

"Are you all right, Mr. Cooper?" I asked, and he nodded slowly, as though contemplating the infinite vagaries of my question.

"It's a bit chillier today than it has been all week," I said, sidling nearer to him. "You'll catch pneumonia out here, being drenched in this cool air."

He cast a distant smile in my direction and shook his head. "A man who can't enjoy his own life," he said, "has already contracted the most grievous disease."

I began to respond, to ask whether he, in fact, gleaned no joy from his pastoral existence, when he launched into a new line of thought.

"Let me tell you a story, Mrs. Locker," he said. "Franklin wouldn't like me to tell this tale to a guest, but I believe you'll appreciate it. I can feel something of the wanderer in the tides of your eyes and this is certainly a story that appeals to those who wander, those who search after the deepest, most unsettling mysteries."

"Go on," I said. "I'm intrigued." And I was. You know how I've always been, Beth. Do you remember the summer I got lost in the caves out by Archlane Ridge and father and Uncle Gavin spent half a day searching for me? Remember what I was doing in those caves? I wanted to ride a dragon, so I was desperately searching for one that I might tame. And remember when I spent that night in the old, supposedly haunted Campbell place and told mother and father I was at Lucy Hand's? Do you know why I went there, alone? I wanted to sleep beside a ghost. I wanted to let its icy fingers graze my skin and let its misty breath freeze the nape of my neck.

Well, Mr. Cooper's offer appealed to me in the same way as those dragons and ghosts, so I stood in the cold and let him continue.

"Hundreds of years ago," he said, "a tribe of natives—the Quantenac, for which the area is named—inhabited this valley and the hills to both the north and the east. The Quantenac were a fearless band of hunters and warriors. They drove the far more renowned Mohicans back, into present-day New York, and they forced the coastal tribes throughout New England to hug those coasts tight, for fear of slaughter if they encroached too far inland.

"The Quantenac held an unusual spiritual belief that set the foundation for their ferocity: they believed that the world and all the things in it were inherently parasitic. They conceived of the darkness of space as a primeval purity that, each night, attempted to reclaim the land and the creatures in it. Material reality, they believed, had smeared itself across this nothingness and stained what was an otherwise pristine canvas. As a people, the goal of the Quantenac was to return as much of this world as possible to that state of original darkness, to eradicate the living, who reveled in creating light and who, in sleep, fed off the power of the darkness. Essentially, they were death worshipers, and they believed the ultimate state of the cosmos—the perfect state of the cosmos—was one of serene, unchanging lifelessness.

"Given their beliefs, you might think the Quantenac were unflappable, and for the most part, that's true. They didn't fear other native tribes—rather, they were disgusted by them and squashed them like flies, without moral qualm or hesitation—and they didn't fear any of the usual bugaboos like nature or time or even death. But what they did steer clear of was, inexplicably enough, a natural spring that burbled up in the western reaches of the valley, not far from where we now stand.

"The Quantenac refused to go near the spring, even in times of drought. They claimed it was a cursed place, a place beneath which dwelt something even older than their revered darkness. They had a name for this thing: 'Kintinela.' Translated, the word has no exact meaning, but a close approximation might be 'sickness before the beginning.'

"A few vague legends concerning the Kintinela have filtered down to us. One is about a boy who drowned in the spring but was later heard crying for his parents from under the ground. Another tells of a spider that fell into the spring and became a creature formed of liquid, with twice as many appendages as a normal spider and a size thousands of times greater than any spider known to humankind. But the most important tale deals with the demise of the Quantenac.

"This particular legend tells of a bold Quantenac chieftain who thought he might appease the Kintinela by dumping the corpses of defeated enemy warriors into the spring. After a victorious battle against a nameless, long-forgotten tribe, the chieftain enacted his plan and dragged the bodies of his fallen foes to the spring. There, they were weighted with stones and rolled into the watery pit. And nothing more happened. They weren't spit back out. They didn't rise from the dead. They just sank and remained sunken.

"The Quantenac considered this serenity a good sign and reveled and threw a feast in honor of the defeat of not only their enemies, but the Kintinela as well. The Quantenac had accomplished much cleansing of the world that day and were proud. As night drew on, though, a thick fog drifted into the tribe's encampment and engulfed their jubilations. At first, no one thought much of the fog, as the valley has always been prone to dense, nearly impenetrable mists. But as the evening hours grew longer, the fog grew heavier and more solid. It began to stick to skin and sneak into lungs. It weighed on the Quantenac, both inside and out. And still it grew heavier, more condensed.

"Gasps and rattles of strangulation echoed from within the mist as it congealed ever further, first transforming into a shawl of floating water and then becoming something more viscous, something more mucosal, something like an enormous membrane, glittering as though infused with the glow of distant stars.

"Many Quantenac accepted the fog as an ultimate cleansing of the physical world and met their demise with open arms. But others, quite sensibly, couldn't resist the animal urge to flee. Of those that ran away, some died regardless—the fog having already infiltrated their bodies too fully, smothering them from within as they sprinted through the forests. However, a few, a tiny few, managed to escape the massacre. Those scattered Quantenac never returned to the valley. Instead, they integrated into other tribes and spread the legend of the cursed spring and the Kintinela at its depths. Of the Quantenac campsite, it's said that the entire thing disappeared—bodies and wigwams and weapons and tools all missing alike. When other tribes investigated the area after hearing of the massacre, they found nothing at the location of the encampment other than an expanse of rich topsoil, utterly flensed of flora and fauna."

With this, Mr. Cooper stopped speaking. The sweat had dried from his face and he shivered when a breeze gusted over the field.

"That's an intriguing yarn," I said. "And I've never heard that particular legend before. But I don't see why Mr. Burroughs would take issue with you explaining local folklore."

Mr. Cooper nodded and kicked the ground. "You might. If you knew that these fields are supposedly the fallow land those tribes found. We're standing on the site of the Kintinela's wrath, Mrs. Locker. Or so the legend goes."

I paused to consider whether he was attempting to frighten me or enlighten me. I decided those ideas aren't mutually exclusive.

"And the spring?" I asked. "Shouldn't it be nearby, if your legend bears any truth?"

Mr. Cooper again nodded. He pointed to the western woods. "Oh, the spring is still out there. It was excavated and expanded in the twenties, at great cost of life and resources. But that's another story for another day."

"Wait," I said, "do you mean that the Falmouth reservoir...?"

"Is the spring, torn wide open and fed the lifeblood of several dozen creeks and streams."

Given my experiences at the reservoir the previous day, the hair at the nape of my neck stood to attention and gooseflesh cascaded over the lengths of my arms.

I made a few polite parting noises in Mr. Cooper's direction and excused myself to the farmhouse. I hurried back to Harry's and my bedroom and began to copy down the conversation between myself and Mr. Cooper, so I wouldn't forget any detail. I spent the rest of the afternoon there, in the bedroom, rereading the transcript and composing some lines about the ill-fated Quantenac and the chthonic "sickness" that decimated them. Harry flitted in and out, but seemed generally disinterested in my work, which was nothing unusual.

During dinner, I barely spoke, as the table was already plump with conversation. Harry burbled on and on about his progress for the day and how his characters were shaping up, while Mr. and Mrs. DiNarelli regaled us all with their extended personal and family histories. The DiNarellis are interesting people, yes—Salvatore is a fireman from a long line of firemen and his father was killed in a blaze ten years ago; Dianna is a beautician who immigrated to America with her parents during Mussolini's dictatorial reign—but their stories seemed prosaic in comparison to the bizarre legend Mr. Cooper had told me earlier in the day.

As we ate, the soul-shearing screech again tore through the air, bringing conversation to a gracious halt. Dianna exclaimed that she'd heard a similar sound once before, in a dream. She said it had been the sound of a bright, cloudless sky falling around her in huge, ragged shards. Salvatore asked our hosts what the noise was, and they answered—much as they had when I first asked—that a few industrial factories stood on the opposite end of the reservoir and that sound carried a surprising distance in the valley. Harry, already shrinking from the mystery, chuckled a bit and muttered something about it being our dinner bell.

The Final Correspondence of Sabrina Locker

I retired to the bedroom shortly thereafter. The DiNarellis must think I'm snobbish, but I needed solitude. I needed to sit by the bedroom window and stare into the gloaming. I needed to wait for the haze to wriggle itself through the forest, to reveal itself to me, to dance for me and terrorize me and make me feel that the world wasn't just a cozy, well-lit dinner table and casual conversation. And so I pushed a desk and a chair by the window and I waited, writing you this letter, lovely sister.

Harry returned at some point in the evening and promptly fell asleep on the bed, but I remained vigilant for the unknown and have been rewarded. Right now, as my quivering hand traces these letters, the fog glimmers and undulates and slithers through the fields. It commands my attention, arrests my thought. Is this a sickness from before the beginning? Is this the finger of the Kintinela? I find it difficult to believe. And yet...and yet...there is a definite measure of foreboding in those uncertain waves and swirls.

I wonder where it comes from, what happens to it when it dissipates, and what would become of me if I flew down the stairs and ran through it.

Maybe, before the autumn is too faded, I shall summon my courage and find answers to all my questions.

Love ever and always,
Sabrina

October 16, 1963

Beth—

The past several days have been a trial of both body and spirit, because Salvatore DiNarelli has gone missing. According to Dianna, Salvatore woke an hour before dawn on the morning of the 13th and, as is his habit, ventured outside for a brisk constitutional. Three days later, he still hasn't returned from his sojourn.

Initially, everyone suspected he must have injured himself somewhere along his journey, so we spent the entire morning and afternoon of the 13th traipsing through the fields and the forests adjacent to the inn, calling Salvatore's name. However, we received no response and no one in our small search party—which included Harry, Dianna, Mr. Cooper, and myself—stumbled upon any sign of the man. Mr. Burroughs remained at the inn in case Salvatore returned and happened to be in need of medical treatment, but his wait was as much in vain as our search.

During the search, Dianna explained that Salvatore rarely gave her any indication as to where his morning excursions might take him, and, per the usual, he didn't share his destination plans on the morning of the 13th, either. We had no idea where to begin a genuine manhunt, especially in a rural, heavily wooded setting, so we strode about aimlessly.

When we returned to the inn, tired and defeated, Mr. Cooper mentioned that numerous hikers in the surrounding hills go missing every year and most of them—he emphasized the "most"—turn up alive and well under their own power.

Dianna, to her credit, remained composed. I heard her curse Salvatore beneath her breath several times throughout the afternoon and caught her whispering a tearful prayer in the bathroom just before dusk, but she didn't fly into the hysterical fits of despondency that so many men might believe a woman in her situation would be inclined to. By dinner time, she wanted, quite reasonably, to call the state and local police to aid in our efforts, but Mr. Burroughs discouraged the action. He insisted that missing persons could only be reported after twenty-four hours had elapsed from their time of disappearance and that the local police were generally incompetent anyway, referring to them as "the guardians of a bumbling ethos."

So Dianna waited through a tense night. We all waited. Mr. Cooper volunteered to sit up until dawn, in case Salvatore wandered back to the inn, and no one—not even Dianna—argued.

As I lay in bed, exhausted from the day's trek but unable to sleep due to Harry's incessant rolling beside me, one splintered thought kept niggling at my mind: the mystery creak hadn't pealed across the sky that evening. At least, I hadn't heard it if it did. Certainly, the day had been stuffed full of drama and distraction, but it was

The Final Correspondence of Sabrina Locker

impossible to ignore the noise, as booming and cacophonous as it was.

Disturbed by the meaning of the silence and all those things it might hide, I rose from the mattress and moved to the window. Outside, a fog had crept from the woods as usual, but it was not the fog of previous nights. Gone was the luminescence; gone was the membranous solidity; gone was the motion of oceans and single-celled beasts. The fog was thick, no doubt, but as unremarkable as a Gothic potboiler. I wanted to smash the window and scream into those dead mists, but resisted the urge, instead returning to bed and staring at the ceiling until slumber finally collapsed upon me.

By the time I was up and about the next morning, Dianna had already telephoned the police and they had arrived at the inn. Two middle-aged officers—one bald and stocky, the other mustachioed and exceedingly tall—stood in the dining room, conversing with Mr. Burroughs. Positioned between them, Mr. Burroughs seemed little more than a filament of a man, glowing pale and steady. As I wandered by, I overheard phrases like "damn fool thing to hike before dawn," "city people just don't understand," and "bet the missus nags him like hell" float up from the trio. I also heard one of the police ask "What does that make this year? Five?"

I found Harry seated in the living room, scribbling away at his science fiction epic. He murmured something about the police asking him "a few pointless questions" then returned to his work.

I shrugged on my coat and headed outdoors, not knowing where I wanted to go, but sure I needed to distance myself from the stifling air of the inn.

Without conscious purpose, I meandered in the direction of the reservoir. As I entered the wooded path through the western forest, a multitude of voices burbled up in the distance and I caught sight of Dianna, Mr. Cooper, and two more police officers—one of whom held the leash of a German shepherd—striding toward me from further along the path.

Dianna dashed to me, threw her arms around my neck, and began sobbing. Her tears gave way to words and the words gave strength to despair.

"He can't swim," she cried. "The scent. The lake. He can't swim. Why would he? Why would he go in?"

I hugged her tight until the officer without the dog grabbed her by the arm and led her to the inn. Mr. Cooper stayed behind, with me, and watched her go.

"The dog found a scent?" I ventured. "And it led to the reservoir?"

Mr. Cooper nodded. "And Mr. DiNarelli is unfamiliar with even the most basic of the aquatic arts."

"It doesn't mean anything," I said. "He could've waded in where the trail ended and waded back out somewhere else."

Mr. Cooper drew a circle in the air, then another larger circle around it and still another even more expansive circle around the second.

"We traced the shoreline for a mile in either direction. No trace. No ripple. No Mr. DiNarelli."

"And what do the police believe may have happened?" I asked.

Mr. Cooper shrugged.

"The police don't believe. They act. And in the current situation, there's no action to be taken yet."

Incensed by the general lack of concern for the DiNarellis from all parties, I huffed and tried to push past Mr. Cooper, but he sidestepped to block my progress.

"Mrs. Locker, before you continue down this path, let me tell you the other story I mentioned a few days ago—the one about the construction of the reservoir."

I stood before him infinitely curious, even as my eyes narrowed with the sting of empathy for Dianna.

"Fine," I said. "Go on."

"During the twenties," he began, "an entrepreneur from Balington named Clark Falmouth decided that the city needed to find alternative sources of energy besides coal—sources of energy Mr. Falmouth could control. Given that Balington isn't situated near any significant body of running water, it seemed the only other major alternative of the time—hydroelectricity—wouldn't be an option. But Falmouth had vision, of a sort. He determined that if the old Quantenac spring could be expanded to the size of a lake by channeling dozens of small streams and creeks into it, then he could dam the spring, carve an outlet, and, essentially, create a sizable river where there hadn't been one before. Somehow, he sold this insanity to the Balington town council and, even more impressive, to the state department of energy.

"So, in 1927, a massive terraforming project went into action. Falmouth brought in construction crews from across New England to restructure the waterways and force their drainage into the spring. At the same time, he oversaw the expansion of the spring's basin—a process which included digging out a vast portion of the low-lying forest lands to the west and dynamiting open the underground channels that fed the spring.

"At first, the project appeared to be running smooth and steady, but within a few months, the construction crews around the spring worksite began to suffer inexplicable accidents. Two men were crushed by a rockslide that supposedly defied the laws of physics and rushed uphill. A surveyor working in the basin was supposedly sucked into a quicksand-like pit that turned hard as steel after he had been pulled completely under. One foreman was found dead with blisters and burns covering his body both inside and out, as though his very blood had reached boiling temperatures. Perhaps most bizarre of all, however, many of the laborers contracted an unknown infection that caused them to break out in milky white pustules and hear babbling, whispering voices that no one else could hear. Many of these men ended up in psychiatric wards, where they lived out the rest of their days under a barrage of tests and treatments.

"Due to the risk of infection and the growing sense that the spring might truly be cursed, the turnover rate for workmen at the dig site was high. Thus, by late 1928, work on the project had slowed to a crawl. Dozens of tributaries flowed into the spring's expanded basin, creating a deep reservoir several miles long and several miles wide, but an outlet hadn't yet been excavated nor had a dam or a hydroelectric plant been constructed. And none of them ever would be.

"In 1929, Clark Falmouth committed suicide. Drowned himself in his own bathtub, or so the papers said. Later that same year, the stock market crashed and Falmouth's businesses crumbled. The project ground to a halt and has remained in limbo for over thirty-four years, though it retained Falmouth's name. His only legacy is the reservoir—a cursed spring expanded beyond its natural borders and fed new waters so that it might never die."

Mr. Cooper moved to my side and held out his arm, as though to usher me to my destination. I ignored the offer.

"And the lesson here is what, exactly?" I asked, still angered by the nonchalance toward Dianna's suffering but equally enthralled by the new mysteries and horrors Mr. Cooper had let loose. "What does any of this have to do with Mr. DiNarelli?"

Mr. Cooper smiled and spread his hands wide, in entreaty. "There is no lesson or correlation," he said. "There's only a story about what is, what was, and what may be. Which is to say, there is only a story, and that story may not yet be ended."

I stared at the forest trail that led to the reservoir. Still festooned in its oranges, yellows, and reds, it wasn't difficult to imagine the pathway as a tunnel of fire, the umbilicus between this world and a dimension of possibilities both terrible and divine.

"Of course there's no correlation," I murmured, and pushed past Mr. Cooper to continue on my way. Again, sister, I was chasing dragons and hunting ghosts. Mr. Cooper didn't follow. Perhaps he'd already found his monsters.

Further along the trail, after several minutes of walking, I discovered a pile of the white, fungus-like nodules I'd seen before lying upon the forest floor. They'd been hacked from the trees upon which they had grown. An attempt had been made to smash them, but they retained much of their original shape. I stopped and prodded one with my foot and, in response, it quivered like gelatin and latched onto my boot. Initially, I thought that the sac might've had adhesive properties and had merely stuck to my shoe when I poked at it, but as I shook my foot in an effort to loose myself from the thing, it began to wriggle and worm its way toward my ankle.

I can't lie—I screamed and kicked my leg into the air like a spastic can-can dancer. The fungus-thing went flying. It smacked against a tree trunk with a wet splosh and burst apart in a spray of water and pulp.

I forced myself to calm, then bent to examine the other fungal polyps scattered amongst the woodland detritus. As I passed my hand over them, each one squirmed and strained to touch my flesh. I still don't know if these things are part of a rare branch of invertebrate taxonomy or an undiscovered form of plant life or something else entirely too bizarre to comprehend, but I wasn't about to risk picking one up to take back to the inn for further inspection. Concerned for the potential toxins or infectious agents they might harbor, I left the half-destroyed buboes lying along the path and headed back to the farmhouse, the day growing colder and my teeth already chattering.

Later that evening, after the policemen had driven away and Dianna had taken some Valium prescribed to Mr. Burroughs for reasons he wouldn't discuss, Harry and I and our hosts slouched around the dining room table sipping coffee and picking at food that only Harry seemed interested in eating. Mr. Burroughs, grim-faced and preternaturally still, said little. Several times during the evening he walked to the windows and the dark corners of the room and blotted them with a dish towel. When Harry laughed at him and asked "What are you doing there? Dusting for prints?" Mr. Burroughs glared in return and answered "This time of year we tend to find a significant buildup of condensation at the joints and seams of the house. We don't need mildew, mold, or fungus taking up residence here."

Mr. Cooper raised a glass as though to toast and added, "Or anything even more invasive."

As Mr. Cooper's remark hung in the air like a noose drawn tight around my thoughts, an unexpected guest returned: the creaking rapture from beyond the woods. It suddenly blasted out of the dusk, rolling over the forest and the fields and into our dining room enclave. My flesh crawled and my nerve endings tingled despite myself. The sound's return was like the caress of a resentful god who wants nothing more than to break ties with its creation forever.

Once the creaking had ended, Harry, mouth stuffed with meat and rolls, mumbled "You really should lodge a complaint about that noise. It ruins the atmosphere."

Just as Harry finished his criticism, another sound—this one softer, muffled, as though issued not from the air but from somewhere deep beneath us—drifted into the room. And this sound, this new melody of the unknown, was far worse than the godlike creaking, because it was, quite unmistakably, the distant scream of a tormented man.

I leaped from my chair and, without thinking, called out "Salvatore?" Whether the anguished man was or wasn't Salvatore, he didn't respond. Harry dropped his utensils, eyes bulging. Mr. Burroughs gripped the edges of the table hard, his knuckles close to tearing through his paper-thin skin. Mr. Cooper merely raised an eyebrow. Dianna, thankfully, remained in Valium's gossamer cocoon, so she didn't wake to hear the horror.

As abruptly as the scream had torn through our lives, so, too, it dissolved to silence.

"We have to go find him," I said to no one in particular.

Harry shook his head and lanced a chunk of beef with entirely too much violence. "That was just the house settling."

Mr. Burroughs released the table and slapped his hands upon its top. "Exactly, Mr. Locker. This place is nearly one hundred years old. When the temperature drops, it complains, as those with old bones have every right to do."

"You must be joking," I implored. "That sound wasn't the house, unless this house has lungs and a mouth and the capacity to feel pain."

The Final Correspondence of Sabrina Locker

Mr. Burroughs drummed his fingers on the tabletop. "Just the house, Mrs. Locker. Just the house."

I locked eyes with Mr. Cooper, hoping for counsel, hoping for an ally, but he only shrugged and whispered, "One cannot rescue echoes."

The remainder of the night I hid away in the bedroom and contemplated the vagaries of willful ignorance. Reason and rationality are remarkable blades, dear sister. They dissect the universe so expertly, with so much assurance. But when rational men refuse to interrogate their own perceptions for fear of the outré knowledge that such interrogation may return, those same blades become implements of digging. Before long, rational men find themselves standing at the bottom of a deep pit, safe and sure in the depth of their understanding, yes, but unable to see anything beyond the contours of the narrow space they've bored for themselves.

So many people are content in their pits, satisfied to know only as much as might give them the illusion of mastery over the world. But I'd rather wander in the fog than live in a pit.

This morning—just a few hours ago, actually—Dianna left the inn with the police. She carried out her luggage and hasn't returned since. Before she slid into the police car, I embraced her and told her to never stop searching. She leaned in close and whispered in my ear, "I had a dream that we were all tiny ants caught in a flood and we were drowning and we were rushing faster, faster, faster to a circling drain that poured into the center of the earth."

Something tells me Dianna's not coming back to this farm. Something tells me she might never come back to herself. Her aura of supernatural fertility now seems more tragic than divine. Perhaps, for someone like her, a pit might be the last bastion of sanity.

Until my next letter,
Sabrina

Kurt Fawver

OCTOBER 19, 1963

Dearest Bethany,

Last night, long after everyone had retired to bed for the evening, I was awoken by the sound of shuffling feet outside the bedroom door. I assumed it had to be either Mr. Burroughs or Mr. Cooper, so I wasn't alarmed. But as the shuffling continued it took on a different timbre, growing slower, more ponderous, more viscid—almost like the tread of boots through heavy, clinging mud.

Still, I didn't worry. Perhaps one of our hosts spilled a glass of water in his slippers. Perhaps he suffered insomnia and was mopping the hallway late into the haunting hours.

I waited for the sound to abate, but rather than simply ending, it receded to the stairwell. After another minute or two, I heard the back door creak open and, moments later, click shut.

In bravery or foolhardiness—I can never quite grasp the distinction between the two—I rose from bed, threw on some clothes, and left the bedroom. Despite the moist noises I'd heard, the hallway was inexplicably dry. Across the hallway, the doors of our hosts' rooms stood wide open for the first time since Harry and I arrived at the inn.

Think of me as a common voyeur or peeping Tom if you must, sister, but I couldn't resist the temptation to explore. The open doorways beckoned like the Cave of Thieves, and I didn't even need to utter a secret password to enter.

I quickly stole into Mr. Cooper's room and began to catalogue everything in sight. Though the sanctum was illuminated by nothing more than a single desk lamp, I discerned an astonishing array of trinkets and personal ephemera scattered along a system of shelves that lined the room's walls from ceiling to floor.

By the room's sole window hunched a behemoth oak desk, atop which stood the lonesome lamp and a veritable mountain range of books and newspapers and loose-leaf sheets of paper. The books dealt in a variety of topics: microbiology, parasitology, geophysical structures and sedimentary layering, New England history, water tables, ancient folklore, ecosystems, evolution, extraterrestrial life, and even theosophy. The sheets of paper were filled with intricate diagrams of what looked like tree root systems, extended screeds written in near-illegible script, and individual thoughts set off in block lettering. Some of those block-lettered words and phrases that I remember include "RHIZOMATIC," "INFECTION IS A MEANS, NOT AN END," "PROTIST? DIATOM? VIRUS? SPORE?" and, most intriguing, "THERE IS NO HUMAN LOGIC TO EXPLAIN THE BEHAVIOR."

Also lying open on the desk was a notebook that I took to be a journal. I read one of the exposed entries, which was dated 10-18-60—exactly three years past. The entry read: "Only by the grace of this diary do I still remember who I am, where I come from, why I exist in this place, and why I must continue the research. Every day is a struggle to recall. The recitation of the stories helps, but even they only help me constitute myself so much. Frank has been gone so long. So very long. Some diluted portion of him remains, I'm certain, but the Frank I knew is no longer. He's now more THING than Frank. I miss him dearly. I miss being able to remember WHY I miss him."

I moved to the shelves and took stock of their inventory. Mr. Cooper had assembled a museum of American history in his room, or so it appeared. Among the varied items that ringed the room, I found a yellowing postcard from Florida signed by an "E.L." and dated "Nov. 1927," a program to the 1912 World Series in Boston, a bronze buckle emblazoned with the words "U.S. Cavalry," a bouquet of dried bluebells and baby's breath wrapped with lace, a penny issued by the Confederate States of America, an antique flintlock pistol, a brochure from a clothier in Worcester dated 1799, a string of glass beads, several dozen arrowheads, a block of wood carved to resemble a raccoon or a bear, and a series of geodes. Hundreds more items of a similar nature nestled on the shelves.

Not knowing when Mr. Cooper and Mr. Burroughs might return but wanting to investigate Mr. Burroughs' room before I lost the opportunity, I sneaked from one sanctum to the next.

Though I could find no radiator, Mr. Burroughs' room was, strangely, much warmer than Mr. Cooper's. Gentle blue moonbeams flowed in through the window, providing the only source of light and casting an unusual pall over the space. As though in direct opposition to Mr. Cooper, Mr. Burroughs had no knickknacks or pieces of personal memorabilia on display—not even a photograph of a loved one or a generic painting hung upon the wall. An acute loneliness puddled within his room, and it was all I could do to not shed a tear for the man, despite his perpetually brusque attitude.

I circled the room once and, noticing nothing unusual upon first glance, was about to leave when an unmistakable splash arose from beneath Mr. Burroughs' narrow, single bed. I dropped to my hands and knees and spotted a glass bowl filled with clear liquid sitting under the head of the bed. I grabbed it and began to slide it out to gain a better view of its contents, but as I did so, I felt something shift within the bowl, as though a weighted pulley were dragging it back into its recess. Still, I didn't let go.

I managed to tug the container free from the grip of the shadowy undercarriage and hold it up to the light that spilled from the window. There, as the substance sluiced about the bowl with a torpid movement more reserved for oils or bodily fluids, I could see that it was much thicker than water.

I sniffed at the stuff, but it had no particular odor, no unusual tang. Ready to write it off as perhaps a mere saline solution of some unknown medicinal use, I poised one of my index fingers over the liquid and thought to stir it. As I did so, the substance began to glow white with some internal flame. A bizarre form suddenly coalesced within the liquid—or from the liquid—and reached up from the bowl to touch my waiting digit.

I gasped and let the bowl fall from my hands. It shattered against the unforgiving floorboards and the mystery fluid scattered across Mr. Burroughs' floor. The thing that had attempted to touch me disappeared. Whether it had fled when its abode broke apart or again dissolved to liquid and spread itself over the floor, I couldn't say. I scampered from the room and returned to my own, where, shivering, I buried myself beneath the sheets.

Of the thing in the bowl, I can only say that its shape and movement resembled nothing I have ever glimpsed; a skittering spider's leg comprised entirely of small, crystalline pyramids might come closest to an accurate description, but even that does little justice to the uncanny semblance of the thing I saw.

After the incident, I lay in bed, waiting for the return of Mr. Cooper and Mr. Burroughs, waiting to hear voices or footfalls in the hallway. But I heard nothing whatsoever—not even Harry dared snore, for some reason—and, eventually, I fell asleep from nervous exhaustion.

Now, in the dawn's breaking rays, I can let myself admit that I'm scared—mostly for my sanity. But I'm also exhilarated. I can barely comprehend what I've discovered and yet I know it must have great import for our conceptions of science and biology and even reality itself. It may be the height of lunacy, but I feel that tonight, given the willpower and the opportunity, I must investigate further. Save me from myself, dear sister.

 Sabrina

October 21, 1963

B.,

Mr. Burroughs is no fool; he's aware that either Harry or I broke the bowl in his room. Over the past two days, he's quipped that "The mice on the second floor must be growing much more curious this year" and "The ghosts who made a mess of the bedroom need to be exorcised before Christmas." Everywhere I go, he follows me; every movement I make draws his eye. He suspects it all, but he can't confirm anything.

Harry, as usual, remains oblivious. He's entirely given over to his novel, with its pragmatics of tight plotting and realistic characterization. The morning after I found the thing in the bowl, I sat him down on our bed and explained what I'd uncovered. I told the story of the Kintinela and the reservoir construction; I described the throbbing waters I'd seen in the reservoir and the odd, energy-sapping fungus in the forest; and I detailed what I'd found in Mr. Cooper's notes and what I'd found under Mr. Burroughs' bed. And his reaction was to break into laughter—hysterical, belly-busting laughter. Tears ran from his eyes as he gasped "How can you entertain something so ridiculous?"

"You write science fiction," I said. "Is it so difficult to imagine a narrative that might tie together everything I've seen, everything that's happened here?"

Harry, still crying in condescension, waved me off. "No, no. It's not. But that's a narrative. A story. A fiction. You're talking about real life. Real life is governed by rules and reasons, not imagination and crazy unknowns."

"Real life *is* a narrative," I said, growing irritated. "Written by people who want to control it. And if an anomalous phrase or an aberration of theme slinks into that narrative from the margins, it's footnoted or deleted outright. The 'rules' and 'reasons' you're talking about are just editorial guidelines."

Harry's face flushed. "Maybe it was a mistake coming here. I think you might be overstimulated and too deep into that weird Gothicism and supernatural gobbledygook you've been playing at."

"Overstimulated? I'm trying to open you to what's happening around us and you're tightening your blinders," I said. "You might as well just staple your manuscript pages to your eyes." And with that, I left the room—I'd like to say gracefully, but I slammed the door behind me in a huff, leaving Harry muttering to himself.

Truly, Beth, I've thought of divorce. Harry's aloofness, which I once found so mysterious, is merely vacuity. His level-headed outlook on life, which once prevented me from flying too near the sun, now shears even the smallest stub of wings from my back. And his touch, which was always furtive and charmingly boyish, has all but evaporated, leaving behind fingers that abrade my flesh like whipping sand when rarely they do find my body.

The Final Correspondence of Sabrina Locker

I wonder if this is the nature of all distant things, of all mysteries: when afar and unplumbed they offer an abstraction, a slice of infinite potential, but when drawn close and unraveled, they resolve into the bland sameness of everything already quite tired and too well known.

Needless to say, I can't count on Harry. He doesn't want to pick up and come home early, nor does he believe any of the occurrences here have been abnormal, let alone paranormal. If there are dangers here, I'll have to face them alone, and if there are miracles to be seen, I suppose only I'll bear their witness. I'm on my own.

S.

October 24, 1963

Little sister,

This evening started out like so many others since our arrival, with Harry sucked into his manuscript and me at the bedroom window, gazing at the luminous fog as it twisted through the trees and made its mercurial circuits of the farm. Harry ate too much at dinner and eventually drifted off to sleep early, but I remained vigilant, waiting for the next chapter of weirdness to begin either outside my door or my window. I turned off the lights, lit a candle, and let my mind race.

As I watched the fog, occasionally jotting down a few lines for my latest poems, the notion struck me that the vapor's movement wasn't simply an emulation of a living thing; it was a living thing. I mused on the idea for a time and dreamed of the mist's inevitable retreat to the ground or the reservoir every dawn, like some sort of bilious, nocturnal creature scampering back to its burrow. Yet that wasn't right. The thing beyond my window was both more and less than an animal.

If one could distill the consciousness of all the world—from the rending of weak flesh under a predator's gnashing fang to the fragrant bloom of a delicate flower high within the Himalayas—and give it the most appropriate of forms, then the fog would surely be it. Is it the Kintinela of Quantenac lore? Perhaps. I certainly perceive a vague menace and exceeding indifference at its core, as of an earth-annihilating meteor streaking toward us from hundreds of light years away. But, as with such a heavenly destroyer, there also exists around the fog a corona of revelation and awe, a promise of states new and different and charged with potential.

While I sat by the window, entertaining these and many other thoughts, I suddenly caught sight of two figures wading through the mists: Mr. Burroughs and Mr. Cooper, stark naked and covered in a reflective liquid sheen that added a luster to their already luminescent pigmentation. The men moved through the fog with purposeful though furtive steps and I couldn't help but stare. Images of tightrope walkers and soldiers on patrol in hostile lands flashed behind my eyes.

A thick billow of fog rolled toward the men, met their exposed skin, and then, unbelievably, began to spiral in orbit about their bodies. As a pair of glowing cyclones they continued on, deeper into the night, their destination unknown. I watched until their outlines had entirely vanished and the fog resumed its usual undulation.

I pushed my face against the window pane and considered following them. I wanted—no, needed—to know where they were headed. I needed to know why they had disrobed. I needed to know what was out there. But I'm no fool. I had no conception of what might happen if I ran outside and let the mist envelop me, let it fill my lungs and seep into my pores. For all I knew, the same fog that orbited Mr. Burroughs and Mr. Cooper might suffocate me or poison me in an irrevocable way. So, instead of following, I decided to wait by the farmhouse's back door and ambush our hosts upon their return. I'd catch them in the act—whatever act that might be—and demand as much explanation as they could provide.

Thus it was that I still found myself propped on a stool by the farmhouse door at 4:11 in the morning, watching the hands on the kitchen clock recycle infinity. It was then, at that precise minute, that the back door inched open and our hosts—now once again clothed—tiptoed inside. Their hair, soaked as though they'd just stepped from a bath, dripped onto their shoulders.

I cleared my throat and both of them spun to face me.

"Mrs. Locker," Mr. Burroughs said, obviously startled, "what has you up and about so early?"

I shrugged. "I might ask you gentlemen the same question."

Mr. Burroughs stiffened. His lips drew taut, into something like a grimace. "We may not have crops or cows, but we still have many jobs and duties on this farm," he said. "For the pleasure and safety of our guests, some of them must be undertaken at night."

"Surely you don't mean to tell me there's something harmful here, at this lovely inn?" I asked, feigning shock and surprise.

"Every place holds dangers," Mr. Cooper said, with his usual distant tone. "And the older a place, the more deeply ingrained those dangers become."

Here, I thought I'd won. I thought I'd already trapped them. "But what chores could possibly be so tremendously dangerous to the guests yet perfectly accomplished in the dark?" I asked.

Mr. Burroughs dismissively waved a hand. "Too many kinds, Mrs. Locker. Too many to name."

"Such as?" I began to follow up, but was drowned out by Mr. Burroughs.

"And now if you'll excuse me," he said, "I'd like to rest a bit before breakfast."

"Such as?" I repeated. "What chores, Mr. Burroughs?"

But off he went, out of the room and up the stairs without another word or glance in my direction. "What chores, exactly?" I shouted after him, but he didn't respond.

Mr. Cooper didn't follow his partner's lead. Instead, he stared after Mr. Burroughs, then darted toward me, crossing the room in a matter of two steps. I'd never seen the man so animated.

"Do you have time for one last story, Mrs. Locker?" he whispered in a rush. "This one is most important and must be told quickly."

I nodded. What else could I do? The best stories tend toward tripartite form, so a final act was inevitable.

"Listen closely," Mr. Cooper continued in the same hurried, hushed voice. "Eighty years ago, a family by the name of Delbert moved into the Quantenac Valley. Where they originated is something of a mystery—some say they were cannibals on the run from the law in Canada and others claim they were mountain folk who practiced the devil's arts in upstate New York. Regardless of their background, it's indisputable that they arrived in the valley in the mid-1880s and set to work constructing a farm not far from a certain accursed spring of local legend. The other occupants of the valley steered clear of the farm, not only because of its proximity to the spring but also due to the unsettling rumors concerning the Delberts.

"No one knew exactly what the Delberts grew on their farm, though everyone had an opinion based on the gospel of hearsay. Those who threw in with the cannibal lot believed the family was overseen by a maleficent patriarch, Ovid Delbert—a man whom they claimed sired children with his wife and his daughters and his granddaughters so that he might create a sizable breeding pool of offspring that he held as stock animals. Here, those people said, Delbert raised and devoured his own progeny, branding them at birth and penning them up like hogs.

"Others—the witchcraft adherents—said that the Delberts had been drawn to the spring by its vile power and that the clan held bloodletting ceremonies in its basin. Those frightened people were given fodder by the strange lights often seen in the forests near the Delbert farm—lights that they attributed to demonic presences and lost, roving souls called forth by the Delberts. In the witching view, the Delberts used the farm as a mere cover for their true intention—satanic dominion—and sowed nothing upon the land but turmoil and chaos, sustaining themselves on the sorrow of the world.

"Whether cannibals, dark warlocks, or misunderstood outsiders, the Delberts vanished wholesale in 1918. Without so much as a notice or a noise, they completely disappeared. Locals who investigated the farm after the disappearance said the dinner table had been set with a broad complement of uneaten but oddly unspoiled food. They also said that they'd found several full sets of clothing heaped throughout the farmhouse and across the fields, as though whoever had been wearing them had suddenly evaporated. No one could determine where the Delberts had gone. No one cared much to look, either.

"For ten years following the disappearance, the bank that held the deed to the Delbert farm desperately tried to unload it, but no one bit. Every potential buyer described feeling 'shaken,' 'unsettled,' or 'in disarray' after touring the property. In 1930 the place was finally written off as a financial loss and utterly abandoned. Thus it gathered decay and mystique, entering into Quantenac Valley lore as the 'ghost farm.'

"So it remained until ten years ago, when two men from Albany—both ensconced in middle-age and in dire need of an adventure—purchased the place for pennies. They hoped to refurbish the property and open an all-inclusive rural inn that would cater to the rich, the powerful, and the famous.

"These men...these men were fools. They knew nothing of life beyond the city, of the strangeness which clings to unkempt lands. They knew nothing of the unknown, which dwellers of faraway places understand and respect as their own back yards. They knew nothing of farming or animal husbandry or any of the pleasantries that might make a rural inn an attractive resort. They only knew how to fix up a house and cook a satisfying meal. So these things they did, and did them well.

"Their business didn't flourish, but neither did it flounder. With well-placed advertising, they managed to stay afloat and draw clientele from the eastern seaboard, the mid-Atlantic, and even the Midwest. Their inn was never entirely vacant, and for that they were grateful. But something ominous hung over the farm. Both men could feel its presence in the fields and in the forests that surrounded the place, ever watchful, ever yearning to reach out and touch them. Through some long-buried atavistic sense, they gathered that it—whatever it was—inhabited virtually everything around them, even the soil beneath their feet.

"Months passed and the men witnessed unexplainable phenomena as a daily routine. Noises that sounded as though the very universe were collapsing around them, disembodied voices in the hallways of the farmhouse, inexplicable lights slithering from the fields and the forests: all this became the tablet upon which the men chiseled their lives.

"Still, the men could have dealt with living in a paranormal blender. The high strangeness didn't affect business, as guests generally didn't stay long enough to recognize anything awry, and the men *had* been seeking an adventure—albeit of slightly less gravity. They could have made a life of it, were it not for the changes. For, as they had disturbed the unknown by resurrecting the farm, so, too was the unknown in the process of remodeling their reality from, quite literally, the ground up..."

At this point, Mr. Cooper's story was broken by Mr. Burroughs, as he stormed back downstairs and pointed an accusing finger at his co-owner.

"You need to rest, too," Mr. Burroughs snapped. "Or you'll fall to pieces, with as much work as you've done this morning."

Mr. Cooper nodded, made a curt bow in my direction, and whispered two more words before he turned and followed Mr. Burroughs upstairs.

"Reservoir. Tonight."

So, there it is.

The reservoir. Tonight. You know I have to go, little sis. Is it the fruition of a dream? Or is it a willingness to walk into a nightmare? I can't say. But I have to find out. One way or the other, tonight I plan to return with my dragon finally in tow. Pray it doesn't devour me.

Sabrina

The Final Correspondence of Sabrina Locker

October 25, 1963

B—

The history of everything must be rewritten as a series of blank pages. The laws of science and the dictums of religion must be rephrased as jokes, for that's what they are. I feel as a mite would if it had the power to discover that the skin upon which it lives is not a fixed world, but merely the surface of yet another confused creature bound in chains of ever-increasing magnitude and complexity.

Tonight, when Mr. Cooper and Mr. Burroughs again left the inn under darkest nocturnal shroud, I followed. Just as I'd planned, I grabbed a flashlight to guide my path, bundled myself against the gradually deepening cold, and took flight. No fog rolled through the fields this evening, so I wasn't afraid to step foot outside and breathe deep the ancient musk of the earth.

In near darkness, with foliage above and thickets to my sides, the tunnel-like trail to the reservoir had become an esophagus and I a morsel of willingly ingested food. I treaded softly toward my goal, my flashlight beam trained just beyond my feet, and cursed myself and my desires as I went. Few other reasonable individuals would have traipsed into the uncanny woodland. Few other reasonable individuals would have followed two naked men to a cursed spring just to know *why*.

As I neared the reservoir's banks, I heard voices in conversation. I extinguished my light and sneaked closer. A few feet from the end of the trail, I ducked behind a tree and peeked at the muddy shoreline. There, bathed in a sliver of moon glow, Mr. Cooper and Mr. Burroughs sat cross-legged, gazing out onto the reservoir. Against the sable backdrop, they exuded an unmistakable luminescence that couldn't be dismissed as optical illusion.

Buddhas, I thought. Buddhas wreathed in St. Elmo's fire. But what enlightenment had they found?

"...the woman. She's curious," I heard Mr. Burroughs say.

"Curiosity is both a stairway to heaven and a trapdoor to hell," Mr. Cooper responded. "One can never be sure which direction it will lead."

"She must be brought here. She may be a useful extension."

"No. She'd want answers it can't provide. The dissonance would overtake her. Her mind would dissolve into hemorrhage or psychopathy."

Mr. Burroughs considered a moment, then, "Like the old man from last year."

"Yes," Mr. Cooper said, quietly. "Besides, she's already been here."

"I know. She attracted its attention. Now we have to deal with the fallout."

Mr. Cooper sighed. "So spirals the drain of time."

Neither man spoke again for a long while.

In the wood line, I clung to my tree, shivering and uncertain. They had to be referring to me. I had caused some sort of disturbance. Had I been responsible for Mr. DiNarelli's disappearance? Had ripples I created somehow grown into a tsunami wave that swept him off the face of the earth? I worried over this possibility until, finally, Mr. Burroughs broke the silence.

"It's gathering," he said, and both he and Mr. Cooper rose to their feet as the all too familiar cosmic creak split the sky. I looked out across the reservoir and nearly let out an audible gasp.

Deep below the surface of the lake, far beyond the shore, glowed a vortex of the same indescribable silver-blue-violet light that permeated the mists. Stretching at least fifty feet into the air from the center of the vortex were dozens of appendages like the one that had formed within the bowl under Mr. Burroughs' bed, only many magnitudes larger in size. I say "appendages" for lack of a better word. What they are has no name and may not even be nameable within our current framework of knowledge. If I consulted a thesaurus I might be equally tempted to call them "cilia" or "ganglia," and neither term would be any less correct.

The Final Correspondence of Sabrina Locker

Imbued with the same shimmer and coloration as the water below, the appendages whipped through the air noiselessly, hypnotically. I was put in mind of pendulums and mandalas and the gyre of our galaxy through the lonely vacuum of space.

The vortex winked out and the appendages collapsed back into the reservoir with a tremendous splash. Almost instantaneously, however, the thing reappeared closer to the shore—so close that I could see into its depths.

And what did I spy there within?

Imagine someone rapidly switching between channels on a television set that has a million stations. Now imagine that some of those stations are showing the most horrific surgeries ever performed and some of those stations are showing the most adorable puppies ever born; some are showing footage from future wars that will eradicate all life and some are showing innumerable loved ones hugging in a grand ceremony of communion; some are showing a cold pitchblende knife carving up the universe and some are showing a burning needle suturing reality. All these images pour out upon you at once and still infinitely more images come—images of things that you can't possibly apprehend, images no human mind could ever discern. You feel there must be a sequence or an order, but it's beyond you. You're trying to find meaning, to make sense of it all, but it's like catching a song in a jar. You're giddy and riddled with wonder, but you're also terrified and anxious. You want to laugh and make love. You want to cry and rage against the gods. You want to scream and run far, far away. It's all so amazing. It's all so horrible. It's all there is.

That's what I saw, dear sister: Everything. Everything swirled in the abyss.

While I gaped at the spectacle, the appendages again coalesced and resumed their chaotic dance. Without a sound, they shot forth and encircled Mr. Burroughs and Mr. Cooper, both of whom bent and picked up long knives from off the ground where they had been sitting.

I expected battle.

But, instead, Mr. Burroughs and Mr. Cooper brought the knives to their own throats and, in one quick, choreographed movement, slashed across them.

Blood arced into the mud and the men dropped to their knees, gasping, gurgling. The appendages circled closer, twined around the supplicated forms on the shore, and drove themselves deep into the fatal wounds Mr. Burroughs and Mr. Cooper had just opened. As blood sprayed out, reservoir water flowed in and the flesh of the men glowed brighter. Their pallor increased to the point that it stung my eyes.

The ritual apparently finished, the appendages quivered and retracted, resuming their incomprehensible orbit above the vortex. Pumped full of light from the thing in the water, Mr. Burroughs and Mr. Cooper again stood erect, their throats red but otherwise astonishingly unwounded.

Were they now dead? I wondered. Were they ever alive? Or were they now more than alive?

Assuming I'd witnessed all Mr. Cooper had intended, I turned to seek out the trail and find my way back to the inn when I heard a great sucking noise. I hurried back to my hiding spot and again peeked toward the reservoir. What I saw swept the breath from my lungs.

I cannot adequately describe the thing that rose from the depths. Immense and helical, it slowly rotated as it sat in the water. It was like a skyscraper from an alien city or a single-celled organism grown to monstrous proportion. In some way I couldn't grasp, the thing seemed alive and aware, and I felt a profound and utterly indifferent intelligence emanate from it.

The absolute apathy of that vast thing coupled with its tremendous power chilled my bones. I had encountered a god, and it felt nothing. Absolutely nothing.

Unsettled in a way I've never been unsettled, I backed away quietly and sprinted to the farmhouse. The entire time, it seemed as though the earth were disintegrating beneath my feet, as though

The Final Correspondence of Sabrina Locker

all the atoms that comprise reality were both loosening themselves from one another and yet compressing to a singular point.

"The alpha and the omega," I whispered, "and every letter in between."

Heaving for air and for escape, I burst into the farmhouse kitchen and filled a glass with tap water, then scurried upstairs to the bedroom. I grabbed a sleeping pill from the secret stash in Harry's luggage and downed it, chugging the entire glass to coax it down my parched throat. That tiny white pill settled my nerves sufficiently so that I could sit down to write this letter, but it has also begun to cause my eyelids to droop and my thoughts to go fuzzy. I need rest, dear sister. I need rest.

Until tomorrow, if such a distinction even matters any more.

Sabrina

October 26, 1963

Sister,

This morning, I didn't eat breakfast with the men. I sat up in bed, my head heavy and swimming with foreign thoughts. Even now, it's a struggle to focus. In my mind's eye, I keep seeing segments of the room differently—sometimes it appears darker and stripped of all modern convenience, other times it smells of burnt wood and seems to be sagging, and still other times it wholly disappears and I'm left feeling as though I'm floating in a vacuum.

Something is happening to me—has already happened to me.

Mr. Cooper says...he says...well...let me backtrack for a moment.

Harry's been working in the living room today. He told me to get some sleep if I felt ill. So I was alone in bed, trying to maintain focus, when someone knocked on the door an hour ago.

"Come in," I said.

The door opened and Mr. Cooper darted inside. He closed the door behind him and stood with his back against it.

"You were in the forest last night?" he asked.

"Yes," I said.

"So you saw. And you know."

"I don't know what I saw" I said. "And I don't know what I know, either. Explain it, Mr. Cooper. Give me omnipotent narration. How does it all fit together?"

He held out his palms, as though cupping a large sphere. "It...it's..." He shook his head and his hands fell back against his sides. "Could a flea wandering the beach at Normandy have explained what was happening around it when its experiences were suddenly thrust into zones of strangeness on D-Day? We're bound by the limits of our cognition, Mrs. Locker. A greater mind knows greater complexity, makes greater connections, deals in greater concerns. I can't explain how it all fits together. I'm too limited. We're all too limited."

"Then why did you tell me to go to the reservoir?" I asked.

"Because you wanted to know. Because showing you was easier than if you'd stumbled down there some late eve and never come back." A trace of sympathy limned Mr. Cooper's words.

I reached out for my water glass, which had but the tiniest of droplets left in its bottom, and Mr. Cooper's eyes went wide.

"Did you drink from the tap?" he asked.

I nodded. "Last night."

Mr. Cooper balled his hand into a fist and mashed it against his forehead. "How much did you drink? How are you feeling?"

"A glass," I said, taken aback. "One glass. Why?"

"You don't realize yet," he said, profound sadness underscoring his sentence. "You truly don't realize. Why do you think we give you spring water from miles away? Water...water has a habit of... spreading. It washes over. It carves. It seeps. At some depth, it lies beneath us practically everywhere we stand. A lake...a reservoir...it filters into what surrounds it."

Unease invaded my stomach. I wanted to flee the room, flee the inn, flee the entire Quantenac Valley.

"It's in the groundwater, too?" I asked, less a question than a hopeful appeal.

Mr. Cooper sighed and, ever so quietly, said, "What do you think happened to us?"

The Final Correspondence of Sabrina Locker

I felt bile rising up inside my throat. "What do I do now? What can I do? Is it too late? I only had one glass."

Mr. Cooper moved to the bedside and stared into my eyes. In his own, I saw curiosity and suffering. I saw a baby blinking against hospital lights and the dark, hollow sockets of a grinning skull.

"It's inside you now," he said, his usual distant tone returning. "It's going to draw you to it and use you, somehow, some way I can't imagine."

I leaned over the side of the bed and vomited. As I hung there, coughing, Mr. Cooper placed a hand on my back. "You're a part of it. Be ready. Try to remember who you are. Try to remember your story. It's the only way to maintain."

I vomited again and Mr. Cooper took his exit. I couldn't cry. I couldn't scream. I could do nothing but stare at the floor and wonder if tonight was the night I'd finally go walking in the mists.

Now here I am, barely able to concentrate enough to set down another word. The room is shifting, shifting, shifting. The paper is paper, then desk, then air, then cinders, then wood, then paper again.

Nothing makes sense. Nothing but this: I love you, dearest sister. And I love Mother and Father. The next time you see them, hug them for me me, fiercely. And, despite everything, I still love Harry, too. Tell him that.

I don't know if I'll be able to write again. I don't know if you'll ever see me again. I don't know what's about to happen. It's all so sudden and makes no sense. It's the way of life, I suppose.

But Mr. Cooper says I have to remember who I am. He says I have to remember my story. So here goes: I'm Sabrina Persephone Locker, formerly Sabrina Persephone Fields. I'm a poetry writer of exceedingly minor repute and the wife of the well-regarded though abusively aloof science fiction author Harrison X. Locker. I'm from Cincinnati, Ohio. I have a sister—Bethany Helena Fields—who is a secretary at the University of Cincinnati. I like antiquarian books and archaic language. I like starry nights and fireflies. I hate strawberries and Frank Sinatra. When I was a girl, I wanted to hunt monsters. As a woman, I wanted to investigate the unknown. Now, I just want to wake up tomorrow and still be Sabrina Locker.

An Interview with Samuel X. Slayden

Today on Horror Gateway—your source for horror movie, book, and video game news—we have an ultra-exclusive in-depth interview with Samuel X. Slayden, pseudonym of the reclusive owner and managing editor of Tantalus Press. Tantalus is the publisher of the mind-blowing, award-winning, and supposedly cursed anthology *Desire*. As of this interview, four of its contributors have committed suicide, three have been institutionalized, two have altogether retired from writing, and one murdered his entire family.

In the following interview, Slayden explains a bit about the anthology's genesis, its curation, and his take on the misfortune that hangs over its pages.

WARNING: Spoilers ahead for anyone who hasn't yet read Desire.

Horror Gateway: At this point, *Desire* has become one of the most recognized works of horror fiction of the last decade. The

New York Times did a piece on it, it's recently entered its third printing, and it's swept every genre award it's been nominated for. So, how did it all begin?

Samuel X. Slayden: As many anthologies do. With a submissions call.

HG: But I assume the call didn't work out as you'd planned, given that you eventually transitioned to invitation?

SXS: The guidelines couldn't have been any clearer: we wanted stories about wanting. Terrible, erosive wanting. The kind of wanting that launches a thousand ships, that topples kingdoms, that drives men and women to slit throats and burn homes.

We wanted to know how far people would go to fulfill a dream and what tainted colors they might see at the end of their rainbows, after they'd shredded their souls to get there. We wanted horror, torment, infernal desire. We wanted irony and the subversive twist of expectation you never saw coming. We wanted Burgess Meredith crying out "It's not fair!" over a pair of broken glasses amidst apocalyptic rubble.

But what we received in that initial call was dreck. Absolute dreck.

HG: How so?

SXS: Let's start with substance.

The most obvious route of ingress for the project was love, and everyone who had ever been romantically jilted wrote us a story about desperately wanting another person. Not surprisingly, in the vast majority of these tales the object of desire turned out to be a ravenous monster of some sort, and, as love monsters are wont to do, most of them gobbled up the protagonist wholesale or devoured a specific part of the protagonist's body—usually a still-beating heart or a set of engorged genitals. The belabored point was, obviously,

An Interview with Samuel X. Slayden

that love consumes all. We couldn't argue that. Love does consume all, good writing included.

The second most popular source of want was money, and we received so many morality tales of greed gone awry that if each one had been a dollar, we could have printed the entire anthology on 24-karat-gold-leaf paper. Too many of these stories ended with people buried and suffocating beneath mountains of coin or treasure. An equal number—and therefore equally too many—ended with the protagonist mutating into an oozing, inhuman force of corruption. This batch of stories was entirely unoriginal. Yes, we know the path to prosperity is slicked in sleaze. Yes, we know wealth separates us from empathy. Yes, we know the danger of greed lies in its infinite recursion. Money can't buy happiness, you say? It can't buy creative talent, either.

The remainder of the stories we received revolved around unimaginable idiosyncrasies and diabolic pacts. Among them:

—A man who wanted the ultimate pet sews together dogs to create his "perfect" Ur-dog

—A woman who wanted to see everyone in the world be happy becomes a serial killer who carves gaping grins into her victims

—A child who wanted so desperately to grow up that everything and everyone around him begins to age in reverse

—A man who wanted to become the world's greatest lover makes a deal with the devil and eventually goes to hell where he's forced to have nonstop sex for all eternity

—A woman who wanted to become the world's greatest chef makes a deal with the devil and eventually goes to hell where she's forced to eat herself for all eternity

—A man who wanted to write the perfect story makes a deal with the devil and eventually goes to hell where he's forced to inscribe the history of the world on his flesh with a penknife

and my personal favorite:

—A man who wanted to stop wanting literally ends up being sucked into a black hole inside his own head.

These, too, disappointed.

HG: What was wrong with those stories? Some of them sound promising.

SXS: We wanted something more profound, more unsettling. The anthology we'd envisioned broke new ground, set new standards. It won awards—shiny, classy, engraved awards. It would be the kind of anthology people would still be talking about decades into the future and scholars would puzzle over well into the next century. It would be a book to rival the Bible, the Koran, the Bhagavad-Gita—such would be its wisdom and its import. We weren't going to produce that sort of anthology with thematic elements that could have come from any given hack.

HG: So the problem with the original submissions was substance, then?

SXS: Style, too. Even the meaning of all existence would be rendered impotent if it was written in incomprehensible gibberish. There was, as most in human endeavor, a tremendous mound of spastic idiocy.

HG: What did you do then? Since the first submissions call didn't work out as well as you'd planned?

SXS: As champions of genre literature and knights of quality fiction for the ages, we at Tantalus Press did what we felt necessary to create our anthology: we selected several of the most prominent and promising writers from the horror writing world and, to make sure the stories they submitted might contain truth beyond truth and wisdom beyond wisdom, we provided them the rare opportunity to experience the darkest shades of desire at our exclusive Tantalus Writer's Retreat and Workshop.

HG: Which is what, exactly?

An Interview with Samuel X. Slayden

SXS: An all-expenses-paid opportunity for writers to explore the dark corners of themselves and human experience.

HG: Can you give us any details? Did all the writers in *Desire* attend the retreat?

SXS: They did. The first writer we chose to invite to Tantalus was Dane Bushnell. Bushnell was, of course, already quite famous in the horror community, having written the story collections *Cicatrix* and *The Grinding Place* as well as the novel *Bloodstains in a Well-Lit Room*—all of which have been nominated for Stokers and Jacksons and World Fantasy Awards. Bushnell's style is incomparable; he writes like an armored eight-hundred-pound gorilla on a bender, which is to say without reservation and with a brutality rarely seen in prose. His main characters—usually street toughs and aging bouncers—tend to massacre enough people to populate a small city before invariably disintegrating into realms of agonizing netherspace. No one can package nihilism as well. We had to have him in the anthology. But he didn't take our invitation seriously at first.

HG: Bushnell is a burly guy and, like his characters, has something of a reputation as a churlish strongman himself. How did you convince him to come?

SXS: Two darts tipped with horse tranquilizer to the neck and he was comfortably bound and gagged in the back on a van, on his way to the retreat.

HG: Isn't that kidnapping?

SXS: No, it's editing. Of the most complex text.

HG: What text is that?

SXS: "Reality." Notice the quotation marks. We're all flash fiction.

HG: And you say Bushnell's the nihilist. In any case, he arrived at your retreat. What then?

SXS: At the retreat complex, we strapped him face-down to a table and tore the shirt from his back. Once every hour, we let in visitors—hulking, steroid-enhanced visitors with equally hulking fists—to see him. They were paid to massage Mr. Bushnell the way one of his antiheroes might massage a confession out of a weaker character. At first, he held his composure, his portly frame steady and unyielding as a steel plate. But over the course of a week—then two, then three—the bruises on Bushnell's back ruptured and re-ruptured so many times that the color of his flesh changed from talcum white to the purple-black of death's foul tongue. By the fourth week, Mr. Bushnell cried out for mercy when the fists landed against that hump of clotted blood, pulverized muscle, and shattered bone. But we had to keep pushing. We had to make him not just cry for mercy but *desire* mercy in every thought and breath and bead of sweat from his brow. Only then would he be able to pen the sort of story that tilts the axis of the world. So we made sure that Mr. Bushnell's massage therapy continued for another month. It was our solemn obligation to art.

HG: Do you realize what you're describing?

SXS: A writer's retreat and workshop. And a very successful one, at that.

HG: Also, torture.

SXS: Every writer worth reading would admit that sometimes the creative act must necessarily be torture. Art demands it.

An Interview with Samuel X. Slayden

HG: Would you say art is of the highest value to you?

SXS: Art is the only value.

HG: What about human life? Did you cause your authors undue pain and suffering?

SXS: There can be no art without pain, without suffering. It's the great catalyst. Philosophers used to talk about a "Prime Mover" shaping the universe. That mover is suffering.

All our authors eventually signed waivers indemnifying us of all physical or psychological injury sustained while in the performance of workshop activities. For those who signed them early, it's possible that most of them believed "injury" meant carpal-tunnel problems or dredging up old daddy issues, but preconception is a dangerous foundation for action.

But even independent of legal concerns, I believe our actions were justified by the product. Don't you?

HG: *Desire* is an incredible anthology, unlike anything I've ever read. But the cost seems steep.

SXS: Our authors didn't understand the dark depths of yearning when they came to us. When they left, they were masters of want. And now you reap the benefits of their understanding in every story.

HG: But Dane Bushnell shot himself after finishing "Machismo" (his story which appears in *Desire*).

SXS: We wanted art for the ages. He gave us such art. A tale of an effeminate boy beaten by bullies so terribly that he desires to grow to gargantuan proportions. A realization of the boy's wish, and his subsequent transformation to a kaiju of sorts. His rampage, his destruction—of not just his oppressors, but his entire town, his loved ones, everything. And that final scene, where he pounds his fists against Mt. Rainier, bringing it down upon him. *That's* a desire for mercy. It's brilliant. The immortality of Mr. Bushnell's work should be recompense enough for his fate.

NOTE—*"Machismo" has won a Bram Stoker Award for short fiction and a Shirley Jackson Award for best short story and is currently nominated for a World Fantasy Award in the same category.*

HG: I'm not denying the quality of the story—we can feel every ounce of the horrible yearning that throbs from young Tolliver Vix (the main character of "Machismo")—but do you believe your retreat contributed to Mr. Bushnell's suicide?

SXS: As much as anything else in his life. He was a tormented individual.

HG: Did any of the other retreat invitees have an experience similar to Bushnell's?

SXS: Of course. Julian Larchmont was the second writer we invited to the Tantalus workshop.

NOTE—*Larchmont, a professor of creative writing at Cardley College, works exclusively in short form and has released two collections,* Lachrymose Retinae *and* Darwin's Oversight, *both of which have garnered a great deal of praise in critical circles.*

SXS: Larchmont's a man of big ideas in small packages, which means his fiction doesn't sell especially well and is rarely understood, but is always mentioned as some of the most intellectually stimulating in the genre. For instance, in his "Metastasis" he theorizes that all suffering is a result of being born organic in an inorganic yet sentient universe that perceives our existence as a blight upon its sanctity and, therefore, attempts to rid itself of us—and

An Interview with Samuel X. Slayden

life, in general—at every turn. In another story, he writes from the perspective of a dying blood cell that's been drained from its host—a host who, we find out by story's end, is the thirteenth victim of a mysterious serial killer; here, Larchmont weaves microcosm and macrocosm together so masterfully that we don't know whether the victim is the cell or the cell is the victim or whether they're both caught up in a system of violence and destruction so vast that the difference between the two is purely academic.

Needless to say, Larchmont is a curious type. We sent him a letter with the list of other attendees and a vague statement of purpose, and he was intrigued enough to show up at our doors without the slightest coaxing.

HG: What was the writing aid you provided to Larchmont?

SXS: We treated him to what all scholars want: knowledge.

HG: Meaning?

SXS: While Mr. Larchmont reclined in a very plush restraining chair, his eyes were forced open and he was fed a nonstop stream of information from around the globe on a theater screen. Stock tickers, sports highlights, pornography of every variety, Twitter feeds, mass emails, commercials for erectile dysfunction, proceedings of Congress, footage of protests in third-world nations, videos of beheadings posted by militant groups in the Middle East, Instagram selfies of drunken college kids, *New York Times* book reviews, police blotters filled with domestic abuse, clips from sitcom reruns, clips from *The 700 Club*, clips from the nightly news: we let it all rush into him. He couldn't blink it away, couldn't avert his gaze. Media saturated, he held on for weeks without making a sound. Then he saw a news report from somewhere in California. It was about a group of youths that set dogs and cats on fire for sport, and it showed the horrific results of those actions. After that report, he began to want. Truly, *want*. At first, it manifested as nothing more than a low gurgle in the back of his throat, but over the course of several minutes, it grew in volume and intensity until he was screaming louder than the booming screen before him. He'd finally found something to desire in that intricate matrix of suffering and banality.

HG: And what was that?

SXS: The very thing he screamed, over and over: "ENOUGH."

HG: Mr. Larchmont is now a committed psychiatric patient at Pallstown State Hospital in western Michigan. You don't believe your retreat had any influence on his mental degradation? Wasn't Mr. Larchmont's Tantalus workshop essentially the same as the torture and reconditioning that features heavily in Anthony Burgess's *A Clockwork Orange*?

SXS: We didn't create the images we showed Mr. Larchmont. We simply aggregated them and presented them to him in rapid succession. We wanted a serious philosophical story, but we had to pressure his mind to get one that satisfied us. The results were more than worthwhile, wouldn't you say?

HG: "The Second Trimester of a Stillborn Universe" (Larchmont's contribution to *Desire*) is an astounding piece, yes. I wouldn't have thought omniscient second-person point of view could be readable, but Larchmont pulls it off. All that aside, however, if the work made him unstable...

SXS: It's worth the sacrifice. He gave us what we wanted. The way "Second Trimester" expands upon the Platonic allegory of the cave is genius. Plato's cave as womb, the universe as a dead infant, all of us as decaying cells desperately yearning in vain to break away from the shadow world and be born into the light of Forms and Truth—every bit of the story builds a deeper darkness.

An Interview with Samuel X. Slayden

The last thing Larchmont said before he left the retreat was "There's nothing outside. It's shadows of shadows and we'd be better off closing our eyes forever."

HG: Speaking of eyes, two weeks after your retreat, Larchmont gouged out *his* eyes with a shard of plastic from a shattered television set, didn't he? And that was why he was committed to a psychiatric facility?

SXS: I believe those were the circumstances, yes.

HG: And Bushnell and Larchmont were at the Tantalus retreat at the same time?

SXS: Yes. As were all the other contributors. All screaming together, at once. You could walk between rooms and experience the shift in tone and pitch and intensity, and you knew that each writer was working through a distinct agonizing desire. The retreat lodge was an art installation unto itself. We should have recorded that sound, in hindsight.

HG: So Coral Kane and Ronald Case were also at the retreat with Bushnell and Larchmont? They contributed particularly notable stories to the anthology, too. Would you like to say anything about either of them or their experiences at the Tantalus retreat?

NOTE — *Kane's story from the anthology, "Subkaryotes," is currently up for a World Fantasy Award in the short story category and Case's contribution, "This Page Intentionally Left Blank," has already won a Stoker Award for best long fiction.*

SXS: Ms. Kane is a swarm of bees masquerading as a person. Her mind scatters and returns, scatters and returns, always bringing back new and unusual pollens from its journeys. She's also apt to mass her power and sting to death anyone who bumps up against her. Yet her talent is undeniable. She transcends genre, writing horror with as much verve as science fiction or fantasy. And she's won both a Stoker and a Locus Award to prove it.

We knew that Ms. Kane's forte lies in environmental horror and the occulted aspects of the natural world, so that's what we wanted her to write. A short version of her novel *Permafrost*, perhaps.

HG: That's the one about the megaliths that turn out to be fossilized bones of a creature from another universe?

SXS: Yes. She showed up at the workshop with a replica pterodactyl egg, actually. Said it reminded her of the endless cycle of life and the myriad forms it could take.

HG: And Ms. Kane's workshop experience?

SXS: She adores nature, therefore we provided nature. We sequestered her in a five foot by five foot faux-outdoor space covered in a thick bed of rose bushes and poison ivy and granted her audience with a series of inspirational guests. First came the hissing cockroaches and the millipedes. Several thousand of each. At that point, Ms. Kane squirmed and pounded on the glass walls, asking to be let out but remaining remarkably calm for all the legs skittering across her skin.

Next, we added a few hundred vipers drained of their venom—we're not in the business of murder, after all. Ms. Kane weathered those, too. Again, she squirmed and pounded on the walls. She screamed when the vipers struck. But she hadn't fallen into the pit of desire yet. So we let in the camel spiders and the vampire bats, the fire ants and the sewer rats. Then she descended. Then she found *want*.

The ants massed and bit, the rats gnawed and clawed; the spiders sank fangs deep and the bats, sensing loosed blood, dived greedily. Ms. Kane turned on them all, crushing underfoot everything that moved. She snatched up vipers and smashed them against the glass

An Interview with Samuel X. Slayden

walls, squeezed spiders and rats to a pulp, and screamed not of escape or disgust, but destruction.

HG: You harmed animals?

SXS: No. We at Tantalus would never promote such deplorable behavior. What some of our writers do during their workshop time, though, is out of our hands.
  I will say that the violence sparked a new fire in Ms. Kane.

HG: "Subkaryotes" is certainly a total inversion from Kane's normal themes. In most of her work, nature is an ambivalent force, with both a light side and a dark side. But "Subkaryotes" presents a natural world of absolute terror.

SXS: Yes, the conceit of the story is glorious in its terror: insectoid scavengers that exist on a subatomic level in all organic matter and cause its inevitable breakdown, quark by quark. We're eaten alive by the natural world as soon as we're created within it. The scene of mass self-immolation at the end of the tale is equally sublime.

HG: Kane is one of the few authors in the anthology who hasn't stopped writing for one reason or another.

SXS: Nor should she. I believe she now has much to show us as regards the burning of the world. I look forward to her future work.

HG: So what about the grandmaster of horror, Ronald "Basket" Case?

SXS: It should be obvious why we wanted him. He's topped the *New York Times* bestseller list fourteen times, won nine Stokers, and could tile the bathroom of every house in the world with his sheer number of sycophants and imitators. The volume of his output is staggering. He writes in his sleep, some say.

NOTE—*That output is, to date, twenty-four published novels, seven short story collections, five produced screenplays, one graphic novel series, and a nonfiction book of writing advice.*

HG: Case's style has been called "pure Americana"—white picket fences hiding devils, old barns haunted by ghosts, lonesome highways stricken with ancient Native American curses. It's a bit more homespun than that of the other contributors in *Desire*. Case is also close to twenty years older than most of the anthology's roster. How did he weather the retreat?

SXS: Quite well, actually. We hooked an IV drip to his arm and chained him up in what we refer to as "the white room."

The white room is precisely what its name suggests: a room painted the same uniform white color. Through special architectural flourishes it contains no edges or corners. Light constantly floods the room through the walls, which are constructed of a thin but durable plastic and backlit by halogen lamps. We've also never installed furniture in the room, so it's either quite barren or quite austere, depending on your point of view. When one is inside the white room with the door closed, it's very much like being inside a sensory deprivation chamber or a hollow egg or a stereotypical "padded cell" for psychiatric patients.

In his time at the retreat, Mr. Case never left the white room, nor were any visitors allowed in to see him. He received no stimuli beyond the IV in his arm, the omnipresent light, and the whiteness of his surroundings.

At first, he used his time to call for help and struggle against his manacles. But the room works a terrible magic over the human mind. Three weeks in, Case began to talk to himself as though he were a character in a story. "Okay, Ron," he'd say. "You're surveying the room for cracks. You can break out of this prison if you

An Interview with Samuel X. Slayden

just find those cracks. That's our climax, when we smash right on out of here." At five weeks, he was holding discussions with himself in various personas—none of which were Ronald Case. In the sixth week, he sang Pink Floyd's "Comfortably Numb" nonstop for twenty-one hours. By week eight, he'd stopped talking entirely. He simply hung on his wall, staring at no point in particular, and mouthed "Where are you?" over and over again.

He was then ready to write.

HG: But not anymore. Case has officially retired from writing. In a statement, he said that "I've nothing more to say about this world."

SXS: In the spaces of our white room, he discovered a silence he hadn't been in touch with in many, many decades. Fandom had been propelling his fiction for years. His true voice was drowned long ago and he finally realized that at our workshop.

HG: You don't think you drove him into retirement?

SXS: We helped him see what was in his heart and his mind after the fame was muted. That's all. Call it what you want.

HG: I have to ask about one final contributor, and I think you know which one.

SXS: J.V. Brickley. Of course.

HG: What happened to Brickley?

SXS: At what point in his life? I'm sure I don't know all the details. And even if I did, I'm sure they'd be too sordid to share here.

HG: What happened to him at the Tantalus retreat?

SXS: Well, as you're aware, Brickley is something of an also-ran in the writing world. Before the retreat, he'd released one short story collection that garnered lukewarm reviews and edited two self-published anthologies filled with undistinguished authors. He wasn't setting the world on fire by any means. But we believed he had a spark of genius, perhaps. At very least, he had an interesting rage within him that we thought we could tap. His story "Straw Men," for instance, revolves around a character who's able to construct indestructible scarecrows that, when seen by other people, cause those people to go mad with uncontrollable anger and lash out at everything within striking distance. The main character moves from city to city, sowing chaos and destruction. We never know why. We only know, from the points of view of other characters, that his arrival in a town is feared above all else.

HG: So you realized he had anger-management issues?

SXS: We surmised as much. Brickley was delighted to receive an invitation to the retreat. He told us that he truly believed he deserved the honor, that his writing was of the same stock as Bushnell and Larchmont, Kane and Case. We smiled and laughed with him and patted him on the back. We massaged his ego. Then we locked him in a pitch-black closet with speakers embedded in the walls and turned on a loop of pre-recorded—and entirely faked—messages about how terrible he was as a writer and a person. Through those speakers, he heard his wife calling him a "talentless hack" and his children—so adorable—calling him a "loser daddy." He heard Bushnell whispering that he was a "shit stain upon the ancient tapestry of art," Larchmont saying his writing was "amateurish by the standards of lower order primates," Kane explaining how she thought "Brickley's best writing is probably his weekly grocery list," and Case describing how he felt that "Brickley's first collection has a great deal of worth as kindling for your fireplace." He heard these and many other similar voice recordings nonstop for two months.

An Interview with Samuel X. Slayden

I should also note that we didn't clean the bodily waste out his closet. We let him wade in his own filth. We wanted to immerse him in rejection, dejection, abjection.

It worked. Too well, perhaps. By the time we let him out, he certainly knew desire. We'd hoped it was for renewal or cleanliness, but, alas...

HG: It was for revenge. He wrote a flash fiction story for you...

SXS: A *superb* flash fiction story.

HG: ...a *superb* flash fiction story, then went home and, within a day of leaving your retreat, stabbed to death his entire family. You don't believe there's any causation between those events?

SXS: We wanted Mr. Brickley to write an outstanding story and we helped him do so. His horrific acts beyond that authorship are his own.

HG: I'm tempted to call you the devil.

SXS: That's quite the compliment.

HG: So you have no regrets over the retreat?

SXS: None. Look at *Desire*. Read it again. It's the essence of want. It's a remarkable achievement for all its authors.

HG: And for you?

SXS: For everyone at Tantalus Press, myself included, it's the true fulfillment of our desire.

HG: Seven people dead. More than a half dozen careers in ruins. Your desire seems to have birthed more than a book.

SXS: Perhaps. But we have no time to dwell. We're already moving forward, into our next project.

HG: You believe writers will participate in another anthology, even after *Desire*'s "curse?" Even after this interview?

SXS: Writers are already lining up to come to the next retreat. They email us every day. I don't predict that will change. Success in a world that cultivates failure is a great temptation and an even greater reward. People will kill for it. People will die for it. We hope to give some of our authors those opportunities. It's what any worthwhile publisher would do.

NOTE—*As of this interview,* Desire *has received a starred review from* Publishers Weekly, *maintained the number one bestseller spot in the "Horror" subgenre on Amazon (both in paperback and Kindle versions) for fifteen consecutive weeks, won a Stoker Award for Best Anthology, a Shirley Jackson Award for Edited Anthology, and is nominated for a World Fantasy Award in the Anthology category.*

Samuel X. Slayden and Tantalus Press are at work on their second edited collection, Sacrifice, *due out next fall.*

All That Is Thrown Away

As he emptied a trash can into his rolling refuse cart, Torrance cursed the lords of janitorial scheduling.

"Third week in a row," he mumbled, hands trembling ever so slightly. "Third week in a row for this crap. Late-shift nonsense."

Everything about the university after midnight bespoke an unsettling emptiness, a sense of lost potential and cosmic futility. The darkened classrooms with their empty desks, the lonely, fluorescent-lit hallways, the shelves of unopened books and rows of blank computers: it all felt haunted by some distant, tremulous future that had already shattered under the weight of its own failed possibilities. One of Torrance's co-workers called the vacuous presence "the ghost of an apocalypse," and Torrance thought that seemed just about right.

Slamming the trash can back into a corner, switching off the lights, and locking Holloway Hall's room 358 behind him, Torrance exhaled a puff of anxiety. He stared at the laminated map of the building that hung from his cart and the photograph of a young woman in graduation cap and gown that he'd taped beside it.

He pressed a finger to the picture. "359. Last stop tonight. Top floor, end of the corridor. I hope you're not up all night in a lonely classroom, too."

Torrance sighed and glanced ahead, to the darkened room further down the hallway. Its refuse called his name and promised at least a ragged, fleeting freedom.

He wheeled his cart to the room, unlocked the door, and scooted inside, grabbing a wastebasket that squatted just beyond the room's threshold. He jogged back to his cart and dumped out the mucus-laden tissues of students whose single-semester tuition cost was greater than his salary for an entire year. *I should bottle that snot and sell it as a magic lotion for success,* he thought. *Rub it on your hands and face three times a day and all your dreams will come true. Somebody somewhere has gotta believe that.*

Torrance paused and wondered at his latex-gloved hands and the garbage can they held. Sometimes he found it difficult to believe he'd been working at Kelland University for fifteen years. Fifteen years he'd tossed out the same blank answer sheets, the same crumpled questions. Fifteen years he'd meandered over cobblestone pathways that led to knowledge he might be able to understand but could never afford.

He shook his head and surveyed the mountain of refuse in his cart. At its very bottom, known only to Torrance, rested the shredded greetings of an acceptance letter to a local community college— the second one this year.

"I might as well be piling it on myself," he mumbled, readying himself to sprint back into 359 and end his nocturnal drudgery. "I might as well just crawl under all this junk and die."

And he might have, if not for the muted scream that punctured the floor beneath him.

"So you're not coming this weekend?"

Laced with the infection of normalcy, the question cut sideways, leaving Torrance's stomach sour and his confidence ragged and seeping. He closed his eyes and squeezed one of the arms of his battered couch, a refugee from a curbside giveaway. Foam lining burst up through a tear in the arm's fabric as Torrance gripped it harder.

"I wish I could. I just can't afford a flight right now. Everyone's hours are getting cut back because the board of trustees slashed the budget and..."

"Yeah, okay." Same volume. Same tone. More distance than the Earth to the moon.

"I really want to be there. You know I do. I'm so proud of you. But it's two thousand miles. If your mother hadn't decided to move all the way across..."

"Dad. Don't make this about Mom again. Okay?"

Torrance's fingers burrowed into the couch arm. One of them struck something pointed and sharp embedded within. He grimaced and pulled his hand to his chest, a droplet of blood welling up on his index finger.

"It wasn't my decision to move you to the other side of the country. That's all I'm saying."

"I know. But it was your decision to not follow."

A thorn, already sunk well and true inside Torrance's chest, inched deeper.

"It's not that easy." A whisper. A plea.

Torrance thought he heard something tear, but he wasn't sure if it was on his end of the line or hers.

"Okay. I have to go. I'll talk to you later, Dad."

The call cut to unspoken words and regret. Torrance dropped the phone to the floor and cradled his head in his hands, the blood from his finger smearing his brow like a blessing.

A scream. A young man's scream. Not rage, not struggle. Terror. A scream of terror.

Torrance dropped the wastebasket, which clattered to his feet and rolled away. He stood motionless, his back to his cart, waiting for he knew not what while muttering, "No, no, no, no, no, no."

From the floor leaked another scream, even more muffled, and the sound of thrashing.

Torrance reached under his cart and grabbed a dustpan—its scooping edge secretly sharpened to a razor tip for situations just as this—then crept toward the stairwell.

"God damn late shift," he whispered to himself as he peered over the balustrade that overlooked the shadow-limned stairs. Nothing flew from the darkness. Nothing leaped for his throat. And so, gathering a deep breath, Torrance began to descend the stairs.

Upon reaching the second-floor landing, he cautiously stepped into the hallway. He brandished the dustpan before him and shouted, "Hello? Anyone here need help?"

No answer.

Torrance squinted into the shadows of the half-lit corridor, but spied no one.

"Hello?" he called again.

His voice rang unrefined through the hallway.

A disembodied scream wouldn't be the strangest incident he'd heard about in his twenty years at Kelland. Not by a long shot.

The university was dense with dried blood and unsettled bones. Torrance often said that if you attended a meeting of the university's board of trustees, you'd probably see gods, devils, and Death itself all sitting in honorary chairs. The truth might have been even more wondrous and terrifying than that.

In the past hundred years, dozens of students, staff, and faculty had been inexplicably found dead on campus; even more had simply disappeared, never to be seen again. The university's dark history meant that sightings of specters and monsters—whether real or imagined—were not uncommon at Kelland. As a result, innumerable legends of the bizarre and preternatural sneaked into the vernacular of anyone connected to Kelland. Mad science and alien

All That is Thrown Away

intervention, occult conjuration and mass insanity: they all had deep roots at KU if you believed the stories.

As he crept along the second floor hallway, the hair on Torrance's arms standing at attention, Torrance hoped he wasn't about to enter into legend himself.

"It's nothing," he muttered as consoling mantra. "It's nothing. It's nothing. It's nothing."

Then, suddenly, it was something.

There, in the middle of the floor just outside the offices of the Physics Department, lay an essay smeared in an oily brown substance.

Torrance bent and picked it up. Its title page read: "Christopher Cobb. Dr. Panchal. PHY 375. 'On the Feasibility of Subatomic Infinite Regression.'"

A stripe of the slick, brown gel ran further down the corridor, away from the discarded paper.

Torrance reached into his pocket, snagged his phone, and dialed campus security. No one answered. After six rings and an automated messaging system that instructed Torrance to "calmly describe the nature and location of the incident or emergency," he ended the call.

He shook his head at the brown trail on the floor.

"Shit," he groaned, "this is not my job."

Despite that fact, he followed the trail anyway, bladed dustpan held two-handed at his shoulder like a readied sword; the ooze led him in a straight, unbroken line to a low-lying heating vent whose metal grate had been smashed through.

Torrance crouched and glanced inside the vent. Viscous russet liquid coated every surface of the ductwork beyond and slid down, down, to the boiler room in the basement. The heat kicked on and blew a stream of crisp decay into his face. Crushed leaves, ancient parchment, decomposing flesh, and rusted iron all commingled in the gust. It was the fragrance of the end.

Something's down there, Torrance thought. *Something besides boiling water and hot pipes. Something old. Something between life and death.*

A noise—perhaps a hoary voice that crackled the words "We dine" or perhaps just the settling of outdated machinery—echoed up the vent.

Torrance shivered and tried campus security again. Still no answer.

"Never where you need 'em," he sighed as he stood erect.

He glanced at the vent, then at his latex-wrapped hands. Vent. Hands. Vent. Hands. He was a janitor. He cleaned the university. He scrubbed toilets and washed windows. He soaked up spilled coffee and waxed marble floors. For nine dollars per hour, he wasn't obligated to descend into the bowels of Holloway Hall to discover the source of a preternatural stench, let alone track a screaming student through the night.

But descend he did. Because he was a janitor. Because he cleaned the university. Because this was where life, however fair or unfair, had left him.

"Mr. Speers? Torrance Speers?"

Heart hammering rivets into his chest walls, Torrance jumped up from his seat and shook hands with the man in the crisp, white button-down shirt and dark green tie.

"Mark Vivendi, financial aid specialist." The man waved at one of the chairs in his office. "Please have a seat, Mr. Speers."

Torrance chose a chair—it didn't matter which one he sat in, the upholstery on all of them was sagging and stained—and waited. The man from financial aid slid in behind his desk, a packet of papers ruffling in his hand.

"So, Mr. Speers, let me start with the bad news and get it out of the way. We can't offer you any federal or state aid. Your income is too high, unfortunately."

"Too high?" Torrance laughed. "Too high? I only make twenty-four thousand a year. Rent's eight-hundred per month and it's for just a one-bedroom apartment. Alimony and child support's about the same. That doesn't leave me much to live on."

All That is Thrown Away

The man from financial aid shuffled the papers as though to reaffirm his statement.

"I'm sure it doesn't," he said, "but for a single-person household it's well above what we consider in-need. Your felony conviction precludes you from many alternative options, too."

The man said it as so much a throwaway statement, a wispy nothing in his day. It fluttered against the back of Torrance's neck, a moth with wings tipped in the frost of deepest space.

"That was almost twenty years ago. I was nineteen and I paid my debt with twenty-four months of my life."

"Even so, Mr. Speers, it remains a part of your record. If you and another candidate without such a conviction have relatively equal need, well, I hate to say it, but..."

The man from financial aid trailed off, apparently unwilling to speak a full truth.

"You do have private options, of course."

"You mean fall into even more debt."

Again with the unnecessary shuffling of Torrance's paperwork.

"Well, yes, but it's good debt, assuming you can find a lender with good interest rates and..."

Torrance felt a pit opening beneath his feet. He felt rough tongues licking at his calves, snaking upward, along his thighs.

"So there's nothing you can do for me?" he asked.

The man from financial aid shrugged. "We can help you seek out private loans, but..."

Torrance stood and extended his hand, which was not taken this time.

"Thank you," he said, and exited the room before he fell headlong into the chasm that was always waiting to swallow him whole.

Wandering into the bowels of the building and finally touching down at the door that led into the boiler room, Torrance fished his key ring from off his belt and whispered a quick prayer to any deity that might offer aid.

Muscles tensed and mind spinning with scenes from countless horror movies (mostly those in which a nameless nobody bumbles upon his or her grisly demise), he unlocked the door and threw it wide open. Putrid amber light and the same decayed odor he'd smelled in the heating duct spilled from the doorway. He inched into the boiler room on the balls of his feet, ready to lash out or take flight. He nudged past maintenance equipment that sat stacked in organized piles along the walls and ducked beneath a maze of pipes and vents that crisscrossed toward the ceiling. The boiler growled out more steam and he jumped, reflexively taking a wicked swipe at empty space.

Imagining demon dead, he moved on, squeezing around the massive, antediluvian furnace that squatted ever-burning, ever-consuming, ever-transforming in the middle of the room. Once on the other side of its bulk, he saw the source of the squalid light: a door set into the opposite wall, a door that should not have—and technically did not—exist. Illumined colors of stale urine, spat tobacco, and refried grease leaked from around its frame.

As Torrance approached the door, his feet squished on something in the dark below. He assumed—and hoped—it was only more of the strange liquid.

Close enough to discern details in the shadows, he now saw a rusted metal plate mounted upon the door. Its surface contained only a simple, unadorned zero.

I do not have to do this, he thought, staring at the door. *I do not have to see who holds class in Room 0. It's not my responsibility to save some kid that will just shit all over my days and puke all over my nights and then end up sending his own kids here to do the same.*

A sound like a million essays simultaneously crumpled in angry fists crashed against the other side of the door.

Torrance stomped his foot and snorted.

No, he argued with himself. *You have to go in. You know what's on the underside of this place. You're the only future that kid has right now.*

He wiped a dribble of sweat from his eyes. Entrance to nowhere or exit to everywhere, the door, so innocuous, so much like any other on campus but for its placement and labeling, frightened him. And yet, despite logic and better judgment, he reached out, hand trembling, and, ever so gradually, opened Room 0.

Peeking inside, he couldn't help but gasp. The interior of the room wasn't a room at all, but an infinite scrapscape, a world fashioned entirely from detritus, from trash, from hoary thoughts and dying dreams. Rather than desks and chairs, dry-erase boards and computer podiums, the room led onto a wide, off-brown valley spread full with rotting fruits and silver wrappers, grease-stained cardboard and mold-encrusted cloth. A stream of raw black sewage cut a bubbling line through the middle of the valley and Everests of broken glass and twisted metal towered along its flanks, casting pale shadows over the brackish basin. Somewhere overhead, concealed within a liver-spotted caul, hung a withered sun that suffused the entire panorama with the colors of forgotten nursing homes and disused dumpsters.

Torrance stood immobile in the face of a world that so closely embodied the sentiments of his own life. He considered turning back and forgetting the entire experience, but for the possibility that a student with untapped promise and potential had been dragged down here, into this squalid dimension, and needed his help to escape.

Repeatedly whispering "I *do* have to do this," Torrance stepped into the castoff terrain and inhaled the sour-sweet ruin of eternity. Having no idea where to turn or how to proceed, he began to walk through the valley, the ground beneath his feet a miasma of spongy, squishing repugnance. He decided to follow the flow of sewage, hopeful that it might lead to answers or, at very least, a reprieve from this foolhardy quest.

***

"Why did you do it, Dad?"

The question had been dangling from her lips since the day she was born, his own daughter his Sword of Damocles. Torrance had no better answer now, so many years later, than he had when he was young and ignorant and answering the same question posed by his parents and his sentencing judges.

"Because when your mom got pregnant, I didn't know how I'd be able to provide for you or her. I was only a couple years older than you are now. I panicked. I took an easy route. Quick money. Big money. Dangerous money."

A silence. Contemplative or judgmental, Torrance couldn't know. A thin sheen of nervous sweat formed at his hairline.

"So you did it just for us? Really? Not for yourself?"

Torrance paced his tiny kitchen like an ant trying to escape the sunbeam from a child's magnifying glass.

"Of course it was for me. I wanted a good life. I wanted to support you and your mom. But I wanted it to come easy. I didn't want to slog through the day to day like everyone else. I thought I could jump over it or sneak around it. I thought I was so clever."

"Mom always says you did it because you were confused. She says it's the same reason you married her."

Torrance grabbed the refrigerator door, opened it, closed it. Opened it again, closed it again, opened it again.

"But I don't think that's the reason, Dad."

The refrigerator bulb, always too bright, cast a burning light into Torrance's eyes. He caught a whiff of spoilage from somewhere in the fridge's recesses.

"I think you did it because you wanted to save something that couldn't be saved, and you didn't know how else to begin doing the impossible."

For Torrance, no response could possibly be adequate. That his daughter believed in him, that she couldn't even conceive of his youthful stupidity as simply that, was more honor than he could ever deserve.

A tear rolled down his cheek, and he wasn't sure whether it was from the searing light in his eyes or a light much brighter, on the other end of the line.

"How did you get to be so smart?" he asked, throat tight. "How did you get to be so smart?"

All That is Thrown Away

■ ■ ■

As he slogged across the wasteland, dustblade gripped so tight his knuckles popped when he tensed or untensed his hand, a flurry of white flakes began to fall from the sky.

Torrance gazed up into the haze of twirling specks and grunted, "The hell? It's gotta be ninety degrees in here. But there's snow. Of course. Makes perfect sense."

Large flakes landed on his arms and shoulders, spun into his eyes and flitted about his cheeks. He swatted them away without second thought, not caring to inspect them, not imagining they were anything more than the nonsensical precipitate of a dysfunctional world. But as he trudged onward, they fell faster, blew harder, and began to stick to his clothes. He brushed them off and squinted against their onslaught, the way forward increasingly wrapped in a whirlwind of white specks.

He swiped at the flakes with his dustpan and crouched low, seeking reprieve from the storm. There, at ground level, partially shielded from the suffocating, twirling mass, Torrance glanced into the scoop of his makeshift weapon and saw that in his quixotic lunging he had collected a mound of the snow. Only it wasn't snow. It was paper.

In his pan, Torrance held shredded college and loan applications, torn up bank statements that began with minus signs, love letters and Dear John letters, foreclosure statements, obituary columns, and crumpled family portraits. Mesmerized by the infinite forms of loss, he sifted through the jumbled confetti until he found what he dreaded he might: fragments of his name and the creased faces of his daughter and his ex-wife. He retrieved the broken and bent images of his family from the pile and tucked them into his shirt, letting them rest just below his heart. He spilled the remains of other lives, other dreams, onto the squalid ground and, stifling an outburst somewhere between a shudder and a sob, plunged blindly onward.

Gradually, the blizzard of sorrow dissipated and Torrance was again able to traverse the scrapscape unimpeded. Though a dusting of flakes still lingered in the air, he could see the entire valley stretched out before him. Unfortunately, the returned clarity also meant that he could see, maybe three hundred yards directly ahead, a trio of humanoid figures hovering around a dark hole in the ground. Suspended above the hole, upside down and floating in midair, was another human shape, limp and crimson-stained.

"This is not happening," Torrance breathed. He began to turn away, to leave the valley and its inhabitants to whatever arcane rituals they be practicing, but for the scratch of his family's picture against his chest.

He stopped, stood firm, and nodded. Not knowing what else to do, Torrance ran—not back toward the door as he could have (and probably should have), but straight at the strange cabal within the valley.

Doubt stabbed at the back of his mind and shouted the mocking refrain "You're too late. You failed again. You're no hero. You failed again," but Torrance hissed, "Shut up," and kept running, muck churning at his heels.

Halfway to the captured student, legs pumping and heart racing, he slipped on a spot of organic slush and tumbled headfirst into the slime, cursing as he went down. The reverberation of his expletive must have carried far, because the three humanoid figures broke from the hole and began to hover—not walk, but clearly hover—toward him.

Picking himself up from the sludge, Torrance froze and held his dustpan-blade at the ready. The things from the valley flew closer, close enough to recognize that *things*, and not human beings, they were indeed. Although their outline was generally that of a human—head, torso, hips, and legs—the advancing things had no arms. Rather, a series of long, black, undulating tubes lined their flanks from shoulder to knee. They had no meaningful features, either; with the exception of the flagella-like tubes, their bodies were entirely wrapped in strips of brown, wet, dripping bandages. And, as a coup de grace, as a last insult to physics and reason, the things levitated above the ground without any obvious means of propulsion.

They halted a few feet in front of Torrance.

"I...uh...I'd like to take the kid back, if that's what you've got there" he said, pointing at the hanging body, having no idea how to speak the language of monsters. "He doesn't belong here."

The things continued to float, impassive, their tubes oscillating in an unfelt breeze.

"I'm...uh...I'm going to go check on him now."

Torrance took a furtive step forward and, almost instantly in response, a tube-arm shot toward his head. He had no time to react, no time to duck or swipe away the appendage. It punched into his mouth, tearing his front teeth from his gums, and snaked down, inside him, through him, feeling every part of his body and soul. His loves, his hatreds, his hard-won successes and his many disappointments were all spread open to the thing. It learned of his misspent youth, his time in prison, his divorce, and his daughter, who lived a thousand miles away, in a world entirely separate from and better than his own. It also learned of his attempts to enroll in community college, his hours spent reading library-borrowed textbooks on mechanical engineering, and the stacks of bills—rent, alimony, power, heating—that prevented him from signing and returning his acceptance letters. It even learned of the ghosts he'd seen at Kelland and the unmarked cemetery he'd uncovered behind Severance Hall.

The thing retracted its limb and Torrance collapsed to the ground, coughing and spitting up blood. He heaved his dustpan at one of the things, but it sailed far wide of its target.

"It contains only dross," one of the things said, its voice a crackle of dead leaves and funeral pyres. "It must leave or be broken and sorted."

"What?" Torrance sputtered, massaging his throat. "Dross? Broken and sorted?"

"Leave or be broken and sorted," the thing repeated. One of its arms slid into the swampy ground and yanked free a yellowed, human skull from under the surface. The thing held the skull out to Torrance.

"Broken and sorted," it crackled.

Torrance wiped his mouth and nodded. Abject truth piled in fragments to his every side. He hadn't saved the kid. He hadn't saved his family. He hadn't even saved himself. So much everything was simply trash swirling high on gusts of delusion.

"I'll...I'll go," he said, holding his hands aloft in deference. "But I'm not going without the kid."

The thing threw down the skull.

"The empty can be taken away," it said. "It has been licked clean."

One of the things flew back to the suspended body, wrapped it in its tentacles, and returned, dropping the inert form of a bespectacled teenaged boy at Torrance's feet. Roseate bile trickled from the kid's gaping mouth; his eyes bulged vacant and dim, like the dual moons of some lifeless planetoid.

"Leave," the thing said. "Clutter the *other* side instead."

Torrance heaved the insensate lump of Christopher Cobb over his shoulder. The kid was heavier than he looked. Torrance felt the muscles in his lower back already pleading for mercy. He shifted the weight of his burden as evenly as he could and trudged back the way he'd come, toward the door, a minuscule dark rectangle cut into the horizon of this entropic dimension.

The things hovered close on his heels, their hose-flagella twitching to strike, waiting to break him apart if his slow march faltered.

Torrance huffed and puffed under the weight of his burden. His shoulders burned. His legs quivered. His pulse hammered hard and erratic. And yet he did not drop young Christopher Cobb. He remained true to his duty, whatever duty that might have been.

◻ ◻ ◻

She reached up to the car window and pressed her tiny palm against it. From the opposite side, Torrance returned the gesture.

"You don't have to go," he said.

All That is Thrown Away

His wife—soon to be ex-wife—stood behind him, waiting for the end of goodbye.

"Yes, we do," she said. "It's time to restart."

"You can restart here."

"No, we can't. There's too much baggage here. Too many anchors. If we stay, we're only going to be dragged deeper. That includes you, Torrance. You need to get out of here, too."

A lawnmower puttered in the distance. Birds sailed above their heads. The lilac bush in front of their apartment building waved in the breeze, its perfume promising lies of white picket fences and family picnics.

Inside the car, his daughter giggled. For her, still innocent at this moment, it was just another car ride.

"Just because we didn't work doesn't mean that you can curl up and die, Torrance. Quit that terrible janitor job and make something of yourself. Do it for her. Do it for yourself."

His wife opened the car door and slid behind the wheel.

Torrance backed away.

"I don't know what to make of myself," he said. "I'm not sure anything *can* be made of me."

The door slammed and the window rolled down.

"Torrance, I'm done. You can be more. You can do more. And I'm sick of telling you so."

The window rolled up halfway, then stopped.

"Remember to call. Your daughter's going to need you, no matter what."

The window slid shut and the car shifted gears.

Torrance waved. He didn't think about his job or his future or his past. All of those things bristled with menace. Instead, he concentrated on his daughter's hand, waving back, greeting him to the last bastion of hope he'd ever inhabit.

After what seemed hours, Torrance lurched through the darkened gate to his own world and passed into the boiler room. The door to Room 0 evaporated behind him. He laid his once-precious cargo on the floor and fell to his knees. He looked into Christopher Cobb's eyes and saw nothing reflected there—no intelligence, no emotion, not even a flicker of recognition. The kid wasn't dead. He was breathing; he had a pulse. But he was, as the things on the other side had said, empty. Whatever had once been Christopher Cobb, physics student at Kelland University, had been drained and devoured. Torrance had rescued a husk.

Torrance turned to the wall where the door had stood and pounded against its unyielding brick, hoping something might answer, hoping maybe he could still fight.

"Come back," he screamed. "Come back. You can't take someone away like this. You can't."

Room 0 did not reappear.

It wasn't fair. None of it was fair. None of it was supposed to be.

Torrance collapsed next to Christopher Cobb. Through tears, he whispered, "I'm just a janitor. I'm sorry. I'm just a janitor," and mourned for all that had been lost this night and all that had never truly been found.

The Convexity of Our Youth

A Disclaimer

    The children of Burke's Point Elementary can't be blamed. When the orange ball rolled onto their playground, they couldn't have known what it was. We didn't discuss the orange ball with them, didn't explain to them its importance, its danger. We didn't even tell them it existed, though some of them had undoubtedly heard vague rumors about it from sadistic older siblings and precocious cousins with little parental supervision. We wanted to turn a blind eye to the orange ball, hoping that what we didn't acknowledge couldn't touch our lives. If we didn't speak of it then surely it would have no reason to seek us out; it would roll past our town and work its horrors somewhere else, somewhere far away. Though it might bounce against the concavities of our skulls, tinting every thought orange, orange, orange, we feared to let its name roll off our tongues. We believed in the prophylactic power of ignorance, that if we provided no magnetic pole of recognition, the ball's compass would never point in our direction. So the children of Burke's Point Elementary—our children—couldn't have guessed that when the orange ball spun its way onto their blacktop and they began kicking it back and forth, shoes slapping rubber, rubber throwing up pebbles and dust, laughter spilling over the schoolyard as the ball seemed to zig and zag of its own volition, it would, for all intents and purposes, kill them all.

A Background

Our town is, in many ways, like any other town. Imagine parallel lines of artisan boutiques running beside a brick-laden boulevard that sprawls outward, onto a few dozen crosshatched streets along which stand sentinel rows of townhomes and condos. Beyond the townhomes and condos, imagine that the streets gain curvature and turn to winding roads that slide by cozy one-story, two-story, and three-story homes replete with manicured yards and picket fences and two-car garages. And on the fringes of it all, where the roads meet the infinite progress and regress of the interstate highway, imagine the dense modern fortifications of commerce—the strip malls and chain stores and supermarkets and fast food parlors and gas stations and motels and casual family eateries all vying for patronage. Our town is, in this, like any other town: the fruition of some sort of dream and the image of some sort of beauty, though neither may be ours.

Just as is the case with our parents and grandparents, most of us have lived here our entire lives, with, perhaps, a brief four-year foray to a college or a university within driving distance during our early adulthood. Occasionally we venture outward, to other towns, other cities, other regions of the world where people speak with intonations different from ours and wear clothes designed more for function than for form, but, though we may be charmed or fascinated or surprised by those other places, we are, inevitably, neither drawn away from our town for long nor tempted to remain elsewhere. We are tethered to our town by a dull, soothing comfort and, with the

The Convexity of Our Youth

lengths of our tethers, have woven complex webs of existence to further secure ourselves here.

Life is, you might say, easy for us. We have no great wealth but also no real poverty, no overwhelming love for our neighbors but also no outstanding hatreds. We are not a people who leave our doors unlocked throughout the night, but neither are we a people who suffer from any crimes worse than petty theft and vandalism. We have achieved a level of contentment and stasis in which our primary worry is losing our contentment and stasis. Thus it is that everything we do, every decision we make, every social, cultural, fiscal, philosophical, theological, and political step we take as adults, as citizens, and as parents is designed to uphold the most sacrosanct of our shared values: security.

A Symptom

After the orange ball had been spotted on the elementary school playground by an astute second-grade teacher, the sixteen boys and girls involved with its play were rushed to a secure hospital facility where, mere hours later, the symptoms of contact began to manifest. We knew what to expect as we huddled by the side of our children's beds. First came the uncontrollable leg spasms that, had the children been upright, would have sent them sprinting into the blustery night at ten or fifteen or however many miles per hour their muscles and ligaments could carry them before completely shearing away from bone or snapping apart. Impervious to muscle relaxants, the spasms lasted for several grueling hours during which our children alternately laughed and cried, sang unfamiliar songs and shouted words we'd never taught them. As they sweated through their bedsheets, we sweated through our clothes, waiting for a resolution that we'd fooled ourselves into believing might arrive.

Once the spasms had run their full course, metabolic exhaustion set in and extreme cramping stole over our children's tender bodies from head to toe. Despite the best efforts of doctors and nurses to rehydrate our children and replenish their depleted electrolytes, chorales of anguish blared from the isolation ward, driving us to near madness with their fiery accusation of our universal impotence. If hell has an anthem, truly we believe it must be the ululation of one's children in hysterical, unending pain.

As our babies screamed and thrashed through a hurricane of tears, we wrung our hands and tore at our hair and prayed to our myriad deities for succor and mercy. We discovered, however, that succor and mercy were in short supply, even for us, even for our town, which we had always assumed must exist as a tiny sparkle in the corner of our gods' eyes. Indeed, only when the doctors pumped the children full of opiate pain killers—so many, in fact, that we feared coma must be near—did the cries subside and our beloved quietus regain temporary control of our lives. Then, only then, with our children in deep chemical slumber, did we again feel safe.

Of course, this was only the first symptom of the ball's infection and, as we understood it, the least severe. There would be two more symptoms yet to come, two more symptoms for which none of us could be properly prepared, unimaginable as they were.

Our peace was, in the end, a fragile lie.

A Realization

We initially learned of the orange ball seven years ago. Rumors of the ball's existence had been spreading across the internet for months prior to our localized revelation, but this spotty information was relegated to fringe news sites, shared social media posts, and obscure discussion forums—none of which registered on our tightly focused radar. We didn't read to the margins of our world; we didn't feel that we needed to. The margins were for those people too unmotivated or too deviant to find their way to a more stable center. Surely, we believed, our town and our lives were near the center of whatever vast page reality had been impressed upon. Thirty minutes curled up with the local nightly news on television, an occasional foray across the main page of a cable

The Convexity of Our Youth

news network's website, a glance at a nationally distributed magazine: these were the energies we deemed it necessary to expend in order to remain informed citizens of greater, polished society. So while the ball rolled on and families in other communities—dust-ridden rural locales and bullet-populated inner city neighborhoods, mostly—dealt with its aftermath and expressed their despondency, their fear, and their anger through peripheral channels, we went about our days in relative peace and naiveté.

It wasn't until the ball passed through a town much like ours, a town sealed tight in its onion-layers of self-satisfaction and supposed normalcy, a town with the anywhere name of "Vernonville," that the mainstream media followed its bounce. In Vernonville, cameras captured grim men in pressed, button-down shirts and sensible khaki pants, quavering women with tasteful makeup in smart, monochrome wrap dresses, and tearful children in all manner of character-emblazoned shirts, pants, and shoes. These were a safe people, an ordinary people, a people with enough time and money and respect for the prescribed social order to arrive for interviews entirely photogenic, even in the face of crisis. We worried over the people of Vernonville, because, in truth, what the cameras in that quaint suburban town captured was nothing less than ourselves, doubled at another point in space.

To the media, the people of Vernonville spoke of an inexplicable childhood illness run rampant in their town, of an orange ball with which the stricken youths had played. They spoke of their outrage, their sadness, their memories, their lack of understanding. They asked for prayers and protection and they insisted that the Centers for Disease Control and the World Health Organization investigate the disease, for, surely, disease it had to be that their children had contracted. To pacify the people of Vernonville, the CDC and WHO did, indeed, finally launch an investigation, but, ultimately, neither found evidence of a pathogen or a wicked foreign invader endlessly multiplying in the blood of the town's children. The lone key fact the doctors and scientists at the CDC and WHO discovered—or what they knew all along, more likely—was that a series of past incidents in other locations mirrored the situation in Vernonville. All the rural nowheres and the urban centers that had cried out for the selfsame recognition and investigation that Vernonville received were at last acknowledged, if only as fragments of a greater pattern and decimals in a ledger.

The situation in Vernonville, combined with the newly revealed information that the incident was not isolated and that the orange ball had spread a sickness to children elsewhere, sent us into a low-boiling panic. We began to discuss the ball at work, at PTA meetings, at the gym, in our bedrooms well after midnight—anywhere that our children wouldn't hear. We drove by our homes and our children's schools during our lunch breaks, just to spot check for orange balls that might be lolling about outside. We threw into the garbage any orange balls that our children or our pets possessed and bought them shiny new blue or green ones for their enjoyment. Even the recreational basketball league at our local YMCA switched from traditional orange and black balls to red, white, and blue Team USA balls.

As days passed, our fear did not abate, but, instead, settled into our routines. We formed a community watch group to buy all the orange balls in the all the stores in town and burn them in pre-selected dumpsters; we gathered up orange traffic cones and hurled them into gutters wherever we passed them; if we were sports fans, we stopped following the NBA and NCAA basketball altogether. We even purchased oranges at the grocery store with less frequency. And yet, despite all our activism, we spoke of the ball less and less, almost as if we didn't give it second thought, almost as if it was something we'd never heard of, almost as if it didn't even exist.

A Second Symptom

After our children's cramps unknotted and melted away, the second symptom began to manifest. Its appearance could have been mistaken for an unusual rash or an off-color bout of jaundice, but we knew better. The circular, orange blotches that

The Convexity of Our Youth

crept over our children's skin had no dermatological precedent except in the history of the towns the ball had visited.

For many of us, this was the most difficult stage of the illness. Though our sons and daughters remained firmly ensconced in cradles of opiates so as to not feel the flesh-peeling inflammation that the children of Vernonville had, we found the mere presence of their infected bodies intolerable. We sat by their beds with our faces turned away, unable to watch as the blotches spread and joined with one another, forming Rorschach patterns we feared to interpret for what they might reveal about ourselves. We were asked by doctors and nurses to comfort our children, to hold their hands and wipe their chins as saliva leaked from their lips, but we could not bring ourselves to touch them. With every new sore, with every new patch of smooth, glistening orange, they drifted from us, becoming less a part of us and more a part of the ball. Theirs was a future we could not countenance, let alone accept.

In the hallways and common areas of the secure facility, we pounded vending machines with our fists though we were not seeking refreshment and we stared into bathroom mirrors for hours though we were not preening. In the facility's lobby, we gave interviews to assembled reporters, our faces properly stoic, our words sufficiently labored. In the facility's parking lot, well-meaning friends and family lit bonfires and invited us to stoke the flames with balls of diverse size and color, balls that they had purchased for precisely that therapeutic kindling purpose. And all the while, as we sulked about the facility in our bubbles of distraction, our children lay in their rooms, alone, transmuting.

The bravest among us eventually worked up the courage to return to our ailing offspring. We pulled up chairs beside the hospital beds and, tears welling at the corners of our eyes, whispered unheard endearments to our sons and daughters while stroking their swollen pumpkin-hued foreheads. Even for those of us with iron resolve, however, the caresses did not last long. We pulled away our fingers and wiped them on our pants, our dresses. We ran to the nearest bathroom and scrubbed our hands under scalding water, so desperate were we to remove the sensation of our children's rashes against our flesh. For what we touched when we stroked their heads was not soft, pliable skin, but a hard, dense surface that barely yielded to the pressure of our fingertips. Where once had been ridges and divots and tiny, perfectly formed imperfections was now an expanse of smooth, featureless orange. Doctors who had biopsied the rashes of children in other towns had long ago determined the nature of this impossible flesh. It was a substance the world knew well, a substance that had no place in human biology, and we shuddered to witness it merging with our children, becoming our children, our children becoming it.

Brave or not, we fled into flasks, into puffs of cigarette smoke, into passionless sex in the hospital bathrooms. We spent our last remaining energies in pursuit of merciful distraction. We refused to contemplate the truth of the situation, and the truth was this: by the time the second symptom had run its course, our children would no longer be copies of ourselves, but products of forces far beyond our control. By the time the second symptom had run its course, our children would be, effectively, rubberized.

A Referendum

When, a few months after Vernonville, the orange ball appeared in another town like ours and the death toll ticked higher in that small burgh than it had in any of the previous places the ball had infected, we experienced a surge in anxiety unlike any we'd known before. Every bounce of a kickball and spin of a bowling ball and hollow plink of a ping-pong ball against a table sent us into cold sweats and caused us to glance over our shoulders to make sure nothing was rolling up behind us. Accident rates in town doubled. 9-1-1 calls reporting suspicious incidents tripled. We became a study in paranoia. So, in conjunction with the PTA and several local religious groups, our mayor called a meeting to discuss "the ball dilemma" and invited all concerned adults from the community to attend. Minors—even teenagers who understood the is-

The Convexity of Our Youth

sue at hand—were strictly prohibited from entering the town hall during the meeting due to the nature of the subject matter.

On the evening of the "ball dilemma" discussion, seating at the town hall was elbow to elbow and hip to hip. It seemed that every person in town over the age of eighteen had come to listen, if not participate. We all wanted resolution. We wanted the mayor or the president of the PTA or a local minister or rabbi or imam to give us instruction, to tell us that our town would be safe if we simply followed an enumerated plan with easily accomplished steps. Instead, we were faced with a coterie of leaders who, through PowerPoint slides and Excel spreadsheets, explained that no feasible protection was possible. We couldn't wall off the town from the rest of the world—though some of us would have surely felt more at ease behind medieval battlements—nor could we afford a video surveillance system for the town's perimeter. We couldn't track the ball's movements—not even the Department of Homeland Security had been able to manage that feat yet, or so it claimed—nor did we have the resources to set up an official ball patrol. We couldn't even print informational posters because we had no information to convey that might have been of use in case of the ball's appearance. For all intents and purposes, we lacked any meaningful choice of action.

It was, therefore, not surprising that when the presentations ended and the mayor opened the floor for questions, the town hall broke into a silence reserved for sepulchers. We dared not speak or move, as speaking and moving would imply that the meeting was truly nearing its conclusion, that our authorities had failed us and left us without plan or direction. The notion of confronting such a limbo we could not abide. So we sat and waited in the anticipation of one last key address or instructional video. Our leaders fidgeted, unsure of the silence's tenor. We held our breaths, unsure of the question to ask. And, somewhere, the ball kept bouncing, entirely sure we could not stop it.

Finally, after the tension had grown so sharp it could slice through the hall's concrete walls, one of us—Marcus Jefferson, the proprietor of our town's used bookstore—stood and asked the question that would govern our lives for years to come.

"If you don't have a plan to deal with it," he said, "and we can't prevent it from happening, then why are we even talking about it?"

The question provoked no answers from our leaders, but it did raise applause and echoes.

Other voices in the crowd, our voices, yelled at the stage, asking "Why? Why? Why do we need to discuss it? Why should we even bring it up?"

The mayor responded the only way she could. She asked us what we wanted to do about "the ball problem." She asked what our democratic solution might be.

Again we slid into silence. We'd never imagined the decision might fall to us. We had no idea how to prevent the ball's coming; we had no special information, no learned insight. We only knew that we were frightened. So when Jessica Cadiz—a manager at one of our town's three banks—stood and said, "Let's try to ignore it. Let's imagine it doesn't exist. Let's push it away as best we can. Let's strike it from our vocabularies and close the browser windows when we see stories about it online and turn off the TVs if newscasters start yammering on about it. And, for the love of God, let's never allow the kids to know what it is, to know that it's out there. At least not until they're older," we all understood why.

The applause for Cadiz's suggestion shook the floor and rattled the windows. A chant of "ignore it, ignore it, ignore it" erupted from the crowd. We, the people, had spoken. Shortly thereafter, our mayor called for a vote, a referendum, and what would become known as the Cadiz Proposition unanimously passed into our town charter and into our law.

A Final Symptom

A child whose skin has remolded itself into a two-inch thick layer of orange rubber can barely be referred to as a parent's "flesh and blood," yet this is how, even after the second

The Convexity of Our Youth

stage of the ball's impact, we still thought of our children. The doctors at the secure facility kept them under constant sedation, so it was impossible to know how much the transformation had affected their perception of the world. Did they still think like our children? Would our fumbling hugs still soothe them? Did they still feel the warmth of sunlight and cool breezes the way we did? Was a kitten's fur softer or harder under the stroke of their new skin? Would they still look at us and call us "father" or "mother" or would they now refer to us by words we couldn't understand? We didn't ask, and they couldn't tell.

The doctors claimed that the sedation was imperative, not because the rubberized flesh by itself would necessarily cause pain, but because the final stage of the ball's infection involved a horror for which there was no cognate in the annals of medical literature. Ushered from the treatment rooms due to what the medical staff called "the unpredictability of the final stage," we watched our children on monitors from areas within the facility labeled only as "safe zones." Vaguely scented like fresh carpet, these areas resembled bizarrely arranged discount furniture store show rooms, with disparate couches and loveseats and plush recliners and end tables encircling central banks of computer monitors and television sets. The walls of the "safe zones" were also entirely lined in mirrors, which both lent to the commercial effect and led many of us to believe that as we watched our children, so too were we being watched from behind those mirrors.

Over the course of the three days following our children's dermal mutation, we sat in these safe zones in relative silence. Occasionally, we would leave and find our way to the hospital's roof. There, six stories from the ground, we would consider leaping off the edge, into a more certain madness. However, none of us had the energy or the willpower to actually make the jump. Instead, we would simply stand on the rooftop ledge and wonder what revelations the air between the tips of our toes and the tarmac below might hold. Perhaps the wind whipping by our faces in that two or three second plunge might speak to us of death's mysteries. Perhaps the very ground below might whisper wisdom as it collapsed our forms. We would never know.

If we did not head to the rooftop, we would leave the safe zones and wander through the dark wards that sprawled under our children. We would pass skeletal figures hooked to spider webs of IV tubes, bodies suspended in vats of brightly hued gels, and other children stuffed inside windowed copper tubes, clearly suffering from a dread malady different from that of our own children. We would continue downward, downward, until we reached the basement of the facility, where we discovered the morgue and its seemingly infinite rows of tabled corpses, some of which were wrapped in thin, clear plastic sheets and others which were encased in silver mylar bags. To this room we would take our husbands, our wives, our boyfriends and girlfriends and secret lovers and there, amongst the plenitude of the dead, we would explode into a molten flow of volcanic sex, entwining with our partners in as many configurations as we could devise, often knocking bodies to the floor with the force of our writhing and tumbling naked after them. We didn't care that the dead watched us, were part of the act. Indeed, we wanted them to see. We wanted them to know. Why, we couldn't explain.

So, mostly, we remained in the safe zones, silent and unmoving, unless, of course, we didn't. All of which is to say that we knew not what to do with ourselves or how to act as our children, for all intents and purposes, died. While we sat in silence, every one of our children's bones and internal organs were evaporating. They did not liquefy or explode or turn putrescent and rot; they just evaporated, into air, leaving behind nothing but an expanding bubble of space and increased pressure. Brain and heart, spine and scapula: it all dissolved to nothing. As our children's brainwaves diminished and their heartbeats flatlined, the space within them grew larger and more rounded. Their tiny bodies expanded and inflated and gained contours no human shape was ever meant to contain. Their shoulders and torsos became one with their heads, with any trace of their necks disappearing; their legs and arms descended into the vastness of their abdomens. With every passing hour, they took on new

The Convexity of Our Youth

convexities, new spheroid shapes. They were all Violet Beauregarde, eternally trapped in Wonka's chocolate factory.

Over the final symptom's three day reign, our children continued to expand, to inflate, until, when all was said and done, there were no more bones or organs left to dissolve. What lay in our children's beds then were no longer our children, but enormous orange rubber balls with the distorted and elongated faces of our individual sons and daughters imprinted upon one of their sides. Somehow, even after this, even after the final symptom had run its course, the worst had not yet arrived, for, when the life-giving machines were shuttled away and times of death were officially stamped on certificates, our children, whatever they now were, began to move once again. They began to bounce. They began to roll from side to side. They began to roll toward us. And we, more fearful than we'd ever been, more uncertain and filled with shame than we thought possible, clawed at our eyes and wished that we had never tried to hide the ball from our children or ourselves in the first place.

A Scientific Inquiry

Epidemiologists have studied the effects of the orange ball and have determined with certainty that the symptoms it causes cannot be traced to a viral, bacterial, fungal, or parasitic source. Despite extensive tests of our children's every conceivable tissue and bodily secretion, there is, they say, no detectable pathogen present in their bodies either pre-transformation or post-transformation. This conclusion has led numerous researchers to suggest that the vector for transmission may lie on the molecular or atomic level—a potentially provable proposition, but one that will require many more years of study.

Another faction of scientists—mostly biophysicists—have conjectured that what occurs to the infected children has little basis in any macrocosmic discipline. These experts have advanced a hypothesis that the wholesale restructuring of an organism can only find its catalyst in the quantum realm, amidst probabilities so infinitesimally small and possibilities so strange they might be thought impossible. Therefore, in their view, it is far better to approach the issue as a problem of fundamental forces and abstract equations than cellular division and genetic re-encoding. Intriguing though the concept may be, it is untestable with current medical technology.

Still another segment of the scientific community washes their hands of the entire matter, choosing to believe that the orange ball and its accompanying syndrome must be either grossly misreported or an outright hoax. To the myriad MDs and PhDs in this camp—none of whom have seen a ball-child in person—the situation is undeserving of serious attention and, in their assessment, a blemish upon those scientists willing to examine the phenomenon.

Needless to say, the underlying reason for the changes to our children remains unknown and we are forced to wonder not just "Why?" but also "How?"

A Treatment

The symptoms having finished their grotesque parade, we were left with their result—a roomful of huge rubber balls bouncing and rolling about the hospital ward under what appeared to be their own volition. We watched, fascinated and horrified, as the faces of our children, forever frozen in a dilated sleep, spun about the balls' surfaces. The doctors assured us that the balls were not our children, could not be our children, as our children had surely died when the dual hemispheres of their brains evaporated. Time and again they explained that, clinically, our children were gone. And yet, for all the explanation and entirely rational assurances, the movement of the balls—nonstop and just a degree under total chaos—reminded us of our daughters and our sons and their feverish orbits of play. When we gazed through the windows of the secure ward, we saw both our children cavorting in a schoolyard and utterly alien beings performing a dance we could not understand, and, in truth, we could not distinguish between the two despite our best efforts. We watched the balls for many weeks

The Convexity of Our Youth

this way, our terror becoming familiar, our sense of certainty in the world further eroding.

Thus it was that by the time the doctors at the facility presented us with two options for the balls' futures—to leave them in the facility for continued study or to take them home with us—we chose to take them home. The doctors, the facility's administrators, and a panel of high-level bureaucrats from various government agencies all attempted to convince us that turning over guardianship of the balls to the facility would be in everyone's best interest. These things, they said, should not exist—by all rights, cannot exist—yet they do. These things, they reiterated, were not our children. These things, they warned, would be well beyond our control and may even pose a danger to others. Of course, we knew the doctors were right. We knew that we would never be able to touch our children again without shivering, that we would never be able to look at those child-sized orange balls without worrying that unknown intelligences might be looking back. We knew that we could never talk to them again without nervously contemplating all the unfathomable thoughts and incomprehensible plots that might be incubating beneath their surfaces. We understood that the balls were not our children anymore. Yet, by the same token, we could not shake the impression that the balls were not *not* our children, either. Somewhere within them still floated fragments of our DNA and, therefore, we believed that somewhere within them surely floated remnants of our children. However fleeting or memorial those remnants might be, we could not leave them to the emptiness of the facility and its doctors clinical probing. So, instead, we took them home with us. In this decision we were sorely unprepared.

Once in our houses, the balls went wild. Brimming with an unnatural energy, they slammed against our walls and bounced from our floors to our ceilings in rapid, machine gun succession, perhaps testing the boundaries of our homes. They cracked our windows and shattered our lighting fixtures, knocked over our tables and splintered our chairs. They rolled throughout our houses every minute of every day, always in motion, always progressing toward a destination we could seemingly not provide. Sometimes they even bounced against *us*—often with enough force to make us stumble or send us sprawling to the ground—and we, unsure of what else to do, fled from their advances, scraped and bruised as we were. Whether the bouncings were attacks or gestures of play or symbolic movements beyond our guessing, their violence caused us to worry for our lives, especially after several of us suffered concussions and broken bones. Therefore, in order to protect ourselves, we did what any reasonable community would do—we instituted a treatment plan for our ball-children's unchecked mania.

Our options to this end were admittedly limited. We owned no golden egg with which to bankroll a major project and we received no meaningful guidance in our planning. At secret meetings held in neutral locations, we brainstormed and we deliberated and, ultimately, we embarked upon a plan that we thought most effective under the circumstances. Laughable though it may seem, we bought high-end treadmills and, between their arms, rigged leather harnesses that would support the weight and girth of our transmuted children. Into these harnesses we wrestled the frenetic balls, locking them in place with a variety of straps and buckles while making sure that they could still spin freely within their binds. We provided a modicum of leeway in the harnesses' lengths so that the rubbery dynamos could also bounce a few inches into the air, off the treadmill track, if they needed to bounce at all.

Once we were certain that the ball-children had been firmly restrained and fully introduced to their new living arrangements, we turned on the treadmills and set them rolling at a sprinter's pace. There, in those harnesses, we'd planned that they would spend every moment of the rest of their strange existences, safe and secure, locked in place yet spinning ever forward, on a path we'd made for them, a path that could cause no damage or destruction. We would never unfasten their buckles or loosen their straps; we would never lift them out of their bindings or wash the residue of the treadmills' rubber belts from their orange sides. We would not even pause the treadmills' circulation unless their motors burned out. We were too

The Convexity of Our Youth

frightened to do anything other than maintain the ball-children as surreal conversation pieces and monuments to our parental failure. We were not offering a cure to our children, but a palliative to ourselves. And, in this, we were relatively satisfied, at least for a time.

A Divide

Other towns deal with the orange ball and their own infected offspring in other ways.

In Mercury, Ohio, the citizens have built a windowless, private gymnasium the size of an entire office complex for their ball-children. Within this gym the ball-children permanently reside, never allowed to exit the building's triple-locked steel doors, even with supervision. The people of Mercury reason that their ball-children should never want to leave the gym, given that it's equipped with a dizzying array of tubes and chutes and mazes and wheels in myriad sizes and shapes. It is, after all, designed to be a ball's veritable paradise. And yet, when questioned about the usual movements of the ball-children within their unique enclave, Mercury residents recite an odd fact: no matter how often the ball-children run their mazes or blast through their chutes, no matter how much exuberance they seem to emit as they slide and bounce and roll, they always end their day by congregating around the doors, rebounding against them lightly.

Elsewhere, in Sutter's Glen, Tennessee, every family of a ball-child owns an oversized, triple-reinforced bouncy castle which their individual ball-child inhabits. These bouncy castles are a significant source of revenue for the people of Sutter's Glen, as they allow the families of ball-children to offer wealthy curiosity-seekers the opportunity to purchase exclusive admissions to view their ball-children. It's rumored that, for the right price, the people of Sutter's Glen will even allow patrons to enter the bouncy castles and play with their ball-children. Through this trade, the community has grown quite wealthy—so much so that Jaguars and Porsches and Ferraris are now common sights on the streets of Sutter's Glen. It should be little surprise then, that, privately, many of the town's citizens whisper a desire for the orange ball to return, to transform the rest of their children, to help them erect more bouncy castles in their backyards.

In yet another locale—Kylersburg, Wyoming—the ball-children are herded onto a ranch with absurdly high, electrified fences. There, after they have been stamped with a unique number and fitted with a tiny tracking device, they are given free reign of the open fields and sky. On the ranch, they are treated much as any other herd of livestock; they are frequently rounded up and counted, often driven from one area of the ranch to another so as to evenly wear on the land, and occasionally used in special rodeos during which ranch hands attempt to rope and tie them or ride them like angry steer. The people of Kylersburg contend that, as a whole, their treatment method is by far the most natural and humane of all known treatment methods. Perhaps surprisingly, few outsiders argue with the assertion.

Finally, in Vernonville, Texas, in the town that ignited our initial fears, the people have no ongoing treatment plan, as the treatment they eventually instituted was of a singular and final variety. "Shots from heaven," some of the citizens of Vernonville call their particular treatment. Others refer to it more modestly as "A mercy." No matter what moniker they choose, the people of Vernonville claim they feel no remorse or guilt over their actions. They say they simply copied the treatment from their traditional methods for handling lame horses and terminally ill pets. They say that the greatest kindness they could show to their children was to let the dead lie down. Whether or not this statement rings true, one thing is certain: the people of Vernonville no longer need to worry about their ball-children, because there are no longer any ball-children in Vernonville to worry about. Considering this outcome, some might argue that their treatment has been the most successful of all.

The Convexity of Our Youth

A Revelation

After our treatment plan went into effect, we returned to lives of relative normalcy. We went to work and complained about paperwork and bosses rather than silently hunching at our desks, worrying over what the balls might be doing to our possessions and our loved ones while we were away. We attended movies and ate at fine dining establishments. We went out for drinks with our friends and argued politics and sports with our families. We walked about our homes with confidence, with surety, with the peace of mind that no weighty orange ball might be tracking us from behind, waiting to pounce upon us and send us careening down a flight of stairs or through a window to our certain dooms. Gradually, we returned to our blissful old routines and, in a sense, the sharp edges of our lives once again began to wear smooth.

Meanwhile, however, the treadmills kept running in the background.

The ambient thrum and whir of treads cycling around and around became as ubiquitous to us as the soft whistle of breath from our own nostrils. We avoided the rooms in which we'd placed the ball-children—often keeping the doors to those rooms closed, if not altogether locked—but no matter which room or closet or hidden alcove of our homes we might try to hide away inside, we could hear the treadmills spinning. Music, sound machines, televisions blared at painful volumes: nothing entirely muted the noise. It became clear that if we were in our homes, we could not escape the treadmills' flat song, and because we could not escape we were perpetually on the verge of remembering why they ran nonstop. Even when we were not at home, many of us heard the treadmills' rhythmic drone, as though it had somehow recorded a loop of itself upon the very drums in our ears. Animated luncheons with friends, meetings with important business clients, birthday parties for significant others: all of it played out with the soundtrack of the treadmills whispering in the background. Our lives may have been returning to a state of normalcy, but it was certainly not the normalcy we'd known before the ball.

It wasn't long before the noise from the treadmills took its toll. In small ways that would have been imperceptible to anyone unfamiliar with our community, we began to wear thin. Our laughter at even the best-told jokes faded faster. Our goodnight kisses took on an unexpected hardness. Our footsteps came faster, lighter, as though we were trying to outrun a looming danger without showing any appearance of panic. We began to suffer from insomnia and panic attacks, which would lead us to pace in our yards during the witching hours of the night and, trembling, stare at the starlit sky. We lost weight—small amounts at first, healthy amounts we should have lost anyway, but eventually enough to make strangers wonder which wasting disease we must have developed and how many months we had left to live. Worst of all, we began to let our thoughts float away from us. We began to consider the balls as our children. We began to imagine what they might do if they weren't on the treadmills, speeding to nowhere. We began to try to grasp their needs and intentions and desires, impossible though the task might be.

Through our unrelenting contemplation, we were slowly drawn back to the rooms in which we'd placed the treadmills. At first, we stole into the rooms for the briefest of seconds, barely glimpsing even a flash of orange. But seconds stretched to minutes and minutes stretched to hours. Soon, we were spending entire evenings in the treadmill rooms. We watched the ball-children roll in place, our thoughts rolling with them. We could not stop envisioning new scenarios for them, were we to set them free of their shackles. Some of us conjured wild fantasies about the ball-children forming utopian ball-societies that operated without prejudice or hatred or any of the plagues of our human society. Some of us sketched nightmares of ball invasions, with our spherical overlords inflating us to bursting in an effort to assimilate us to their ways of being. And some of us simply hoped that the ball-children might roll to the ends of the earth and back, collecting experiences and perceptions and loves and dreams along their journeys.

No matter their substance, beneath all our thoughts settled an abiding sense of guilt. When no one else was home, we curled up in the treadmill rooms and we wept. We cried for the children we'd lost and we cried for the things they'd become that we'd never let live. We knew we'd wronged the ball-children. We knew we'd trapped what was not ours to trap, held on too tightly to a control we never really had in the first place. If the balls were to save us, we knew it was right. If they were to destroy us, we knew that was right, too. And if they bounced off to distant futures not meant for us at all, we knew that would be best, for in those futures we would find a sanctuary that we'd been missing for quite some time.

So we conferred with one another and we decided to engage in a final treatment so shocking, so revelatory, that no other town had even considered it. We decided to unbuckle the ball-children, open wide the doors to our houses, and, with no small amount of commingled anxiety and excitement and regret, let them roll past us and out of our town. Our final treatment, the only treatment we could justify in the end, was to simply let them roll away.

A Mystery

There exists even less data on the nature of the orange ball itself than its terrible effects on our children. Its first documented appearance occurred in a rural farming community in the heartland of the nation—a place called Goldenrod, Nebraska—where, eight years before our own tragedy, it infected its first three children. Its trajectory since then has followed no discernible pattern or logical progression, thus making any prediction of its present or future movement an exercise in pure divination. Its origin is equally the province of speculation and often involves theories that touch on fantastical notions of extraterrestrial intervention, interdimensional slippage, demonic corruption, and clandestine military projects gone awry. Beyond firsthand accounts, visual evidence of the ball itself is also utterly nil, as every attempt to photograph it or record it to video has resulted in nothing but blurred or fuzzy images. Though numerous adults have seen the ball in person and can attest to its physical reality, it has, as far as we or anyone else knows, never been so much as grazed by an adult hand. Many people, ourselves included, wonder what might happen if such an interaction were to occur. Would we, too, be transformed into balls, dead in humanity but vibrant and alive in a new state of being? Is the transformation a curse exclusive to our children? Or have we adults already been cursed in a less tangible way? About any of this, we may never know.

Acknowledgments

My deepest thanks to all the people who have helped my writing dreams become reality: the writers who have inspired me, whose names would fill a book longer than this one; the brave souls who have encouraged me online and in person to keep writing and to keep publishing better, including but not limited to Simon Strantzas, Joe Zanetti, Michael Wehunt, Justin Steele, Sam Cowan, Christopher Slatsky, Christopher Ropes, Matthew Bartlett, C.M. Muller, Brian O'Connell, Barry Lee Dejasu, Casey Frechette, and Christopher Mountenay; the outstanding editors who have believed in my stories enough to publish them, especially Justin Steele, Sam Cowan, Richard Thomas, C.C. Finlay, Jon Padgett, Matt Cardin, Michael Kelly, Robert Shearman, Stephen Jones, Mark Morris, Jordan Krall, S.J. Bagley, Kate Jonez, Kelly Young, Mike Davis, C.M. Muller, Joseph Nassise, Benjamin Holesapple, Alex Scully, and Michael Cieslak; the wonderful publishers and publishing crews who make the idea of "my books" possible, namely Steve Berman and Alex Jeffers at Lethe Press, Sam Cowan at Dim Shores Publishing, Jordan Krall at Dunham's Manor Press, and Matt Edginton, Michael Parker, and Syndey Leigh at Villipede Publications; the artists who have lent their talents to my books, Varsam Kurnia and Luke Spooner; my family, Sharen, Dave, Barb, Rob, Kenz, Beth, Josh, Gatsby, Daisy, and, above all others, Erin, without whom I would have dissolved many, many times; and my readers—always my readers—who take time out of their lives to step into my little worlds, no matter how disturbing they may be.

Publication Credits

"All that is Thrown Away" copyright © 2016, first appeared in *Strange Aeons* #20 / "The Cone of Heaven" copyright © 2016, first appeared in *The Lovecraft eZine* #37 / "The Convexity of Our Youth" copyright © 2017, first appeared in *Looming Low*, Volume I, ed. by Justin Steele and Sam Cowan, Dim Shores / "Do You Hear What I Hear?" copyright © 2018, original to this volume / "Ensoulment" copyright © 2013, first appeared in *Into the Darkness*, eds. C. Dennis Moore & David G. Barnett, Necro Publications / "Every Weeknight at Seven and Seven-Thirty" copyright © 2014, first appeared in *Desolation: 21 Tales for Tails*, ed. Michael Cieslak, Dragon's Roost Press / "The Final Correspondence of Sabrina Locker" copyright © 2018, original to this volume / "From the Ground, the Souls Burnt Clean" copyright © 2014, first appeared in *Visiak's Mirror*, 2014) / "The Gods in Their Seats, Unblinking" copyright © 2017, first appeared in *Vastarien* #1, ed. Matt Cardin / "An Interview with Samuel X. Slayden" copyright © 2015, first appeared in *Enter at Your Own Risk: Dreamscapes into Darkness*, ed. Alex Scully, Firbolg Publishing / "The Kindness of Surrender" copyright © 2015, first appeared in *Midian Unmade*, eds. Joseph Nassise and Del Howison, Tor Publishing / "Marrowvale" copyright © 2015, first appeared in *The Spectral Book of Horror Stories*, Vol. 2, ed. Mark Morris, Spectral Press, reprinted in *Best New Horror* #27, ed. Stephen Jones, PS Publishing / "The Myth of You" copyright © 2018, original to this collection / "A Silence of Starlings" copyright © 2016, first appeared in *Nightscript* 2, ed. C.M. Muller, Cthonic Matter Press / "Special Collections" copyright © 2016, first appeared in *The Magazine of Fantasy and Science Fiction*, Nov./Dec. 2016

About the Author

Kurt Fawver is a writer of horror, weird fiction, and dark fantasy. His short fiction has previously appeared in venues such as *The Magazine of Fantasy & Science Fiction, Strange Aeons,* the *Lovecraft eZine, Weird Tales, Gamut,* and has been selected for inclusion in *Best New Horror* and *The Year's Best Weird Fiction*. He's also released one previous collection of short stories, *Forever, in Pieces,* and one novella, *Burning Witches, Burning Angels*. Kurt has also had nonfiction published in places such as *Thinking Horror* and the *Journal of the Fantastic in the Arts*. He lives in the apocalyptic ruins of Florida and dreams of fleeing to a snow-capped heaven. You can find him online at kurtfawver.com or Facebook.

www.ingramcontent.com/pod-product-compliance
Ingram Content Group UK Ltd.
Pitfield, Milton Keynes, MK11 3LW, UK
UKHW041416180426
11947UKWH00007B/161